Turning the key, her heart sunk, there were too many hours left until dawn. She looked out the windshield and froze, her heart lodged in her throat. Afraid to move or breathe, Rayne stared at the animal a few feet away from the headlights. Her brain said dog, but that was no dog. That was a wolf. It had to be a wolf. Were wolves *that* big? It seemed bigger than in any pictures she'd seen.

She sat there staring, not sure if she should honk the horn or just sit and try not collapse in hysterics. The car may be metal, but the roof was something this animal could probably get through. As she continued to stare she couldn't help noticing that it was a beautiful. Its grey and brown fur looked soft and thick, not that she'd dare to find out. It was the haunting grey eyes watching her that helped her decide not to honk the horn or scream, which had crossed her mind. Rayne was fairly certain it was as surprised to see her as she was to see it. Didn't wolves travel as group? A pack? She wanted to look around and see if there were more in the trees, but logic said she was better off not knowing. Never argue with logic.

Also by Jacqueline

ANIMAL SENSES
1 *Heart*
2 *Scent*
3 *Passion*

MAGIC SEASONS ROMANCE
1 *Beltane Magic*
2 *Solstice Heat*
3 *Harvest Dreams*
4 *Autumn Dance*
5 *Winter Mist*

Dreams
Three steamy stories that started with a dream

Curses
Two tales of curses.

After the Silence
Volume 1 Bree

SINGLE TITLES
Solitary Witchling
Salvation

<u>**Writing As: J. Risk**</u>

THE ALTEREALM SERIES
1 *The Huntress*
2 *The Seer*
3 *The Empath*
4 *The Witch*
5 *The Chronos*
6 *The Warrior*
7 *The Telepath*

HEART

Animal Senses Book 1

Jacqueline Paige

Published by FRP
Copyright © 2017 Roxane Kerr
Edited by Gaele L. Hince
Cover art by: Off the Wall Creations

Previous edition released in 2012
Updated 2020

ISBN (paperback): 978-1-7773723-2-3
ISBN (digital) 978-1-7773723-3-0

DEDICATION

For A.J.

You're my number one fan, that loves every word I write. My number one (first) son—who to this day still thinks I'm an invincible, superhuman mom. All mothers should be as lucky as I am.

Author's note:

When *Heart* was first published I had a trilogy in mind. After writing the second book, I knew there were too many wonderful, intriguing characters to stop at three stories. The trilogy has been reworked to become the *Animal Senses Series*. Find a comfortable corner and hang on… this is going to be quite the ride. I hope you enjoy reading it as much as I do writing it!

Jacqueline

Stopping in mid-stride, every muscle in her body tensed, she knew that voice. What she didn't recognize was the tone.

"I don't care if you have to slice pieces off a little at a time. He will tell you who did that to me—to us. My father hasn't been in the ground six months. No one will disrespect his memory like that—no one!" The voice hissed.

Rayne's heart was now resting in her throat, each violent pump threatening to choke her. She crept back out of the room being careful to not make a sound, debating for half a second whether she should close the door or just leave it.

She left it. Every instinct was telling her to get out of there, fast.

Clutching her purse against her chest like a lifeline, she forced her body to move back toward the elevator. If her legs weren't shaking, she would have run to it.

By the time Rayne reached the elevator door, her hands were shaking and it took all of her concentration to make her hand push the button. Banging it repeatedly wishing the doors would open allowing her escape.

She was barely able to breathe by the time the door opened, her heart was racing so fast every vein throbbed, she had to move. She looked back in the direction of the office one last time, then stumbled through the elevator doors, throwing most of her weight on the button to close them.

Chapter One

Blinking, Rayne glanced around. She was in the underground parking space in her apartment building and didn't even remember the drive. Her chest hurt, hands were vibrating and reality felt far away. Three times, she tried to extract the keys from the ignition, finally after fumbling she managed. *Come on, Rayne, get it together. Think!*

Her mind didn't want to accept the words that had come from Aiden's mouth, her fiancé. In all the years she'd known him, never had he used that tone. Scared her enough to send chills through her spine. She believed he meant every word. *I am not an idiot, I've always known he was a hard man, but the words turned my blood to ice and a part of me knows I'll never feel the same for him again.*

Taking a shaky breath, she groped around for her purse, feeling like she was moving through mud. Somehow, she managed to move and get out of the car. Her legs still felt like rubber, but she couldn't stay in the parking garage all day. Turning, she forced herself to move to the door.

What am I going to do? I can't marry a man like that. I'm not even sure if I can look at him now.

Stopping, she looked at the elevator door. Just the

thought of stepping inside left her feeling suffocated and trapped. Hugging the purse again, she turned toward the stairwell. *Keep moving*—she had to.

Trapped, I am, aren't I? Trapped in a relationship. Just that one word showed her the next move. She had to get out of this relationship. Aiden was not her dream man, if such a thing existed, but he had been comfortable. Admitting that, she now accepted that the relationship was too comfortable to be real.

When she reached her third-floor apartment, she wasn't out of breath. But, as numb as she felt, she wasn't sure if she *was* breathing. Maybe this was just a dream and she'd wake up any second now. Giving herself a small reprieve, she let that thought marinate for a few seconds before reality came crashing back.

It took her two tries to get the key into the lock. *What had his associate said just before my world darkened? "We haven't found a body or any sign of him, Aiden."* Him, who? A body? *A body!*

As Rayne stepped inside her apartment the dreamlike veil lifted away, revealing reality. *A reality I'm not sure how I can live with.* She quickly locked the door, all three locks. Not it would protect her, Aiden had keys. Leaning back against the door she tried to calm down and think.

Aiden was some sort of mob, mafia...*whatever?* Standing there she waited to feel her doubts were unsubstantiated, but it didn't happen. Her fear *was* the truth. This explained the dangerous looking misfits he had in his employ. They had never quite *fit* she thought. Aiden wasn't a boy scout—she knew that. He was a powerful man, as his father had been, but what kind of power was now very clear to her. Closing her eyes, Rayne held a trembling hand over her heart, it was still beating too heavily. *I can't look at him again. Ever.* This only meant one thing...

She looked around the pretty apartment for a moment, taking two steps towards the kitchen before stopping. She had to leave, now. Everything was *his*. *He* paid for everything in this apartment, she worked in *his* gallery. Her whole world was controlled by *him*…

Moving in a slow circle, Rayne studied everything in sight.

Every. Single. Thing.

Bought by him, in one way or another. Taking a deep breath, she tried to exhale slowly. Failing, her breath huffed out in one loud whoosh. There was no alternative, she had to get out of here.

Today.

Right now.

Kicking off her shoes, she bent down, scooped them up, and headed towards the bedroom.

Faster than she ever changed before, the skirt was stripped off and tossed on the bed. Barely having both legs in her jeans, Rayne began pulling open drawers and cabinets, dumping the contests all over the bed. All she really owned were clothes, her beloved camera, laptop and a few mementos to remind her of her parents. All of it was going in her car. A thought made her freeze as she held the empty drawer over the bed— her car was in *his* name. Dropping the drawer on the pile, Rayne sat on the bed, defeated. In the mirror, a frightened woman stared back. Seeing herself was enough to jolt her back into action. Giving the frail looking reflection a determined nod, she made a solid decision. To hell with him. She was taking the car. He hated it, called it girlie, and complained it wasn't comfortable. *The car is now mine.*

Forty-five minutes later Rayne surveyed the bedroom. There was nothing left that she wanted. Leaning down and picking up the last bag, she went to set it with the rest. "This is pathetic, Rayne Andrews. Your entire life fits in six cases and a couple of purses."

She walked through the apartment for the last time, working out how to get all of the cases downstairs to the car without causing suspicion, when the ring of her cell phone pierced the silence. She looked over at her purse, the ringtone was Aiden's. A few seconds after it stopped, the phone on the table began to ring. *Can I do this?* Taking a deep breath, "Buy some time," she whispered aloud just before answering it.

"Hello?"

"There you are. You didn't answer your cell."

He may be using that soft tone, but she now *knew* what he was. "Oh, I was taking the garbage to the garbage room." Her hand shook as she held the phone and prayed that her voice didn't give anything away.

"Where the hell is that girl I pay to do that?"

Just the way he said it made her tremble. "I-it's Wednesday, Aiden. She doesn't come in today."

"Right. Listen baby, I may be here awhile. Could be most of the night..."

"That's—fine. I was heading to the spa shortly." Closing her eyes, she waited to see if he questioned that.

"Do you want me to come by in the morning to pick you up?"

For what? "Pick me up?"

He chuckled. "We have a brunch with Donny and his wife."

Letting out the silent breath she'd been holding. "Oh, yes please." *Please let me sound normal.*

"Okay baby. You go get all beautiful for me and I'll see you in the morning. Ten o'clock."

"Okay, Aiden."

"Love ya, baby."

"Me too." She hung up quickly. Suddenly gasping for air, Rayne tried to settle her nerves again. *Ten o'clock.* Looking over at the clock and doing the math, she had seventeen hours to disappear.

It took almost as long to get all the bags down as it had for her to pack them. Of course, if you're planning to pack your whole life up and vanishing, it would probably be easier if you didn't drive a *Cabriolet*. Fitting everything into the micro-sized car had taken more than one attempt. In the time it took to finish, she was much calmer about her decision to leave. Not that she had a choice, but she could always have a mini breakdown and cry her heart out, later. Right now, she needed a plan to figure out the next step.

The first stop was the gas station. Getting out of the car, she looked around, checking for Aiden or one of his men. *Great, paranoia already.* After she assured herself that he couldn't possibly know yet, Rayne walked over to the pump. As she lifted the card up to the slot, she realized that he could track her cards. As if the machine was going to grab it, she jerked her hand back and turned to get her purse. She'd need all the cash she had available. Looking over her shoulder again, she walked to the cash machine. This location was close enough to the apartment to not point in any direction—when she finally decided on which direction. Her hands weren't the steadiest as she punched in the numbers and requested the limit the machine would allow, the shaking increased when she grabbed the cash and stuffed it in her wallet.

Glancing around, she walked back to the pump, inserting a card to pay for the gas. It only took her a few minutes to decide she would hit a few more cash machines in the area to bypass withdrawal limits. Aiden might not drive by, but now she suspected he had people everywhere that would recognize her.

After the gas was pumped, she thought that a map would be a good thing, unless she planned to drive around Chicago endlessly—because that's the only place she'd ever driven. Reaching down, Rayne pulled out the nearest one, only to put it right back, it was a map of the one place she knew. Bending down, she studied the title of each map before spotting an oversized atlas with Canada in it. She grabbed that one. Before she could second guess the decision, she set it on the counter and waited for the clerk to ring it in.

With the receipt and atlas clutched in her vibrating hand,

she went back to the car, hoping she could get through the next few moments without questioning what she was going to do next.

An hour later, she sat in an empty parking lot, trying to force a bagel down her throat. The atlas she'd purchased was propped against the steering wheel, endless lines of varying colors stared back at her. So many places and no idea where to go. She looked over at the glove box where she'd put her money—in a make-up bag no less. It had taken five different bank machines to empty her accounts of every cent she had. Her cards were now at their limits, accounts were empty and on a whim, Rayne had taken out a cash advance on the card Aiden had given her for emergencies. If this wasn't considered an emergency, she didn't know what was.

Focus, Rayne. Looking back at the map, she tried to wash down a bite with the lukewarm coffee. She knew making maps took a lot of work and was complicated in a way she didn't really care to understand, but they really weren't telling her anything. She needed her laptop and the internet to make a decision that the squiggly color coordinated lines weren't telling her. Sighing, she glanced around the parking lot. A hotel was at the far end. She reached down to pull the laptop case off the floor. Setting it on the passenger's seat, she opened it and hit the power button, praying for it to pick up a signal as she flipped through another few pages. There was a signal, not a strong one, but it would do. Bringing up a mapping site, she entered Chicago as the starting point. *Now what?* A starting point generally meant you needed a destination and that she didn't have. Flipping a few more pages, Rayne picked the first name that jumped off the page. Destination? Timmins, Ontario, Canada. Her heart was pounding as she hit enter.

Strangely, she felt relieved knowing she had decided on a location. Her resolve only faltered for a few seconds when she discovered there was a fourteen-hour drive to get there.

Biting her lip, she looked out the windshield, not really focusing on anything. Was she ready for a fourteen-hour drive that would take her far away from Aiden? If she had translated the map correctly, where she was heading was right in the middle of nowhere. That meant there was less chance of her being found. Yes, she was ready. Picking up the notebook that was waiting for the details of *the* game plan, she started to jot down the directions, deciding after a few lines that she'd only write down the first five hours and then reassess her route from that point. She had no idea what it was going to be like driving this far.

Closing the laptop, she put it back on the floor and just sat there. Was she crazy for doing this? Yes, but she couldn't stay here and that left few options. She was alone, just like when her parents died. This time all the decisions to be made were going to be her own.

❦

Her eyes felt completely dried out. Was such a thing even possible? She didn't know, but at the first drug store, she was getting some eye drops. Glancing at the time— again, Rayne squinted back at the road. *How long have I been driving now?* Four hours? No, closer to five, she needed to stop soon. A few hours ago, she had foolishly thought she would be across the border before planning a stop, but that wasn't going to happen. Driving at this speed meant she still had at least an hour and a half to go before reaching Mackinaw City and then another hour to the border. Considering the longest she'd ever driven passed an hour back, Rayne knew she wasn't going to make it. She had a newfound respect for people that drove for a living. The quick bathroom stop a few hours before hadn't been long enough. If she didn't stop soon, she was going to make mistakes and end up lost, or worse. Stopping would be for the best.

Blinking quickly, she tried to make her eyes not feel as dry and then focused on the sign she was coming to. A motel was thirty miles from here. Looking at the speedometer, Rayne attempted to do the math and calculate how long that would take, less than a minute later she gave up and decided it wasn't important. As long as she arrived at the motel before falling asleep. A few hours of rest, something to eat and a shower became the new goal.

After what felt like ten hours she could see the hotel's sign not too far ahead. Elation and a bit of pride filled her as she realized she'd made it to here without help. She was slowing down when she noticed two police cars sitting at the motel. All the hair on the back of her neck stood up. Aiden couldn't know she was gone already, could he? Would he involve police? Biting down on her lip, she thought he probably wouldn't, but she wasn't going to take any chances. Gripping the steering wheel tighter, her heart was crashing against her ribs at the thought that Aiden might find her. There would be more motels further away, and another chance to take a break.

It took several seconds for the sign she'd just passed to register. *I've done it!* She was almost to Mackinaw, at least that's what the sign had said. Taking a deep breath and fighting the grogginess that had been closing in for hours, she forced herself to keep going. Maybe a little air would help, not that it had a half hour ago, but it couldn't hurt. She rolled the window down, hoping it would help. Seven hours of driving, minus two very brief bathroom breaks and a stop for gas, and she'd managed to keep going. If she wasn't ready to pass out, she would be pretty impressed with what she'd managed.

After a few minutes of taking deep breaths she groaned, the open window wasn't working. Reaching for the radio, she fumbled with the buttons and flicked through the few stations that were clear, anything to sing to or even pretending to sing might work. She scowled at the radio.

Turning it off, she stared at the road once again. "Okay," she tried to ignore how slurred her voice sounded. "Use your brain, get the blood pumping and drive." Wiggling a bit, she tried to sit straighter. "Great, my brain is already sleeping," she yawned while trying to see the sign that was getting closer. "Oh. Interstate one twenty-seven. I've been looking at that for what seems like forever," she mumbled to the eyes in the mirror. "And before that it was I31." She bobbed her head and tried to recall the roads before that. "One ninety…something, not that it matters really—It's not like I'm going to be going on the return trip," Rayne snorted and then laughed, not sure if it was delirium or exhaustion that had her talking to herself. "And what are you going to do when you reach your middle of nowhere in Canada, Ms. Andrews?" She glanced at the speedometer, even though she had no idea what it had said on the Mackinaw sign she'd just driven past. Clearing her throat, she looked at the reflection again. "I have no idea what I'm going to do. I didn't sit down and plot out a course of action before fleeing," she giggled quietly this time and then squealed as she drove by another sign. "What–ah, miles..." biting her lip a couple of times, she looked at the time. "Oh! A half hour!" Gripping the steering wheel with the very last of her energy, she focused on the road. "You did it. And the reward?" She attempted to smile, but yawned and erased what would have been the smile. "The reward is sleep."

Rayne stood, clutching the room key in her hand and looking at the car, deciding. With the way she'd stuffed the cases into the car, there was no easy way to get to the one that had the clothes she wanted, without taking everything out of the car. Did she care if she slept in something fresh? At this point, no, she would come back out later and sort out what to change into. As she started to head for the room, her brain flashed a warning. She wasn't feeling very trusting now. Turning back, she unlocked the car and reached in to grab her purse, money, camera and laptop. If anyone decided to pick up the tiny car and carry it away, she could get by with just this.

Stumbling into the dark room, she kicked the door closed. Her shoes were off in two steps, it felt glorious. Her leg smacked into the bed. Setting the precious items down on it, she shoved them to the other side and flopped down, face first. Had she asked for a wakeup call? The chances of a yes were high, but there was no way she could summon the energy to find out.

Chapter Two

After an hour, her nerves were settled or possibly just lulled as the peaceful scenery rolled by. She glanced at the clock, something that seemed to be happening too frequently. How far now? It had been four in the morning when she'd crossed the border—which left her possibly six hours before Aiden arrived to pick her up and discover she wasn't there. During the drive, she had second-guessed her decision to not leave a note, but each time she had the same answer. No.

The scenery was visible in daylight, even with the overcast sky, it was far better than driving through the constant darkness. While it was dark, she worried about missing things to look at, but now she knew there wasn't much to see. If the map was accurate, she had selected an area that was so remote that if she wanted to drive further North, she would have to fly. Beyond her destination there weren't many roads. Part of her hoped the maps were in need of updating, but the other part— a very small part, was quite pleased. She needed to get her life together, or find a new life now, she supposed. Doing that would require some time alone to come up with a plan of action. Hopefully this plan would not involve any more driving, her backside was numb, again.

Her eyes wandered over to her camera that was sitting on the seat. The camera and Rayne had been sharing moments of silent communication since driving away from the border crossing. In a moment of panic, when the guard had asked what brought her to Canada, she said the first thing she could think of, that she was doing a photo journal of Northern Canada. His comment had been appreciative and wished her luck with the bears. She prayed it was just some sort of Canadian humor and she wouldn't need luck with bears. Saying she was a photographer, or hinting at it had just been a way to distract from the truth of her flight. But the longer she sat in the car with her camera beside her, the more she was beginning to think it may be possible for photography to be a part of her future. She wasn't a brilliant photographer or anything like that, yet, but she did have a good eye and could manage to capture things properly. She'd taken a course to learn how to use her rather pricey camera once she realized the days of point-and-shoot were long gone.

Catching herself looking at the clock again, Rayne groaned. *Am I far enough away that I could stop more often and relax a bit?* The searches she'd done after her nap at the motel had shown that she still had roughly ten more hours of driving before reaching the furthest point she was willing to go. The furthest point she was brave enough to go. Of course, the fact that she didn't even know how to pronounce where she was going still seemed a little ridiculous.

I have to stop. Her legs were cramping and mind was wandering again. After the long drive last night, she just wanted to get out of the car. While the scenery was beautiful in the daylight it was becoming repetitive. There were trees, rocks, swampy lakes and more trees— repeat and that was it.

Pulling into the restaurant, which had boasted on a sign miles before that it had the best all day breakfast around, not that food was her only reason for stopping. What they didn't mention was it was the *only* restaurant around for many miles… or was that kilometers now that she was in Canada?

Not realizing how stiff her legs were, Rayne almost fell out of the car. If there had been other cars in the parking lot she would have been embarrassed. Reaching in, she put her camera on the floor and tossed her jacket over it and then grabbed her laptop bag and turned to head towards the door. Roughly three steps later she turned back to get the atlas. Intuition suggested that this establishment probably didn't have free Wi-Fi.

Rayne went to the furthest table in a corner and sat down, facing a window. *What am I going to do once this trip ends? That was the million-dollar question that she really needed to answer while here. What was it my mother used to say? Things are never as bad as they seem? Well they are this time. I am in the middle of nowhere, with my whole world packed into a compact car that doesn't belong to me, with no real destination or a plan once I find it. I plan on living on the money I have, including the amount I'd borrowed without asking. Yep, things were pretty bad.*

She realized a few hours later that it would be best if she didn't stay in a motel when she reached her destination. If she registered, then she could be traced and found. The problem with that was she wasn't sure what other options that left.

Spotting a store called the Trading Post, she pulled into the parking lot. Maybe getting out for a few minutes would help her come up with a solution.

Walking through the store, Rayne was in awe. The amount of merchandise stuffed into the tiny building was unreal. It was a grocery store, fishing and hunting supply and a drug store all stacked and packed into one small space.

"Can I help you find something?"

Turning, she came face to face with a blue-haired boy, at least she was fairly certain he was just a boy, judging by the piercings and pimples. "I'm not sure what I need." Which was the truth, she had no clue.

He gave her a lopsided grin, causing the lip piercing to pop out further. "Are you looking for camping gear?"

Was I? She tried not to focus on his blue spiked hair. "I've never been camping, so I don't know what I need, exactly."

"You're not from around here, are you? The way you talk, your accent, it's kind of cool."

Why hadn't I thought of that? Will my Chicago accent make me stand out to everyone? Offering what she hoped looked like a real smile. "Uh, thank you."

He motioned to the far wall of the store. "Everything you need is over here. We'll get you all set up."

He may just be a boy, but he probably had more camping experience than she did shopping experience, so she'd have to trust his judgement. Rayne didn't know who he meant by *we*, but she followed him despite doubting if she *really* wanted to go camping with each step. It would be a solution. By carrying everything she'd need with her, she could move when necessary. How hard could camping be?

"So where are you going camping?" He pulled a box down from the shelf.

"Somewhere quiet." She watched as he piled a few more things on the box.

"Quiet is all we have here." He picked up another small box. "I can give you a few suggestions if you want." He smirked at her, "but unless you're interested in fishing and hunting, your choices are limited."

"Oh, I see." *Did I want to drive further?* "Is there anywhere past Timmins?" She couldn't even guess at pronouncing most of the locations on the map, so playing ignorant probably was the best choice at this point.

Clearing his throat, he shrugged. "I know a deserted campground, it would definitely be quiet. It's about three hours away though."

Biting her lip, Rayne tried to decide. What's three more hours of driving after the last seventeen? "You'll have to write down the directions for me."

He nodded as he tapped his fingers on a box on the shelf. "No problem. What kind of car are you driving?" The confusion must have shown on my face because I received another lopsided grin. "So, I know what supplies will fit."

She cringed. Fitting anything else into the car was going to take a skill she didn't possess. "It's very small."

He nodded again and turned back to the shelf. "We can take things out of the boxes if it's a tight squeeze."

Nodding like she understood, Rayne waited until he turned away again before frowning. Boxes of what?.

It was over an hour later before she was back on the road. It had taken that long to buy everything anyone could possibly need or want, and fit it into the car. Rayne hadn't even known the back seat of the car folded down. It made the trunk much larger and, she'd like to say easier, to pack everything in, but easy hadn't been any part of it. The passenger seat slid forward and the floor in front was packed with her purse, laptop and camera and anything she'd need to access on the rest of the trip. A coffee maker and a miniature stove were belted into the seat, for safety. Although when suggested it, he had mentioned bears or other animals, like moose running across the road. Unfortunately, from the way he said it, she didn't think he was joking. Having gone her whole life without seeing a bear, she really hoped it would remain that way. She just wasn't *that* brave.

Glancing in the mirror, the expression on her face said it all. "You are in *way* over your head, Rayne," she said out loud. Thinking of everything that was now in the car, it was surprising it moved with the extra weight. Six hundred dollars later and she was now carrying her own portable home. The boy at the store had lost her when explaining what everything was for, but she could figure that out later. She knew absolutely nothing about camping. The closest she'd ever been to camping was when Aiden and she had gone to a cabin at an elite resort. Come to think of it, the 'cabin' was bigger than the store she had just been in. Overall, that trip had been a disaster. Fish flies, which Rayne had never heard of before in her life, had invaded the resort, and most of the guests were complaining or leaving. It was laughable that the guests blamed the resort manager for this incident. How was it his fault that the insects had selected that location to hang out?

If blue boys' directions were accurate, she still had quite a way to go. There had been nothing but trees for the last half hour. She had wanted quiet, and it appeared it couldn't get any quieter than this. Surely she was safe enough to stop more often, far enough away from Aiden that getting out to stretch her legs and wander around a bit was doable. Then again, it would only be for a bit if the possibility of bears was more fact than fiction. A close encounter with a small bird or squirrel she could handle, a bear, not so much.

Trying to keep her mind busy to stop boredom setting in again, she thought about everything she'd bought, and wondered how long it would take to set it up. Hopefully, if she arrived before dark, it shouldn't take too long to figure it out. Right?

Miscalculating how often she should stop and for how long, she'd added more than two hours to her drive. She also hadn't anticipated the sky darkening with a storm—the one and only radio station she could bring in hadn't mentioned the impending storm either. Frowning, she leaned as far forward as she could to peer closely at the surface she was driving on. He had said a rough road, but rough didn't even begin to describe this. The holes in the dirt path were bigger than her tires. A few times there was no choice but to creep through the crevices, dragging the bottom of the car. The car empty was only five or so inches off the ground, which meant filled to the top, as it was now, she was close to tearing off bits that probably should remain attached.

Following the directions, she drove past the main gate, somewhere up here was supposed to be the second entrance to this campsite. It was darker now, making everything harder to see clearly. She may have missed the second entrance all together. Stopping, she looked at what may have been a road at one time. Putting the car into park, she opened the door and got out slowly. Weeds had grown over, making it more of a path than a road. Walking over, she stared at what lay beyond the small opening. If the car survived driving through that she'd be shocked. It was too late to drive all the way back. In the other direction, the so-called road she was traveling on ended no more than thirty feet from where she stood—and beyond that, nothing except trees and more trees. A rumble in the distance drew her attention to the sky, black clouds rolled across it like they were on a conveyor belt. Having no great choices, she needed to find somewhere to stay until morning.

Before she changed her mind and went to search for the nearest motel, she got back in the car. A motel was probably three hours away, back in the direction she had just come from. Rayne was too tired, she knew she would never make it that far right now. Instead of reaching civilization she'd spend the night in the car on the side of the road hoping the bears, moose and any other creatures were nowhere nearby.

The car made it, at least she hoped it had. Though noisy, the scraping of something along the bottom of the car hadn't sounded too serious, and everything seemed to still function. The rain hadn't even waited until she could look around. She had crept around through trees and rocks looking for some sort of shelter, moving slower while driving than she thought possible. Thunder echoed loudly, and with each *boom* her heart sped up just a little more. *Why was it that storms didn't seem too bad while inside a nice large, thick walled building, but as soon as you were in a small car they were terrifying?* Finally admitting to herself that even *if* she found somewhere to camp, she wouldn't be brave enough to get out of the car, Rayne parked beside what looked like a little run-down shack and turned off the car.

The rain was slamming against the cloth top of the car and she hoped that was why it sounded louder than she'd ever heard before. The windows were completely fogged over, she thought about opening the window for a little air, but decided waiting until the rain slowed would be better. There were no street lights, it was so dark that the sound of the rain was starting to freak her out more than she cared to admit. To make an impossible situation worse, she had to go to the bathroom and getting out of the car in this rain was not an option.

Biting her lip, she fought the tears that now decided they couldn't wait another second. The pain and betrayal caught up to her all at once, emotions swamped, tempting her to wish for numbness—for just a little longer. *How could I think I loved a man like that?* Rayne was alone, completely, utterly alone in this world with no idea of what comes next. Fumbling around on the floor trying to locate the flashlight, she continued to fight the tears threatening to overwhelm. Not that the light would chase away the tears, but because it was one of the few things she knew where to locate and use, and right now she needed a distraction. When she couldn't find it, she turned on the interior light, which seemed like a giant spotlight aimed right at her face. When the first tear escaped without her permission and rolled down her cheek she swatted at it, determined not to break down. Turning as much as she could in the seat, she looked at the mess jammed in the car. Having no idea what she would need to get her through until dawn, she randomly poked her hand in between the packed items to feel around, hoping to recognize something useful.

With the sleeping bag, flashlight, some granola bars and a few bottles of water now piled on her lap, she turned to try and face forward again. Setting the water bottles on the dash, she lightened the pile on her lap. First up – figuring out where to find a bathroom. *A bathroom?* Would there even be a bathroom of some sort here? *What am I doing here?*

In the time it took her to get settled again the tears were streaming down her face as fast as the rain on the windshield. She was feeling sorry for herself, and didn't have time for that. A new wave of tears started when she realized she had nothing but time. Reaching back to push items away from behind the seat, she thought she would recline the driver's seat and create more space. She held her breath and pulled the lever. The seat didn't go back as far as she would have liked, but at least it moved back a bit. *What I really want to do is curl up and stay that way until everything is all right again.* Why was that something you did while crying? Curl up?

Now she was sniffling in that annoying way, the way that only comes with tears. Turning off the interior light she sat quietly, hugging the flashlight to her chest. "Day one, drive more miles than I ever have driven in my entire life." She wiped at the window with a shaking hand. "Day two begins with me sitting in my over-full car, in the middle of a forest, in the middle of nowhere, at the end of the earth in the pouring rain, crying to myself." She shivered, feeling the dampness. "While freezing, and wanting nothing more than to pee." Squinting, she tried to see the small building beside her. "If there are Gods out there, please let that be a bathroom." Even as she said it, Rayne knew it wasn't. Why is it when you're cold or upset, it made things worse if you needed to use the bathroom? She didn't have any scientific answers, just knew that she had to stop crying and start thinking, or sleeping—which seemed less likely.

Shifting around in the little space was a challenge as she wrestled with the sleeping bag to cover the seat beneath her. Fumbling around trying to find the cords that tied it together, she wished for a pair of scissors to remedy the problem. When she finally found the right end, she tugged at them and neither would come undone, which meant trying to pull the cord towards the end of the rolled bag, hoping it would slip off.

Once she did manage that, trying to get it underneath her was like moving around in a cardboard box, her elbows hitting the seat and door at every attempt.

Rayne felt like she had won a small battle once her legs were finally inside the sleeping bag.

Of course, when she did manage to zip up she discovered it was turned sideways and the hooded part would be over her face if she continued. Resting her head against the seat, she debated twisting the bag around to face the right way, then deciding it was just fine the way it was. She was too tired and upset to try any yoga-like contortions just for the sake of a sleeping bag.

If nothing else happened, at least she was warmer now. How long would the rain last? *Do I want to wait it out and then try to find a bathroom – in the dark?* Rayne shook her head before she could go any further with that thought. There was no way she was getting out of this car until it was light, rain or no rain. How many hours until daylight? She wondered whether she could squirm around to reach her purse and get her phone. Highly doubtful. Cocooned in the puffy material, reaching was impossible and the phone was off for a reason. Turning it on just to check the time wasn't worth the risk of Aiden being able to trace her. She didn't know if that was possible, not really, even though all the movies referenced it, but realizing what type of man Aiden was, she wasn't taking any chances.

Working one arm free, she shifted far enough forward to reach the ignition, he couldn't track the car's clock. Turning the key, her heart sunk, there were too many hours left until dawn. She looked out the windshield and froze, her heart lodged in her throat. Afraid to move or breathe, Rayne stared at the animal a few feet away from the headlights. Her brain said dog, but that was no dog. That was a wolf. It had to be a wolf. Were wolves *that* big? It seemed bigger than in any pictures she'd seen.

She sat there staring, not sure if she should honk the horn or just sit and try not collapse in hysterics. The car may be metal, but the roof was something this animal could probably get through. As she continued to stare she couldn't help noticing that it was a beautiful. Its grey and brown fur looked soft and thick, not that she'd dare to find out. It was the haunting grey eyes watching her that helped her decide not to honk the horn or scream, which had crossed her mind. Rayne was fairly certain it was as surprised to see her as she was to see it. Didn't wolves travel as group? A pack? She wanted to look around and see if there were more in the trees, but logic said she was better off not knowing. Never argue with logic.

She was sure she stopped breathing when it took a step closer to the car, then turned quickly heading toward the trees. As she was reaching for the keys, it stopped and looked at her for the longest few seconds in history, before bolting into the trees and disappearing.

Turning the key in the ignition to off, she flopped back against the seat while trying to remind her body to take air in. In this moment, with her heart beating so loud she could hear it, or it felt that way, Rayne reaffirmed her decision to not get out of the car until full daylight, and even that was questionable. She also decided to not turn the lights on again, she was much better off not knowing what was outside the car. She checked to make sure the doors were locked, she didn't think a wolf would walk up and use the door handle, but she felt better knowing that she was locked in and other things were locked out.

Pulling her arm back into the sleeping bag, Rayne scooted down as far as she could and closed her eyes. The sooner she slept, the sooner daylight would arrive. Over the noise of the rain beating on the car, she thought she heard a howl. She slid down further into the sleeping bag and squeezed her eyes shut, wishing for morning to hurry up and arrive.

Chapter Three

Leaning back against the windowsill, his mother continued to give her number one lecture on the other end of the phone. *Does she remember I'm a grown man and not eight years old?* Devin wondered, often. Inhaling deeply, he knew, without looking out the window, that a storm wasn't far off. With a lot of effort, he wrestled his focus back to Mother.

"...you really need to socialize more, Devin, to find someone. Your Father won't push you, but you know you're the last in our family line and we..."

Expect you to take over and rule one day. Or something very similar. He knew his obligations all too well. He inhaled as the wind picked up, the dampness of the impending rain filling his system. Summer storms were one of his favorite things.

"...your sister married outside so we'll..." she sighed loudly. "You won't find someone hiding there alone."

Hiding? I am not hiding. My mother, the very definition of a wolf in sheep's clothing. "I am aware of all of this, Mother." Pushing at his hair to keep it out of his eyes, Devin tried to stay calm. "You're talking as if I'm too old. I'm only thirty, barely thirty, there's time. I just need my space..."

"You've had *space* for five years, Devin! So, you lost

control a few times when you were younger, everyone does..."

That cued her to start on lecture number two of the maternal lecture series. A gust of wind blew through the window just as the sky opened up and water pelted the earth in heavy raindrops. He took the scent into his system and found something he was not expecting—the smell of car exhaust. Impossible. No one ventured this far when dark was falling, and definitely not when a storm was brewing. Those facts settled, why did he smell exhaust and something else...gardenias? *Why do I smell a flower that isn't on my land?* "I'll call soon, Mother. Give Father my best." He hung up without waiting for a response.

Tossing the phone over to the chair, he shrugged off the feelings of guilt from hanging up on his own Mother and leaned over the window ledge. He inhaled once more. It was gardenias and another faint scent he couldn't quite define in the rain. Someone was on his land, and unless his nose was wrong, they were female. The phone rang as he headed for the door. Knowing better, he didn't answer it. Letting his Mother cool off before he apologized for being rude always went better than trying to soothe her when her teeth were bared.

Stepping out into the night, he stopped and stood in the rain that was now coming down so hard it almost hurt. The storm clouds completely covered the sky, black and unforgiving. This storm was staying for the night. Inhaling a few more times as he turned his head, he was able to locate a direction. The scent hung in the rain, not moving. After three steps toward the intruder, he picked up the pace and blindly ran into the densest area of the bush. Someone having car trouble was the only answer his mind could generate for a person to stop here. No one came without an invitation, and those were few and very far between.

The darkness wasn't a problem, his sight was better in the low light than in the daylight most days. Devin knew each tree and rock on this land, could have run through unscathed, with his eyes closed. The rain was a steady downpour now and hard enough to still land on him despite the thick stands of trees. Without pause, he dodged around a small cluster of trees and knew, without looking to jump—now, or he would stumble over the decaying tree lying on the ground. Landing without a sound he slowed and took the smell of the wild, his wild, inside of him.

How can my mother expect me to give this up? Freedom to be who he was, without any outside interference was what these hundred acres meant to him. There was no part of him that wished to go back to the city where the streetlights blanked out the stars and moon. No, he was staying here for good. Someday soon he had to find the best way to tell his parents that he would pass on the honor of being next in line to the family legacy.

Stopping, Devin turned his face towards the sky, his breath steady despite the run. The rain that the leaves and branches couldn't catch hit him in the face gently, the touch of each drop recharging him, a gift he desperately needed. Pausing, he turned his head towards the back road, the rain was echoing off something normally not here, something not part of his territory. The scent of gardenias was coming from there as well. Turning, he took off running in that direction. Whoever it was, they had better have a damn good reason for trespassing.

Within moments Devin was at the edge of the bush, peering out while staying hidden to assess the intruder. A small white car was parked beside one of the single cabin units. A light was on inside the car and someone was moving around in there. Making sure to stay in the shadows, he circled around until he was closer. He couldn't smell the gardenias over the other wet scents that assaulted him, but he knew the source of the gardenias was inside the car. If he was hearing correctly through the rain she was upset and—talking to herself. *Do I reveal my presence and offer assistance?* Clearly, she was lost and distraught. Why that mattered to him, he didn't know. Cautiously moving closer, Devin watched the movements through the fogging windows. The small car shifted slightly with whatever she was doing in there. If he wasn't going to help, what else was he supposed to do? Stepping out from the trees he moved towards the vehicle. Scaring her any further wasn't going to accomplish anything. He would just have an upset, hysterical and lost female on his property. *That* he didn't need.

The interior light went out but there were more sounds as she moved around. He should leave until morning and check to make sure she found her way out of here. So why was he moving closer to the car? He wasn't sure, but kept going. The headlights came on, momentarily blinding him. When his eyes adjusted, he could see the long blonde hair as the lights on the dash reflected off her. His stomach tightened as he studied her. A blonde that smelled of gardenias was not what he needed in his life right now. Turning, he took a few steps toward the tree line, his head was telling him to keep going and never look back, yet he turned and looked once more. Huffing out a breath that sounded more like a growl, he forced his legs to run back into the shelter of the trees. He was going back to his house and pretend she wasn't there. Throwing his head back, he called to the night.

It didn't answer, not that he had expected it to.

Devin shook his head as he walked back into the house, sending water scattering across the kitchen. It hadn't taken him long to get back, aggravation had goaded him into a full run. She had until daylight to be off his land. No later.

Dropping the wet jeans and shirt that he grabbed off the step, he stomped over to the dresser and pulled out a pair of old sweatpants. The calm he normally felt during a storm had fled, leaving him raging inside with as much intensity as the storm outside. Only one thing was going to help him settle down now.

Anger coursed through Devin as he stomped towards the studio, flinging the doors open. It took only three strides to cross the room and grab a blank canvas from the stack.

With practiced movements, it was up onto the easel. By the time it was prepped he would know what he needed to paint.

Devin's stomach still clenched and he paused in mid-stroke, brush in hand. *Why am I reacting this way? I haven't spoken to her, hell I was barely able to see her. Maybe I have been holed up here a little too long.* Usually he forced himself to go out in public and associate every few weeks. Being alone all the time suited him perfectly, but to maintain a basic level of humanity, he admitted, he needed people around him from time to time.

That made him snort out loud, disgusted with his own behavior. *Whereas my mother was the wolf in the sheep's clothing, I am the prototype of a lone wolf, and plan to stay that way.*

Hands on hips, Devin glared at the canvas. Hours had passed since it was a brilliant empty white and now the image on it caused his throat to clench. *I didn't set out to paint this! Where did this come from? An overactive imagination? Not likely.* The only thing he could blame this on was being celibate for far too long, it was finally affecting his creative thought process.

Swatting the hair back from his eyes, he studied what the brushes had created, and let out a long sigh. The forest was dark, as it had been tonight. The wet and rain on the canvas—he understood where that had come from. It was the ethereal woman standing just far enough outside the tree line, with some unseen light source glowing off her light, smooth complexion that he didn't understand. It was the woman that smelled of gardenias. She was beautiful with long straight blonde hair, which fell almost to her waist, she had the perfect body of petite femininity, with curves that begged to be explored.

The hair color had stemmed from, the truth of what he'd seen and even the sexy body wasn't too hard to picture, he was male after all. It was her eyes that disturbed him the most, causing his stomach to tauten in a pulsing manner. They were light blue, to his artist's eye the truest hue he'd ever glimpsed. In his mind, warning shots were going off, that hue meant something he didn't want to think about. Overall, the painting was extraordinary and pride should be his only feeling with the result. *Then why do I feel like I should rinse the whole damn canvas with paint thinner and then burn it?*

Rolling his shoulders, trying to ease the tension, Devin let out a few calming breaths, he wasn't going to make any decisions right at this moment. Sleeping on it and deciding in the morning sounded reasonable. He looked out the window, the storm seemed to have almost exhausted itself and only drizzle fell sporadically now. Walking from the studio, flicking off every light switch he passed, he just wanted to go to sleep and forget tonight happened.

He thought about taking a shower and rinsing some of the paint off, he always wore what was aimed at the canvas, but he didn't have the energy to bother. Dropping down onto the bed, he looked out the window. Had she calmed down? In the darkness, his face tensed into a scowl, this concern was a very new emotion. Closing his eyes tightly Devin attempted to breathe it away.

Less than a minute later that he was out of the bed, flinging the covers to the floor in frustration. *How am I supposed to sleep with an uninvited stranger on my land? I can't.* Whether she had calmed down wasn't the issue, at least he was trying to convince himself of that. It was the fact that she was here that disturbed him enough to need to check on her. Again.

As Devin headed through the trees for the second time in one night, cursing inside his head with almost each step, he tried to rationalize why. *She could do something crazy, like run her car and die from carbon monoxide poisoning—or something... it's my duty to check on her, after all I don't need a dead blonde woman that smells like gardenias on my hands, or my land.* The internal argument had his brain so distracted, he stumbled over the same trees he'd flawlessly cleared earlier. Anger flared as he rolled his lip back in a snarl for the rest of the distance.

Stopping in the same spot in the trees, he watched the white car. It wasn't lit or running. *Was she all right?* Inhaling deeply, the smell of gardenias filled his nostrils and his stomach spasmed at the exact moment the fragrance hit him. *Why can I smell gardenias now, with her inside the car? Had she gotten out?* This scent was feminine and enticing in a way he didn't recognize. Moving closer cautiously, the scent got stronger. Devin inhaled warmth and had to stop to just absorb the feeling for a few moments.

A foot from the driver's door he noticed she had rolled the window down an inch, no more. That explained how he could smell her so vividly—but didn't she understand how damp she was going to get with the cool night air filtering into the vehicle? More importantly, why did *he* care? He came to make sure she wasn't doing something brainless, and she wasn't, so he should just go home and back to bed, now.

A sound in the trees had him turning and immediately alert. Inhaling the night air, Devin tried to detect what had caused it. No threatening scent, wild or otherwise came back to him. Probably just something shifting and settling from the heavy rain. The trees on this land weren't tamed and manicured, but left it to be what they were meant to be. He moved to the front of the car and listened. There was nothing out there that felt alarming, just the forest, being a forest.

Turning back to the car, he took the floral fragrance into his body once more, not sure why he felt compelled to. His stomach constricted so hard this time he wasn't even sure he was going to be able to go back to the house. *Maybe I should just stay here awhile and keep watch while she rested...*

He shook his head angrily as soon as the thought went through his mind. *What is wrong with me?* She was leaving in the morning, he would make sure of it, so why did it matter that she rest safely tonight? Looking towards the sky, he wished for the rain again. The clouds were rolling away with no more in sight. A small sliver of the moon was visible, it made him long for the full moon, when the forest and lake were alive with life—anything to distract him would be welcome.

Devin turned so he wouldn't look back and ordered his body to follow his nose and go back toward the trees. He'd go get some sleep and when he woke, chances were, she would be gone.

Several steps later he realized he was not heading towards the lake and was not going in the direction of his bed. He moved faster, maybe the long way home would tire him and he'd be able to sleep.

A slight breeze started to blow over his hair and ruffle it, even though it should be impossible at this speed, he could still smell gardenias. It had to be in his head, not real at all, so he was going to pick up the pace and exhaust it right out of there.

Chapter Four

Rayne's eyes popped open as soon as it was light. She heaved out a sigh of relief to see the rain had stopped and it was bright outside the car. For several moments, she struggled with the zipper in the sleeping bag before having enough freedom to sit up. Her body ached. Everywhere. She could definitely confirm that *Cabriolet's* were not comfortable for sleeping. As she started to move about, she realized there were certain priorities to deal with, now.

Finally, the zipper co-operated and Rayne was able to get out of the car in record time. Was she afraid after her wildlife encounter last night? Yes, but the first thing she desperately needed to do was find somewhere to go to the bathroom.

After attempting a few brief, very brief stretches when she fell out of the door extracting her feet from the sleeping bag, she decided her bladder was more important than working out a few kinks. Surveying the area, she looked for anything that might resemble a bathroom. It had been a campground, so surely there would be one somewhere, right? Popping open the trunk, she dug around in the bags until she found a necessary item. Toilet paper would have not been on her list if the boy hadn't tossed it in with the pile of purchases. *Thank goodness for the blue-haired boy.*

Hugging a bottle of water and a roll of toilet paper, Rayne started to move away from where she drove in. It had been raining, but she was almost certain there weren't any buildings hidden in the thick trees she'd passed the night before.

Three small buildings later, chanting inside her head, *please be a bathroom,* she looked through the filth covered windows to find out they were small cabins like the one by the car. She was just convincing herself of the possibility of having to hide behind a tree and try, which she really wasn't sure how, when she spotted a larger building with a faded sign barely hanging above the door. It said showers, which meant there should be a bathroom in there too.

If her brain hadn't been so focused at that moment, the protesting door and the loud squeak it made as she pushed with her whole body to open it, may have frightened her. Rayne was at her wit's end though, so she really didn't have time to be leery, any choice in the matter would be moot only for a few moments longer. The door stayed open enough that a little bit of light filtered into the dirty space.

Old plastic shower curtains hung lifelessly in four shower stalls, she hesitantly peeked in and hoped it was just the dim light and they weren't as dirty as they appeared. Not important right now, she'd go exploring later with the flashlight. Not being a woodsy kind of person she had no idea how long the campground had been abandoned, but the building didn't appear to be decaying as much as neglected, not that she was any sort of expert. As she passed the shower stalls, trying not to notice that is was darker the further into the building she went, relief filled her when five stalls with doors sat just beyond the showers.

Biting her lip, concentrating on not thinking of how much she really needed to pee, she opened one of the stalls. There was a toilet, which spurred a new chant in her head of *please work, please work.* Why are we prone to chant silently at moments like this? She really didn't know, but with no flashlight she was a little concerned with the state of it, unable to make out the condition. She glanced at the small window above and then back down at the toilet. Forget how much she needed to use it, she *had* to see it first. Stretching up on her toes, acknowledging that was a bad movement to make at that moment, Rayne grabbed the handle of the window and threw her weight back, praying it would open. Two more yanks and it popped open, giving way to leaves and dirt that drifted to the floor. It didn't provide as much light as she wanted, but she could see the toilet more clearly now.

She held her breath as she lifted the seat. Nothing appeared to be living in there. *Do I attempt to flush?* Rayne cringed as she pushed the lever down and a loud echoing noise churned through the wall. The water went down. No water refilled it, but that was okay with her right now. She was only a few seconds away from prancing, so she opened the water and splashed it over the seat, setting the bottle down quickly, she used a handful of tissue to wipe it off. Normally she would never have just dropped the handful of damp tissue on the floor, but this wasn't a normal time. Waiting was no longer an option.

As she opened the door again, she felt like she might make it. Well, at least until the next time she had to use the bathroom. Rayne took a few moments and looked around the room, taking more time for details now. There was a door at the end, and feeling a little braver she went over and pulled it open slowly. It was like a large closet with a water tank in it. Sticking her head in, and into cobwebs, she looked around. There were taps, was the solution to running water that simple? She didn't have anything to lose in trying. Stepping all the way in she gripped the top tap and tried to turn it. It wouldn't budge. Maybe she needed a wrench or something, not that she knew how to use one, but they always used one on TV. Rayne gave up and stepped back out again. All of this could wait, right now she just wanted coffee.

She had to backtrack twice to find her way back to the car, obviously, she hadn't paid enough attention on her earlier quest. She did notice how quiet it was, something she hadn't remembered experiencing for a long time. A small squirrel skittered across the path in front of her, and Rayne stopped to watch it run on fast little legs, its tail moving almost as fast as its body when it ran up a tree. Smiling at the tiny creature, it came to her that this may turn out to be a wonderful retreat while she figured out what to do to fix her life.

Rayne stood still, just listening to all the sounds around her. A bird, at least she was almost certain it was a bird made an echoing call that seemed to travel all around her. A steady tap against wood she identified as a woodpecker sounded off behind her. With the breeze blowing, the leaves on the trees could almost be a waterfall. The place was alive with various chirps, tweets and fluttering, just a few of the sounds. In truth, there were so many differences that it could take her an hour or more to sort out each one, and she planned to, just as soon as she had coffee.

Rayne wanted to stomp on the box in her hand. She read the instructions once more for the little converter do-dad thingy. Apparently, she had to select the right voltage, plug it into the car lighter and then she could plug her new travel coffee maker into it. Simple, if she knew what the correct voltage was. She just wanted coffee and would be more than willing to solve puzzles after that.

Opening the box, she went back around to the opened driver's door and plugged it into the lighter outlet and turned back to look at the coffee maker. If she blew it up, she was going to be devastated—no coffee was a very bad thing. Picking up the brewer, Rayne set it on the floor of the car and slowly plugged it in. A light lit up on the converter thing, but that was it. Blowing out a breath, she hoped that meant it was going to function. She had water— now if she just knew where the boy had put the coffee, the world would be right once more.

Going back, she looked in the trunk. She had to take it all out might as well start now. Rayne started pulling things out, still amazed that this much had fit into the car. Besides her clothes, he had packed a tent, a small folding table and chair, and food all squished into a cooler, which could also plug into the converter. There were several cans of food scattered in nooks and crannies to conserve space. She even had an air mattress, and after sleeping in the car last night, it sounded *really* good right now. It plugged into the lighter to be inflated. Who knew a car lighter could do so many things? She felt around under one of the bags of clothes and touched something that felt like a can of coffee, of course she stood there grinning as she pulled it out and hugged it. Coffee. The day was looking better now.

Roughly ten minutes later, Rayne held her travel mug of hot steaming coffee. Inhaling the aroma was almost as gratifying as drinking it. She paused and looked at the mess she'd made pulling out a bit of this and a few of that. Was she looking forward to setting up her little camp? Yes, now she was. It could be fun. The boy had saved all the instructions, so it should be fairly simple to set up. She turned around and tried to decide, while savoring the coffee, where she was going to set up her tent. He'd said something about the morning sun, but she couldn't remember for sure. Shelter it from the sunrise or face the sunrise? Wouldn't it be better to have the warm sun at dawn? *Oh, dawn light.* So, the East—she should make sure it wasn't in the open to the East. Turning in a complete circle, she frowned, if she knew which way was East, it would be easier. Had she bought a compass? Honestly, she didn't know. He had been packing stuff and ringing it up all while she stood there wondering if she should even be thinking of camping alone.

Not ready to admit she was awake enough to work, Rayne wandered over to the little building and pushed the door open. She didn't step inside, just remained standing outside looking in. It was very dirty from what she could see. There were a few areas where daylight showed through the holes in the walls. Rayne sipped the coffee while debating on cleaning and using it instead of the tent. No, that would be too easy and a waste of money. The sales boy had told her to keep the food locked away from where she slept, so it didn't attract animals—an idea she didn't want to think about and the little cabin seemed the best place to store it all. It would be easier than digging around in the car every time she wanted something. She could even use it with the little table and chair if weather turned stormy again.

Nodding at her first definite idea of the day, Rayne went to pull out the small stack of instruction sheets. *How hard can it be to set up one tent? Can't be that difficult, right?*

With sweat dripping down her forehead Rayne stood back and eyed the results. *Is it supposed to lean like that?* It had not been as simple as the instructions had implied. Two people probably would have made it easier. Each time she had the one side of the little collapsible poles all in place, she'd go around and hook the other one into its hole and then the first side would jump out and tip over again. At first, she was sure she'd been sold a defective product, but she finally managed to get it upright, mostly. That was when she noticed the entire top of it was screened, but her heart settled back down when she fit the fly thing over the top. Why they didn't just put a roof on was beyond her.

Staking it had been a whole different event, after several attempts, she dragged it close to the little building and tied two of the strings to a post so it wouldn't blow away. Buying a hammer would have been a great idea, well, if she'd known what it took to put the stakes into the ground. For a few brief moments, she debated on tying the other strings to her car, but as she'd already cheated by using the building she wanted to at least partially comply with the instructions. A rock had solved the lack of a hammer, even though the boy had told her to just step on the stakes. Did they need to be completely in the ground? Hopefully not. Either she wasn't heavy enough to use his step technique, or the ground was unusually hard and no amount of hammering was going to push them all the way in. Despite a few little kinks, she had her tent.

It didn't look overly large on the inside and she wondered if the air mattress was going to fit. Glancing at the sky, Rayne decided she should probably clean the little storage cabin next, just in case another storm came through. Somewhere in the car was a hand broom and dustpan. The boy had just smirked at her, saying there wasn't much need to sweep while camping, Rayne felt some gratification knowing he had been wrong about something. Of course, locating it in the clutter of items that were half in the car and piled on the ground was going to take a few minutes of searching.

She hadn't bought cleansers, not even thinking she'd need them, and she was sure the blue haired boy didn't think of cleaning often. How she was going to clean the very dirty window of the cabin? Rayne didn't want to waste her bottled water to do it, which brought her back to trying to turn the taps again in the shower building. She couldn't help laughing at herself, she was a list person and it brought her a small measure of comfort when she decided she needed to start a list to keep things in priority.

As she swept out the building, Rayne realized she was enjoying all of this. Just her and the wilderness, she was roughing it. She giggled, okay, so not including all the luxuries the car lighter brought, she was roughing it as much as she ever would.

By noon the little cabin was all clean and the table was set up inside with her laptop and camera on it. The precious coffee maker earned a place indoors. Her bags were neatly organized. She hadn't bothered to remove the cases with her fancier clothes in the trunk of her car. She doubted it would offend the squirrels if she didn't dress for dinner. She had a list too, it made her feel better having one. On the list, in addition to the water tap and exploring the immediate area was a reminder to start the car for a few minutes after using the converter and car lighter. The last thing she needed was to be stuck here with a dead battery. Bonus camper points for just thinking of that.

Deciding she'd earned a break, Rayne sat in the camping chair beside her tent eating a granola bar and apple. She had the book of plants she'd bought open in her lap, but preferred looking around at the real versions. The few items she had managed to identify that were nearby were a great likeness though. The only reason she had bought it was the mention of poison ivy had her wanting to know if there were any other poisonous plants she should be aware of. It wouldn't be good to end up with a rash out here by herself.

Looking up at the sky, she wondered if there would be a breeze any time soon. She felt hot and sticky after everything she'd done, and dirty in a most uncomfortable way. The water tap was at the top of the list for a reason, she had to find a way to bathe. Was there a lake around? Would she be brave enough to go in if she did find one? She didn't know about that just yet, but this had already been a day of many firsts for her, so it was entirely possible.

Break time over, Rayne got up, she had too much to do and a whole new world to explore.

Chapter Five

Devin strode through the bush, anger fueling his stride. He had only managed an hour of solid sleep well after dawn and was irritated—to put it mildly. After he'd shaken the fog from his brain he'd opened the door and inhaled deeply, only to smell gardenias and fresh brewed coffee. His trespasser hadn't moved on. He was going to make sure she did.

Today. Now.

He slowed when he was closer to her car and listened. Humming? She was humming and talking to herself, unlike the version of her last night. Anger bubbled through his veins. He was exhausted and annoyed and here she was, humming away like she didn't have a care in the world. Devin crossed the last twenty feet to the edge of the tree line and stopped. Glancing around he saw she had moved her car. Beside the cabin was a grey tent that from the looks of it, wouldn't make it through a good gust of wind. Shaking his head, he was able to hear her but not see her. She had to be in the cabin. *Moving right in wasn't she? Why was she still here? I could smell her fear last night and if she was that frightened and distraught, why is she setting up camp? Worse still, why was she here?*

Stepping out into the open, he moved toward the cabin. The smell of her sweat mixed with gardenias burned his nostrils, not a bad thing. His body stirred in ways that caused him to pause and stand there puzzled with his reaction. Yes, it had been many months, he wasn't sure how many, since he'd been with a woman, even near a woman, but the scent making his body respond and harden with wanting, shocked him. He didn't like being caught off-guard and that pissed him off even more.

Shaking off the feeling, Devin moved towards the cabin again. He was two feet from it when she came through the door and shrieked, dropping whatever she'd been carrying to the ground with a loud clatter.

Huge, pale blue eyes looked at him. "Oh! I'm...I..." she swallowed and placed a hand over her heart. "I didn't know someone else was here."

Those eyes were the ones from the painting. *How?* "I live here." His voice was so deep it surprised him. Clearing his throat, he tried again. "My question is, what are *you* doing here on my property?" Her long blonde hair was the same shade he had painted it and that annoyed him too.

She hugged her waist and stepped out the door. "I... you own this?" She looked around quickly. "All of this?" Her voice was a soft appealing whisper.

He didn't recognize the accent she spoke with but found that appealing as well, and didn't want to.

"I was told it was abandoned..."

Trying to keep his hands off her, Devin placed them on his hips and scowled down at her. "By whom?" He tried to ignore the smudge of dirt on her pale cheek. He shoved his hands into his back pockets before he did something stupid like lean over and wipe it off. *Did she have to smell so damn enticing?*

"A boy, uh, man that worked at a store..."

Her scent was making his blood hum through his body at an accelerated rate. Devin cocked an eyebrow at her. "Blue, spiked hair?"

She nodded, her eyes lighting up. "Yes. You know him?"

Sighing an annoyed breath, he studied her. "Yes, and sending you here would be *his* way of riling me." He found himself stepping closer, even though he told his legs no. When he stopped, he was only a half foot away from her, and it took every ounce of restraint to not move any closer.

She stood there looking at him, panic in her eyes. Part of him wanted to reach out and pull her into his arms. Crossing his arms over his chest, Devin attempted to maintain an annoyed look.

"Oh. I'll leave." Her eyes skimmed over her tent and then back to him. "Just give me..." She moved by him with quick jerky movements and went to her car. The trunk popped open as the keys jingled in her hands. "I'll p-pack up now," she whispered with a voice filled with so much emotion Devin's chest suddenly felt tight.

Devin could smell her fear, how distraught she was at the thought of leaving. He watched her flip her long hair over her shoulder as she bent to move something in the trunk. The jeans tightened across the most appealing ass he'd ever seen. Uncrossing his arms, he started to move towards her. Clenching his jaw, he stopped. "Fine," he barked at her and then turned back to the trees.

He ordered his body to keep moving and come back later to make sure she'd cleared out. It was only a short moment later that he realized he had only circled the area, and was in no way moving away from her. Stopping, he huffed out a breath and leaned against the nearest tree. Watching through the trees, Devin could still see her. He could smell her too, and his body tightened when her scent wafted by his nose and into his system. That was just what he needed, a throbbing hard on from a small appealing woman that clearly had a lot of issues. *What am I now, a teenager? I can control my own body—or had been able to until I'd smelled those god damned gardenias through my window last night!*

Crossing his arms again, he leaned back to watch. She had all the doors on the car open and was leaning over the hood of the car looking at what he assumed was a map. She sniffled and wiped a shaking hand over her face. She was crying, and for some unknown reason that called to him. The urge to go and shelter her, promising he'd make her world right again came over him. That scared him, to have thoughts like that about a woman he'd never met before. His mind wandered back to the painting he'd created last night. *How was I able to paint an exact likeness without having seen her?*

Devin ran his hand through his hair in frustration and continued to watch her. So many questions plagued him. She was standing beside her car, looking around with her back to him, but he could see her shoulders shaking. *Dammit all to hell!* He started walking back. The scent of gardenias has apparently turned him into a soft-hearted pup.

As he approached he could smell her tears. Devin could sense her confusion, she didn't know what to do. The idea of her being alone and upset gnawed at him in a way he didn't think he'd ever felt. *What is going on with me? Yesterday everything had been normal, and now everything I thought I knew is unclear.*

Chapter Six

Tears ran down her face, but she didn't care. *What am I going to do?* She didn't know where to go and wasn't sure if she wanted to go somewhere else. Here, she was hidden and out of Aiden's reach. The man that had just appeared out of nowhere had scared her half out of her mind and now she had to start over. Again.

Taking a shaky breath, she wiped her hands over her wet face and turned back towards the cabin. Rayne froze. He was coming back and looked angrier than he had before. Not knowing what else to do, she just stood there as he came towards her, his long legs eating up the distance in no more than a few seconds.

He went over to the tent and undid one of the ropes she'd tied to the building. Rayne just stood there, shocked. She knew she was technically trespassing, but hadn't she just told him she'd leave? Not sure what else to do she went over and tried to pull the rope out of his hand. "I can take it down, thank you." He stopped and looked down at her, not releasing the rope or pulling it from her hand. He stood like that for an eternity, even though it was probably only a few seconds. Rayne swallowed, not feeling as certain now.

As he stepped closer she moved to take a step back. He

tilted his head to the side and studied her for another tense moment. "I'm fixing it," he finally said, so quietly it took her a second to realize what he'd said.

She let go of the rope and looked up into grey eyes, which felt so familiar she almost forgot that she didn't know the man. "Fixing it?" she finally managed to mumble. He turned away from her and continued to do something with the rope as he spoke over his shoulder.

"If it storms again, the way you have it, there's a good chance you're going to blow away or get very wet..."

Rayne stepped around him so she could see his face and those eyes again. "I thought you wanted me to leave?" *Did I miss something?*

Stopping, he sighed. "I may have been a bit—abrupt." He looked at her and the expression in his eyes completely contradicting the hardness etched on his face. "Stay for a few days if you need to." He motioned to the cabin. "If the storms get severe, as they often do at this time of year, hide out in there until it passes or your car..." He looked at the car for a moment and then shook his head. "Probably better off in the cabin." With a jerky movement, he bent down and pulled up a stake that had taken her too long to beat into the ground. With quick, sure movements he slipped the rope through it and shoved it back into the ground completely, with just his hand.

Rayne stood there without comment as he repeated the action with the other three ropes. He was used to being outside, she could tell by the way he moved, as if he were part of the natural landscape that surrounded them. When he finished and came to stand near her, she hadn't moved while watching him. She could only watch, not sure if she should speak in case she said the wrong thing and made him change his mind.

He was silent too, giving her more time to notice more than his drawing eyes. He had high cheek bones and a square jaw, her first thought as silly as it was, was he looked like a beautiful animal with an untamed wildness beneath. She blinked, realizing her thoughts were bordering on crazy.

"There's a shower in the small building by the East end, near the lake—the water is on there." The expression on her face must have told him that she had no clue which way was East, or where the lake was, as he gave her an odd look and then pointed in toward the east. "My place is up the hill over on the Nor..." he pointed in another direction, "that way. You stay clear of my place and I don't see us having any problems." He paused and then reached forward so slowly it was as if he was afraid his hand was going to pass right through her. His thumb brushed gently down over her cheek, his fingers tickling against the side of her neck as he did, as a tingling sensation spread through her. "You may want to check that shower out sooner rather than later." With that he dropped his hand and backed up a few feet. Nodding once he turned and started to walk back into the trees.

Wait! She blinked and then rushed after him. "Thank you," she added quickly. "My name is Rayne, by the way." He stopped so suddenly she almost walked into his back. Turning slowly, he looked down at her. "Th-thank you," she said again, not knowing why he was giving her such an odd look.

"Rayne?" He finally asked with a deep whisper. She nodded, wondering if she should thank him again or just leave it there. He smirked, at least she thought it was a smirk and shook his head. He muttered something under his breath and she wasn't positive, but it sounded like 'that figures'.

Clearing his throat, he looked from the ground to her face. "Devin." Then before she could respond, he turned and disappeared into the trees without another word. Rayne stood there for much longer than she intended, looking into the trees that had just swallowed him.

Still glancing back at the trees, she went over to the car. *What had just happened?* She had no idea, but wasn't going to follow him to ask. Closing the car door, she groaned when she saw her own reflection in the window. She looked like she'd been rolling around in the dirt. Well, that helped her understand his shower comment. Shower, oh, she was heading to check that out before she did anything else.

She went into the cabin to find what she'd need. Despite being startled by Devin appearing out of nowhere and barking at her one minute only to turn around and be nice to the next, it hadn't stopped her from appreciating just how gorgeous he was. His height wasn't a surprise, most people were taller than her five foot five, but his wonderfully wide shoulders that had tapered to a perfect waist had been—nice. If she wasn't in the middle of a minor breakdown she'd have bet that he had one of those squeezable butts too. His eyes had been haunting, the pale shade was closer to grey than blue and they had seemed vaguely familiar, and she had no idea why. No one she knew had eyes even remotely similar. She'd figure this out later, right now she was more than ready for a shower to rid herself of the dust and smell.

Chapter Seven

Devin paced by the painting for what was probably the fiftieth time. *Stupid! Stupid! Stupid! What the hell is wrong with me? I went there to get rid of her and instead I fixed her tent and gave her free run of my space.* He stopped and stared at the painting, the exact image of the woman he had just spoke to. Rayne? Not, rain, but the way she pronounced it, Rayne. The summer storm had brought Rayne, which was too ironic—even for him.

He stepped directly in front of the painting and leaned in until he was looking at her face. He squinted at it. *How? How the hell did I paint her so precisely?* It was as if he'd been holding a photo of her in the other hand. *What the hell was going on?* Did he want to know, probably not, but he *was* going to find out.

His eyes, without permission, skimmed over the image of her body. He'd gotten each curved proportion dead on, but that wasn't what had his guts churning like a tornado. This feeling was caused by her eyes. They were so pale, so reflective, so *not* the color normal humans had. *Am I being paranoid?* Most likely. He knew ordinary humans had blue eyes, but hers weren't the normal blue, just as his weren't any typical hue for humans. Yet, he couldn't help but be drawn to

47

her eyes and wonder. His clan had pale eyes, the purebreds that was, and he'd never seen anyone not a part of his gene pool with a shade so pale. *That* shade. He glared at the canvas again.

Shaking his head, Devin tried to rid it of the ridiculous thoughts. He stomped over to the window and leaned on the sill, looking out trying to find peace. *Perfect!* He'd told her where the lake and shower were and now, as he looked out the window to stop thinking about her, there she was, walking along the shore on her way to the shower. His body hardened just seeing her. He looked down, as if it were a foreign thing. Judging by the bulge in the front of his jeans, his body *really* liked her. "What is going on?" He shook his head again, and looked back out the window. "Who are you and why are you messing with me, just by existing?"

Devin scowled as she went into the building. *Dare I open the window, or will I smell her again?* Never having been a flower man, one smelled as sweet as the next, so why did he know she smelled of gardenias and why did it get to him the way it did? Hesitantly, he opened the window and inhaled a quick snort. No gardenias. Good. Fine. That was more like it. So, if he didn't want to smell her or see her, why was he still standing here watching for her to come out of the building? He backed away a few feet, but his traitorous eyes were looking out the pane of glass. *I'm losing my bloody mind, that's it. My mother was right and being here alone this long has affected me adversely.* He drew his brows together to the point it was uncomfortable. The last thing he was going to do was admit his mother was right about anything. Doing that was the same as waving a sign and telling her to start hooking him up with every damned woman that had potential to further their line. Huffing out a loud breath, knowing, just knowing he was on the right track with that thought.

Rolling his shoulders, he tried to get the tension to drop away. He took a few relaxed steps then found himself perched against the window ledge, not to watch for her, just to lounge and think this through. "When I'm ready, I'll find my own woman." He crossed his arms and nodded. "If she's not one of my own, then that's fine." He shrugged, "My sister's mate was accepted and he isn't one of us." Devin rubbed a hand over his forehead. His mind was going in ten directions and he didn't like it. He'd originally left because of women of his own kind. He'd gone away to gain control and a new perspective until he was ready to find a mate that *he* wanted—not just because his body said to. He looked back towards the shower building where the petite Rayne was still inside. "You're undoing my resolve, Rayne. I can't be messing with you and keep my word at the same time." He ran a hand through his hair hoping it would help to settle his mind. She had him so messed up he wasn't able to think straight. "You're not my kind. I'd smell it if you were." He looked back down at the building. "*But* the way you smell does something to me, and until I know why you are going to stay out of my head." He snorted. "Devin, you've lost it and should go back to bed and stay there until your brain has returned." He wasn't in the habit of talking out loud to himself.

Just as he started to turn away from the window a scent drifted in the window. Gardenias, and it was much stronger than before. His vision zoomed to the building to see her standing and looking out at the lake. She was only wearing a towel! *Why hadn't she taken clothes? She couldn't just wander around in a towel for god's sake!* Even as he told his head to turn away, he was taking in every inch of flesh he could see. She had legs that were perfectly shaped and just the right length. Put some heels on those and just her legs alone would be able to stop traffic and have every male mesmerized. *A perfect ass wasn't enough? She had to have legs that I'd love to lick and caress.* His already hard erection pulsed at the thought.

She turned and headed back up the path and he was almost leaning out the window, just to get a closer look. *Dammit!* He turned and headed towards the door. He wasn't going to go see her or get close, he was just—what? Going to spy on her? Ogle her? *I have to figure out why she was getting to me, right?* To do that he'd have to observe her. It was a flimsy reason, but it was the only one he could come up with as he hit the bush at a brisk jog and headed to the spot in the trees he knew she'd have to pass to get back to her car. He paused long enough to pull his shirt over his head. Hanging it quickly on a branch, he unbuckled his belt and worked to make his jeans quickly follow. He muttered a curse when his jeans hit the boots, still on his feet. As he plucked them off and tossed the jeans on top, he wished that movies were the truth and shifting with clothes on was a possibility. Unfortunately, shifting while still dressed didn't turn out that way, the clothes did not stretch, adapt or magically dissolve. Instead they ripped, got tangled in body parts not meant to fit them or just hurt, period.

He smirked before turning to head through the thick treed area. By the time he'd gone no more than four feet, almost at a run, all four paws working with smooth precise motion to take him close enough to see her without being seen. This time he remembered and jumped in time to clear the downed tree without stumbling. As he reached the area he'd been heading to, he stopped and sniffed the air to scent where she was. He'd gotten here before her. Crouching low, he moved over to stand behind the largest trunk in the area, hiding himself in a dark spot, so she could pass without seeing him. Devin focused on his breathing and made sure he wasn't panting loud enough that she might hear.

When he was positive he was hidden, noise moved up the path. She'd thought to wear her shoes with the towel, as the ground echoed her steps. Quickly, he moved down to the ferns covering the ground, almost lying down so he wouldn't be visible even if she was looking around. Hopefully he'd succeeded as he wasn't a small creature to hide. A long piece of the fern was in front of his face, so he had to swipe at it with his nose a few times before he could see under. Briefly, he thought of how ridiculous he looked, a wolf hiding under ferns to spy on an almost naked woman. He thought he should get up and go back to the house and was just about to move when the smell of gardenias filled his senses and he froze. Even in this form she got to him. This wasn't a good thing. He was in control of his wolf, but animal instincts were hard to override, even by someone that had practiced for over a decade.

Devin watched the ground and saw her feet and the cute little white running shoes on them as she stepped in his direction. He moved his eyes, keeping his chin close to the ground and leisurely took in those legs from this perfect height. They were as he'd thought and probably the most appealing, shapely legs ever. She had those cute womanly knees and sexy thighs. He looked at the bottom of the towel and swallowed, she'd stopped with her back to him and was looking at something on the other side of the path.

He swallowed again slowly and let his eyes take in the back of her thighs. If he'd thought she wouldn't freak right out, he'd dart out of his hiding spot, grab that towel and yank it off. The thought evaporated when she bent over slightly to touch one of the... he couldn't even remember what the damn wildflower was called right now, as he got a brief peak of that perfect ass—without a stitch on. Devin knew his jaw was open and his tongue most definitely was hanging out as he could taste fern, but he couldn't move. He was only able to follow her movement with his eyes as she walked right by him, continuing to her little camping area.

He was still lying there when she was out of sight. This was all wrong. His reaction wasn't normal at all. Okay, some of it was very normal, he was male, whether in animal or human form–but this dizzying rush he got just looking at her was, well, he didn't know what, but knew he'd never felt it before.

Huffing out a breath, he finally stood back up and turned to where he'd left his clothes. He looked once in the direction he knew she would be, wanting nothing more than to follow her, just sit and watch —for the rest of the day. He shook his head. No, he was taking his furry ass back to the house and calling his father. If anyone would know what the hell was wrong with him, it would be his father. He is, after all, the alpha and ruler of not just the pack but the entire shifter world, so he would know, wouldn't he?

It was rare that Devin spoke to his father about anything related to their kind. It had always been a sore spot between them. He'd fought being the next in line to take over the pack, but today he needed fatherly wisdom and advice—or answers—before he lost his mind completely. The fact that he was willing to swallow his pride, pride that the Addison family was notorious for, and seek guidance from someone showed he was neck deep in some kind of trouble.

After dressing, he wandered back to the house at a leisurely pace, not wanting to rush and make the call. Just by taking that first step and calling his father, Devin would be giving in to what they wanted for him, in a small way. This alone caused the procrastination. He knew his parents wanted him to step into his so called rightful place as alpha of the pack. If it were just that, Devin may have already agreed by now. By taking over the wolf pack, he was also stepping into the role as the ruler of the Shifter Alliance.

He knew the history behind the Alliance and was all for it, Devin just didn't know if he was *the* one to take on the enormous responsibility. His father believed he was being wise to stop and consider all aspects. Mother's take on it was that he was being irresponsible.

Devin's sister had taken the easy way out. She had mated with a non-shifter, or a one-form as most shifters called them, as they only had one form. He could do that and marry a one-form too, hopefully he would love that person wholly as his sister, Raquel, did. To mate with one of his own left Devin no choice but to take the succession that was his fathers to give. He didn't like having his options removed any more than he liked to think he would take the easy way out.

The shifter world hadn't always been so organized and peaceful. He shook his head, peace was still something that was hard fought for with infighting constantly flaring up among the varying clans in the many species. In the time of his great-grandparents, and for most of his grandparents' lives, each were out for their own. After too many years of bloodshed with certain species being close to extinct, it was decided that the Alliance was necessary to protect them in their human and animal forms from one-forms, hunters and at times the different clans.

It took years to establish the Alliance of the clans. Each clan had a leader and a sub-leader, both of whom were part of the council, but just one clan would rule as the monarch and be *the* ruler of the Alliance. He'd always found it odd that the wolves ended up being the ones elected for this honor. Odd in the way that he knew most of the larger shifters could probably tromp him into the ground when in his wolf form, well, if they could catch him and get past him biting their limbs off. Possibly that was the reason the wolves reigned, their cunning was far more advantageous than the quick temper and brute strength of the larger forms.

Devin glanced up to see his door only a few feet away and regretted that he'd reached it so soon. Yes, he was a Prince in hiding. He could *not* make this phone call and just allow the next in line to take his place, then he thought of his selfish, arrogant cousin, Leon, and Devin made the choice to open the door and go make the call.

With a beer in hand, Devin stared at the phone that he'd just hung up. His father had understood and been tactful enough to not rub it in his face that finally he needed dear old dad. He took another long swig of the beer and swallowed quickly. The fact that he didn't like the answer wasn't the problem. The problem was that he *really* hadn't liked the answers, even though his gut told him that his father was right, and now he didn't know what to do. He didn't like it when he wasn't in control of something and Devin was definitely not in control of this.

He slid further down on the couch and leaned his head back against it. Closing his eyes, Devin thought of the highlights of the conversation, hoping he'd missed something that would prove he had a choice. *'Does she smell like pack, son?"* He'd had to confess he had been afraid to get close enough to smell her, that all he could say for sure was Rayne smelled like gardenias. His father had chuckled and told him that was close enough. *How the hell did smelling like gardenias come close to smelling like pack?* He'd figure that part out later. Devin had asked if he could think of any other reason for her to affect him so completely, other than the reason he didn't want to hear. His father had chuckled again, not something he'd ever done *that* often but he told him no, even if he'd been without sex for a decade—*not happening*—no ordinary woman would get to him that way. That range of emotions was the way he'd tastefully put it. *That was an understatement. In a matter of a few hours I wanted to hug and hold her, shelter and protect her, follow her every movement, fuck her and adore every inch of her in a non-sexual way.* Those emotions were more than enough to deal with.

Devin opened his eyes and drank what was left in the bottle in one swallow. *"You've found your true mate from the sounds of it, Devin, and you can't change that. Only you can decide if you want to bond with her completely or not… if she'll have you."* That was not the answer he wanted. "But she's not one of us." Had been the only defense he had and it was a weak one at that. *"She could be— I'm fairly certain she must be, or you, being who you are, would not react this way."* Again, not even close to what he wanted to hear his father and alpha say. "How can you be sure?" That was when his father had started laughing before he'd regained his composure and cleared his throat to continue. *"You couldn't send her away, could you?"* No, had come out of Devin's mouth, sulky in a way he'd never heard from his own voice. *"I've never known you to have a soft spot for anyone, son, have you?"*

Devin gripped the bottle tight in his hand. *Well, fuck! I have a mate and she smells like gardenias.* Now he sat there trying to figure out if he should go back to bed and try to wake up from this nightmare, or go roll around at her feet and hope she rubbed his belly.

He tipped the bottle back up to his mouth and then remembered it was empty. Lowering it again, he glared. "What if I don't want a mate?" Years ago he had thought that was what he'd wanted, but that fantasy had long ago faded away. One of his best friends had found their mate and had died because of it. He'd seen too many males from the pack, and the rest of the shifter clans lose everything because of a mate that wouldn't accept them. Why was it up to the female? He didn't know. What if he went to her and she rejected him?

Lowering the bottle into his lap, he rolled his head to the side to look at the window. She was out there and the only question pounding inside his skull was did he want her to be? He didn't know. Hormones aside, he honestly didn't know if he wanted to go find out if she was his, or if she was one of his kind and knew it. What he was, Devin decided, was a mess.

The only thing he could do to prevent this disaster from destroying his world was to control it. She was not going to get to him—he was in control. It would be *him* who decided if mating was going on the program, and it would be him and no one else that chose when it would happen.

Chapter Eight

Rayne wandered around exploring after her shower. She'd taken so many pictures she wasn't sure what she would do with all of them. Maybe a photo journal to remember, not that she was likely to forget discovering her fiancé was a thug and then deciding to flee from him. She stopped and looked at the path, wishing she had brought the plant book. For a short second, she debated on asking Devin what some of the plants were, but that would be bothering him and he'd made it quite clear she was to stay far from him.

She headed back towards the camp, deciding to download the pictures onto her laptop and begin a journal. Was there a power outlet at the shower building? Sitting by the lake felt like something she wanted to do. Rayne checked the sky, the clouds off in the distance were nothing to worry about, she hoped.

After she changed into shorts, Rayne gathered her laptop and a blanket then headed for the lake. She stopped when it was in view, wondering how she hadn't realized how big it really was. Not just large but beautiful as well, so serene it wasn't at all surprising that Devin had been upset when she'd trespassed on his land. She wouldn't want to share this with just anyone, either.

Delighted when she found an outlet at the front of the building, she plugged in and set the laptop on the blanket, then sat down to upload the pictures, looking out over the lake. Not taking pictures now would be insane. She walked to the shore, pausing to smile at a family of ducks. They didn't seem bothered by her presence, so she wasn't going to get in their way. Rayne snapped a few pictures of the young ones following mom, she presumed, around in the water in a scattered line. A few ducks landed in the water just away from the family, so she took pictures of them.

Aiming to the opposite shoreline, she began to snap, bringing the focus in and out to get in as many angles as she could. Just as she thought she'd taken enough, a movement on the far side caught her attention. Lowering the camera, she noticed someone in a canoe was heading across the lake. She lifted the camera to zoom in on them. Her breath caught in her throat when she realized it was Devin. He was paddling with long, sure, strong strokes, she hesitated as she noticed that he didn't have a shirt on, before snapping the picture. She didn't want to impose, so she didn't take any more pictures, just used the camera to look at him from this safe distance.

Rayne zoomed the lens in further so she could see his face, the sweat on his brow. He looked troubled, as if he was thinking very deeply about something. The canoe was going fast enough to ruffle his hair as he moved through the water. His hair wasn't scruffy but it wasn't the short, neat haircuts she was used to seeing on men. It fell and framed his face when he put his head down as the canoe coasted through the water in a straight line. He really was very nice to look at. She took a chance and aimed the camera down to look at the rest of him. His sculpted chest was rising and falling as he caught his breath, he had really been working to move through the water at that speed. His arms were just as developed as his chest and for a fanciful second she wondered what it would be like to be held in those strong arms. Heat moved through her as she blushed at her thoughts. *Aren't you in hiding because of a man?* He lifted his head again and started to paddle, slower this time. *Well, it doesn't hurt to just look, does it?* She smiled at that thought as she continued to watch him through the lens.

He stopped paddling and looked right at her. She froze, not lowering the camera. There was no doubt he could see her, those grey eyes were looking right at her. Not sure what else to do, Rayne lowered the camera but continued to stand there and look out at him. He was heading in her direction. *Of course he was, dummy, this is the shore and he'd have to come here wouldn't he?* Did she pack up and run back to her tent or stay? It would be rude to run and hide and she didn't want to be rude. Suddenly nervous, she went back over to the blanket and sat down.

She wasn't going to sit and watch him as he moved closer to the shore, she told herself over and over. Even as she lifted her eyes from the laptop screen to glance in his direction, she tried to convince herself she wasn't watching him, she was just looking around. It took a lot of focus to continue to work on her laptop when he was close enough she could hear him moving through the water. Rayne kept importing the pictures into a folder labelled with the date and tried not to hold her breath, knowing he was almost at the shore now. She was glad for her long hair, it allowed her to look at him and he couldn't catch her.

He maneuvered the canoe onto the shore, bringing it far enough in to not step in the water. Rayne flicked her eyes away from the skin on display and back to the screen for a few seconds. As he was stepping onto the shore she was watching. *There* was a man that made jeans and bare feet work. With one hand, he held the paddle and reached down and picked up the canoe and pulled it completely from the water with the other. It was either really light or he was that strong, she decided it was probably the latter. Not knowing whether to greet him or wait and see if he spoke first, Rayne lowered her head to look at the pictures on the screen. She could hear him moving the canoe and had just begun to think he was going to ignore her, when she was sitting in his shadow. She looked up slowly, trying not to linger on his body before she reached his face. "Hi," she whispered, "sorry to intrude," she motioned to the plug, "I needed power."

He continued to stand silently, looking down at her. She couldn't figure out what the look on his face meant. It wasn't anger, but he didn't look happy with her either. "Is..." she cleared her throat hoping to locate her voice "Is that okay? I'm working on a photo journal..."

"Of?" He finally said.

She looked around the lake and then back at him. "All of this, the trees, animals, plants it's all so beautiful."

"Are you a photographer?"

She bit her lip, shaking her head. "Not professionally, but I can take a good photo or at least recognize them. I am—was, the manager of an art museum." His eyebrows shot up, but it wasn't surprise in his eyes, more like amusement.

"Mind if I take a look?"

A little surprised at his request she hesitated. "Uh—no, not at all." He squatted down beside her as she took a few seconds to drag her eyes away from his sweat covered chest. Coming back to reality she jerked the laptop, adjusting the screen so he could see it as well. "I haven't edited any yet, I was just sorting." She clicked the first one of the trees she'd strolled through. "I'll use the crop and adjust the focus to highlight a bit here and there..." Rayne stopped when he reached across her and hit the arrow key to bring up the next one. His arm was close enough that she could feel heat from it. She held her breath, waiting.

"Good eye," he said quietly.

He was much closer than she realized, for when she turned to look at him his face was only a few inches from hers as he continued to scroll through the photos. She could smell his musky scent, mixed with sweat and had never realized until this moment that the smell held an appeal. Her heart skittered around in her chest. Glancing at his mouth, she wondered what it would be like to be kissed by him. Her eyes were still studying his lips as they turned into a half smirk. Looking back to his eyes, she felt a flush of embarrassment realizing he was watching her while she'd been staring at him.

"Do you swim?" He asked.

She raised both eyebrows at him in question, not sure how that related to the photos. "Yes." *Why is my voice so breathy?* He watched her and she wanted him to, even though she didn't know why.

"You should take some photos from the middle of the lake, you'd get some great shots."

She nodded, not even sure she could trust her voice.

"Do you know how to canoe?" She shook her head. He smirked again. "It's fairly simple. You just paddle and that controls the direction you travel."

Rayne nodded again, still not wanting to speak. He had a soothing voice, she'd heard the bark too, but this—this was much more pleasant. He reached out and moved the hair back from her face with a feather light touch that she was certain happened in slow motion. Her skin tingled just from that brief contact.

"Maybe practice near the shore before you go out too far."

She swallowed. "Okay." He dropped his hand and she felt the loss of his touch. Watching as he straightened up slowly, she made sure to stay right where she was, not wanting to embarrass herself further.

"Enjoy the sun." He looked up at the sky. "The storms will be here by dark."

He continued to stand there and just look at her for a few more moments, but she couldn't figure out what he was thinking. She knew she needed to say something. "Thank you—for everything." Setting the laptop beside her, she knelt there at his feet looking up at him. A strange look crossed his face so briefly she wasn't sure it was real, before he nodded and backed up a step, and then another, not looking anywhere but into her eyes. When he turned and walked the other way she felt let down.

Rayne just sat like a statue watching him walk away. She felt lightheaded and wondered if it was from the sun. Instantly she frowned, it wasn't the sun—it had been the man. The muscles on his back twitched with each step as he moved further away. She allowed herself to look, her eyes wandering down over his jeans. She'd been right about something at least, he did have one of those cute butts that you just wanted to grab. Inhaling deeply, she then blew it out. That was one potent, sexy man. "*Not* what you need to be thinking about right now, Rayne," she looked back down at the laptop and noticed he'd left it open on the picture of him in the canoe. Tilting her head to the side she studied it. It was a good picture, the distant shore in the background and the strong silent man paddling. A picture said a thousand words and these were all words she should not be contemplating. Strong, sexy, appealing, and delicious—words she needed to strike from her mind.

She needed to change the picture or look away, she forced her eyes to look at the canoe. *Could I do that?* He'd made it look so easy, so she knew right then that it wouldn't be. She could do what he'd said and practice near the shore, just see if she wanted to take it out any further. Practicing with the canoe was added to her list, but not for today. Soon though. Forcing her attention back to her laptop screen, she started flipping back through the picture.

Chapter Nine

Devin found himself by the window watching her. She had her head down, bent over the laptop, that long silky hair hanging down over one shoulder and cradling the other side of her face. She was breath-taking. He hadn't even made it to the shower before he found his feet carrying to the window to watch her.

Taking a few minutes to speak gave him more information than he had earlier, so he couldn't be annoyed with her for being on the shore when he'd returned. He now knew, without a doubt, that he affected her just as much as she did him. He could smell her desire, practically taste her pulse when he'd squatted down beside her. It had taken all his control to not lay her down right there and taste her mouth, which is why he'd gotten the hell out of there. His brain had provided too many images when he'd stood there as she knelt before him like a tempting offer.

Shaking his head, Devin sighed and leaned his hip against the windowsill. He needed to know more about her, but the only way to do that would be to get closer, and he wasn't sure if that was a good idea. He'd gone out onto the lake to think and burn off frustration. Physical exertion usually worked well, he'd know because he'd spent more hours than he could count to work through things in the last several years. Today activity hadn't done anything to help. He'd gone out and tried to work her right out of his head and for a few seconds he thought it may have worked, and then he saw her on the shore watching. It was as if he didn't want her out of his head, or space, he just wanted to reach her quickly.

The whole time he'd paddled towards the shore he watched her, observing her every move. The situation stank of obsession, the way he wanted her, couldn't stop thinking of her. It was crazy to be drawn to someone he'd just met. If it was a result of their being mates, then she should feel it too. Devin needed to know there were other logical reasons, not just some pre-ordained animal instinct. If it weren't for the fact that she was his mate, would he still want her this way?

He watched her as she stood up and stretched, his body instantly hardened. She was beautiful and graceful, he could admit that. He knew her eyes were soft and alluring, so alluring he practically fell into them. Her hair was softer than silk, her legs, no—he couldn't think about those for too long. Devin stood there like a lost puppy, rubbing a hand over his stomach—a comfort thing—as he continued to watch her. Yeah, he'd still want her even if she wasn't his mate he admitted. The problem was he'd only want her sexually he wouldn't have this whole array of emotions to go with it, or would there?

Devin watched as she took off her shoes and walked to the shore, daintily dipping one foot into the water's edge before stepping in. The urge to paint her came over him. He straightened away from the window. *Obsessed.* Shaking his head, he turned quickly, placing the window at his back and headed towards the shower. Anger flooded through him. He didn't like not being in control, dammit! She was erasing his resolve. Despite wanting to go back to her, he decided some distance for a few days would help bring him clarity.

Stopping when he reached the bathroom, he looked at the strange man in the mirror. The emotional rollercoaster he was riding wasn't like him. He was cool and non-emotional. He was *the* lone wolf that didn't need hand holding and cuddling to bring him peace. He was perfectly fine walking this path of life alone, with solitary tracks. This was just a thing—something that would end as quickly as it began. And he knew that he was so full of it.

Sighing, he leaned down on the counter, and closed his eyes. The words of a friend he'd lost years before rushed into his mind as if he'd been standing beside him. *Finding your mate is like losing your god damned mind—until you have her.* He looked at his reflection once more. That didn't make him feel any better.

Devin's mind didn't give him a moment's peace, he didn't remember taking a shower but still found himself standing in front of the fogged-up mirror dripping wet. There was no peace inside of him—not that there ever really was. Restlessness was what plagued him, but today it was several miles beyond that. He was running out of arguments to keep him anywhere but near her.

How long was this going to last? Did it get better or worse? He was still trying to sort out whether being near her eased the intensity or made it stronger. He had to force himself to stand in the studio and think about work, and not look at the painting of her—he wasn't succeeding in that area either.

Chapter Ten

Where had the heat gone today? It was July, when did it ever get this cold in July? Clearly Northern Ontario had its own weather rules that were like nothing she'd ever experienced before. She rubbed her hands together and huddled deeper into the sleeping bag. Why hadn't the blue haired boy sold her mitts along with the rest of the store? Fumbling with the flashlight until she found the on switch, she looked around the tent for those little candles. Should she even light one of those to warm up her hands? She looked up at the ceiling of the tent, with the screen covered by that flap thing—wouldn't the smoke just go out that way? Sighing, she clicked off the flashlight, with her luck she'd set the tent on fire.

Rayne shimmied down as far as she could in the sleeping bag and pulled it up over her shoulders. With a lot of grunting and wiggling around she managed to move over by the door. Reaching one hand out, she unzipped the zipper just a few inches and peaked outside. She didn't need to look out to see how hard it was raining, the drops echoing off the tent already told her. Of course she didn't have an umbrella or anything sensible like that, so she couldn't even make a run for the little cabin. Flicking the flashlight back on, she shone it outside, there was a mini river forming and streaming right by the tent. If the rain didn't let up soon it would be in the tent as well. How waterproof was the tent? The driest, warmest place would be the car with the heater on, but did she want to sleep in that seat again? Not really. Turning off the light, Rayne sat there staring out into the dark. Was the rain ever going to stop? It had started before dark and didn't seem to be easing off yet. Did it rain here every night? Next time she fled to a secluded place she was going to research weather patterns first.

Once again, she had no idea what time it was. Had she brought her watch and where would it be? No one wore watches any more, not in this day of cell phones and iPods. She didn't want to make a run for the car to find out how many more hours until the warm sunlight returned. Did she really want to sit here all night shivering?

Another heavy downpour distracted her from pouting, the rain so hard it was deafening. After a few minutes, she could hear each single drop as they hit the tent in the otherwise quiet night. Aiming the light outside, she watched as the little rivers were forming friends as they moved past the tent. She was going to be soaked soon. Her stomach rumbled, reminding her she hadn't eaten. She'd tried to work the little stove just before the rain had started, wanting something hot after a few days of fruit and bars, but the rain changed her plans and here she was, hungry. Rayne groaned aloud when she realized she'd moved all her food into the cabin. She was going to have to go to the cabin, there was no other option. Cold and a little dampness she might be able to handle, but she wouldn't be able be hungry as well. Sometimes being a vegetarian had its trials. Meat eaters could eat a big meal then spend the next eight hours digesting it.

Shrugging out of the sleeping bag, she flashed the light around inside the tent to find a bag to put the sleeping bag to keep it dry while running to the cabin. Her clothes and towels were in the cabin, everything was in the cabin except her bed. Okay, so leaving space in the tent wasn't the most brilliant idea. How was she supposed to know there were mini monsoons here every night, or at least the two she'd been here for? Rayne looked at her shoes, no sense in even putting those on and getting them soaked.

It took her three tries to wrestle the sleeping bag back into its little carrying bag. Why did they make them so small? As she stuffed the little candles into the sleeping bag a loud crack of thunder almost made her faint. Turning off the flashlight, she jammed it into the bag and turned around to unzip the door. Stopping, she looked down at her jeans. It would be easier to dry off skin than to squirm out of soaking wet clothes. It wasn't as if she would be seen running to the cabin without her clothes, the chances of Devin out wandering around in this were slim, not when he had a nice warm home to be in. Before she could chicken out, she pulled the sweat shirt over her head and tossed it into the corner. The t-shirt and jeans followed. Rayne hesitated when she grasped her bra, she wasn't taking it or the thong off. Alone or not, streaking through a thunderstorm naked just wasn't something she was comfortable with.

Taking a deep breath, she unzipped the door, just far enough to squeeze out. The rain was cold on her bare skin. "You're crazy," she whispered into the night slipping out and dragging the bag with her. Squatting as the rain pelted her back, she hugged the bag into her stomach to keep it as dry as possible while trying to zip up the tent. Her hands were already cold, and the cool rain wasn't helping as it took a lot longer than she would have liked to seal the tent up again.

Rising, she hunched over the bag and turned towards the cabin. Her hair was plastered to her head and sticking to her soaked back. A flash of lightning made her jolt into action and lunge for the cabin door. She fumbled to get it open and then tripped through the doorway, slamming it closed behind her. Her heart was pounding in her chest and she was exhilarated. "Okay, that wasn't so bad." Feeling around in the bag she grabbed the flashlight and turned it on, placing it on the floor before digging for the candles. *Matches? Where were the matches?* Groaning, she picked up the light and went over to the bags in the corner.

Rayne dug around through the bags to find the matches then back over to light one of the candles. Clothes were next, her goose bumps now had goose bumps. Stripping off the bra and wet underwear, she wrapped a towel around her while locating something dry and warm.

Dressed once again, she unrolled the sleeping bag and climbed in, holding her hands over the candle. Her hair being wet seemed to defeat the purpose of having warm hands, but the granola bars were a welcome thing.

As Rayne chewed each bite slowly, she stared the candle flame, Camping, was not rating high on her 'fun things to do' list. She took another bite. But, she was doing it all on her own. *How many things can I say that about?* Her parents had coddled and sheltered her all her life, when they had died it had been Aiden's father that looked out for Rayne, then eventually Aiden. This was the first thing she had truly done all on her own. Considering she had no idea how to do any of it, she thought she was doing a good job.

Rayne knew she should blow out the candle and try to sleep, but complete darkness didn't feel comforting. The storm seemed to be louder in the small wooden space, and she admitted that she wasn't *that* brave to be in the dark. She got up to find one of the little pots she'd bought and set the candle right into it. Putting it down safely away from where she was going to sleep, she went back to her warm cocoon. Shimmying all the way to the bottom, she rested her head on the rolled-up blanket. It wasn't as comfy as the air mattress, but there was no way she was making a return trip tonight. At least it was better than the car. No matter, she was exhausted enough that she wouldn't notice in a few minutes' time.

Chapter Eleven

Shaking the water off his coat, Devin padded around the cabin once more. This had to be the tenth time he'd gone around the stupid thing. There hadn't been any movement from inside the for quite some time now. He sat beneath the window and looked up. *Had she fallen asleep?* He'd been shocked when she'd come out of her tent in her underwear and darted in the cabin. *Had she been afraid inside the tent? Is that why she ran out?* And why, his mind wondered for the umpteenth time had she been in her underwear? Or lack of— now that he pictured it again. He could still see her bolting into the cabin and could definitely see her perfect ass in very tiny underwear. *Think of something else...*

He looked up at the window again. Knowing it was wrong, he did it anyways. Without serious thought or focus he shifted back into his two-legged form, gritting his teeth when the water repelling coat was now skin and the cold rain beat off it. Devin looked in the window and his heart surged for a few beats. Candlelight reflected her sleeping form. She was all curled up inside the sleeping bag, hands under her cheek. She was almost angelic in that pose with the flickering light shining over her.

He argued with himself for a moment, wanting nothing

more than to go inside and to carry her back to the house where she would be warm and comfortable. Although, waking up to a naked, wet man carrying you through the dark bush, might not be something she would accept calmly. A shiver ran over his skin as the rain continued to fall in heavy waves from the sky. He'd check on her after the storm passed. Wiping the water from his face, he shifted back to four legs and turned to run through the night.

Several miles later he realized no amount of running was going to stop him from thinking about Rayne. He had to figure out what he was going to do soon, or go insane. Staying away from her wasn't working. Lurking in the shadows and watching her was frustrating, the constant need to see her was a revolving thought that nagged without pause. It pissed him off that he kept giving in, but not enough it seemed, to stop.

Stopping, Devin sat and just stared into the night. He should go home and sleep, something he hadn't really done since Rayne appeared, but he didn't want to leave her unprotected. *How long will I continue to be caught in this whirl of emotions?* He knew the answer or at least the options that applied to the question. He would be like this until he claimed her—and his place of leadership would follow that. Or he could walk away and from the way he was feeling— it would have to be far away and nowhere near where he could smell her scent.

Shaking the rain from his coat, he started a slow pace back to the house. No decisions would be made right now. In the morning, he'd try to resist going right to her and see how that turned out.

Chapter Twelve

Rayne rolled over and stretched, pushing her arms free of the sleeping bag. A good thing about camping was no alarm clock, which she could get used to. Slowly, she opened her eyes and looked towards the window, it was daylight and the storm was gone. She wondered if her tent had floated away. Rayne was congratulating herself for braving it alone when a noise inside the cabin made her stiffen. Turning quickly, she saw something large and furry sticking out of one of the bags. She shrieked and jumped up, kicking free of the sleeping bag and bolting for the door, flinging it open so hard it bounced off the wall behind it. The creature made some sort of noise, she responded with a high-pitched noise of her own and flew out the door, bounding right into a hard chest. Without so much as looking up, she wrapped herself around the solid body and climbed it. "There's something in there!" She tightened her arms around Devin's neck and clung to him.

Devin turned away from the cabin, picking her up with one arm and took a few steps, lifting her with ease. He ran a soothing hand down over her hair and cradled her against his chest for a few seconds. "Stay here, I'll go look."

She nodded against his chest, but didn't let go. He didn't

put her down either, just stood there holding her. Leaning down he whispered in her ear. "You have to let me go so I can check."

Rayne nodded again and reluctantly dropped both feet to the ground, easing her arms from around his neck. Looking up into his grey eyes, she found a tenderness she hadn't expected. Slowly, he stepped back from her and turned back to the cabin door. She heard another movement from inside the building and jumped towards him, hugging his back.

He stopped as she glued herself to his spine and wrapped her arms around his waist. Reaching around, he wrapped a strong arm around her and took the last few steps towards the cabin. She didn't look up, but heard the door bang open and realized he'd gotten close enough to push it open. There was scratching on wood, so Rayne peaked around him just as a large raccoon scurried out the door and ran right past her leg as it headed towards the tree. She screamed just as Devin turned around and she climbed his hard body once more. He stood there and held her tight against him, while she had one leg wrapped around his and her arms squeezing his neck, hiding her face against his chest, every inch of her shaking.

His soft chuckle vibrated through her. "It's okay. I think you successfully scared the hell out of him, he won't be back." He ran his hand down over her hair again. As the shaking slowed, she chanced a glance at him. He watched her silently, as she eased her arms down his chest and rested them there. Rayne could feel his heart pounding against the palm of her hand and now felt a little silly for acting the way she had.

"Sorry," she whispered, "I had just opened my eyes and..."

"It's okay." He continued to run his hand down over her hair while his other one was wrapped firmly around her waist. "You almost stopped my heart with that scream though." He grinned down at her.

She smirked, realizing how it must have seemed to him.

With a gentle touch, he brushed the hair back from her face as his eyes searched mine. "Are you all right now?"

She nodded, still trying to get her heart back under control. She held her breath when he looked at her mouth. Licking her lips, she glanced at his mouth. She wanted him to kiss her though she knew that was something she shouldn't be thinking about, but couldn't help it. As if he could read her mind, he lowered his head slowly towards her, allowing her more than enough time to back away or turn her head. She knew she really should, yet didn't.

His warm breath brushed over her cheek and he stopped there for a few seconds before his mouth lightly touched hers. Electricity flashed through her. He lifted his lips away and she was just about to object when they were against hers again with another feather-soft kiss. It shocked her that it could feel that way. He lifted his mouth away again and ran his tongue over her bottom lip. Rayne heard herself gasp as it sent tingles through her entire body. His eyes met hers before he covered her mouth again in a more demanding kiss. Wrapping her arms around his neck, she gasped when he lifted her feet from the ground.

He parted her lips with his tongue and Rayne's whole body felt like it was engulfed in flames when his tongue rubbed against hers. With one arm, he held her against his hard form as he moved the other into her hair and lightly gripped it, holding her head to continue. It was unlike any kiss she'd ever had. He coaxed her to taste him back. Rayne's heart was beating so fast, but she couldn't stop, not yet.

His body was pressed up against her stomach and she could feel how hard he was and it sent heat shooting between her legs. She moaned against his mouth when he bit her bottom lip gently. Logic appeared and she realized she was kissing a complete stranger in ways she had never kissed another man. He lifted his mouth from hers, almost as if he'd thought the same thing. Devin rested his forehead against hers as she watched him close his eyes for a few seconds. She fought to catch her breath, shocked that she was panting.

His hold loosened slowly as he lowered her to the ground. Her body objected, her brain said 'no' but she stayed silent not knowing what would come out of her mouth.

"I –didn't..." He stopped and looked down at her, still resting lightly against his body.

Rayne slowly slid her hands down his chest until they rested against his waist. What she wanted to do was lift his shirt and run her hands all over his skin. She felt her face flush at the thought and lowered her lashes to hide away from his gaze.

"Are you going to be all right now?" His voice rasped and her body responded with another heat flash. He cleared his throat.

She nodded, but still didn't look back up at him, afraid to see the expression on his face. He probably thought she was a hussy, climbing all over him like that.

His large hand cradled the side of her face as he gently tipped her head up so she would have to look at him. "Are you sure?"

Rayne nodded briefly again. "Thank you–again," she whispered as she watched his eyes move over her face, pausing on her mouth more than once. She knew it wasn't what he wanted, but she wanted nothing more than him to kiss her again, maybe more. She could still feel how hard he was and she wanted to rub into him and persuade him.

He tilted his head to the side. "No problem. I love screaming women jumping into my arms." He smirked at her as she blushed. Dropping his hand away from her, he straightened up to his full height.

Rayne just stood there, holding her breath, watching him.

"I have to go," he said, as his eyes moved over her face. He took a step back. She could only give him a little smile and nod before he turned to stride away.

Shakily, Rayne touched her lips and finally let out a

breath. She wasn't sure how, but she wasn't the same after that kiss. She had never felt like that, even with Aiden. Devin hadn't tried to swallow her face or choke her with his tongue, and she had liked it more than any kiss from Aiden. What did that mean? Somehow she was going to get Devin to kiss her again to see if it was just that one time. It could have been the adrenalin firing from the scary animal in the cabin. Rayne thought of how his body felt against hers and had to bite her lip so she wouldn't sigh. She definitely wanted to kiss him again, but with the way he'd reacted, she wasn't sure the feeling was mutual.

Running both hands back through her hair to distract herself, she looked at the cabin. A fact just decided; she was never sleeping in there again. She headed back inside to see what the raccoon had gotten into.

Chapter Thirteen

Devin paced around the house like a caged animal. He didn't dare go outside, because he knew exactly where he'd end up. *Why did I have to kiss her?* Yes, she'd been in his arms, but it wasn't a warm embrace that had put her there, it had been fear. The wolf inside had loved the fear and all parts of him had loved her body rubbing up against his own. He could still taste her, even after trying to brush the taste from his mouth. He could smell her too, almost as if her scent was the only one in the world. Muttering, he ran his hands through his hair in frustration, he could still remember how she'd felt against him, as if she were still there.

Had he been headed there intentionally before he heard her scream? *Yes, dammit I was.* When she'd screamed, he was close enough to reach her as she'd come charging out of the cabin. Devin looked over at the door. *Stay inside. Get her out of your mind and the taste of her out of your mouth before you go out there.* He snorted and looked down at the hard on that was still very much present. *Yeah, forgetting her was going to be so easy.* He couldn't go outside because he knew he'd go to her. He couldn't paint right now because he'd paint her image. He couldn't even think right now because all he could think of was her. Growling, Devin spun around and headed into the kitchen, he wasn't hungry or thirsty, just knew this was the only room with a window that he couldn't possibly see her. The feeling that he was sunk hit him hard. He didn't like it at all, but at least he was trying to admit to it.

He stopped in the middle of the room and turned around, not sure what he could do to stop from going back to a window to watch for her. Moaning in frustration, he sat down at the table and stared at the wall. *Why did she have to come here?* Devin scowled at the wall, soon realizing the idea of not meeting her bothered him just as much. It doesn't have to change anything. She could work through what ever had brought her here and leave tomorrow. *What had brought her here?* He frowned at his thoughts this time. That would be just his luck, to find his mate, never have her and then she disappears into the darkness as quickly as she had appeared. He slapped his hand down on the table realizing it only annoyed him further that she had him this worked up. Dropping his head, he tried deep breathing to maintain some sort of calm.

Lifting his head, he squinted at the wall. He hadn't been this annoyed or worked up in a long time, and so far, his wolf was under control. Had all the time he'd spent here actually worked? Devin thought about how he would have reacted with her and all the emotional turmoil a few years ago. He knew that he would have lost it, changed and torn something apart. "Congratulations, Devin. You've proved you control your wolf, finally." He should have been elated with this discovery, but he wasn't. Nothing changed the fact that he now had a mate, a too-near-to-him-mate that he couldn't have. He smirked, remembering the kiss, okay, so he *could* have her most likely, but there would never be a true mating. For that to happen, she would have to know who and what he was and accept him, completely. Been there, done that, still have the psychological knife scars on my back. He snarled. He would not think about Leeann, he had enough to deal with right now. Of course, that had him thinking about Leann and, just for a bit of extra entertainment, he was now unintentionally comparing her to Rayne. Devin sighed, he even loved her name. *Rayne. A dark summer storm had brought me Rayne.*

The phone ringing jolted him back to reality, he lunged towards it. Hopefully whoever was calling would be a good distraction. His hand hovered over the phone and he jerked it back and groaned. He knew that number, and was in no mood to talk to his mother right now. No doubt his father had told her about their discussion and now mother would be planning the damn wedding reception.

When his mother's voice came over the answering machine he was halfway to his studio. *Love you mom, but I can't cope with anything you feel the need to tell me right now.* He should take some canvas and brushes and go on a hike, in the opposite direction where he couldn't hear his mother calling. Because she would, again and again.

Chapter Fourteen

As she wandered through the trees, she congratulated herself for not shaking in her shoes. It was daylight, but the area she had wandered into was dark enough that it could have been night. Each time she lowered the camera away from her face and took a few steps, she would see something else that she had to take a picture of. It was truly breathtaking here, the dark woods with a few rays of light shining down through the canopy of leaves.

Memories she thought had long ago faded from came back. The hiking trips with her parents who had loved the outdoors. She always wondered why they had settled in Chicago. Lush, wild forests weren't exactly common there. She really wished they were still here, now when she needed them. More than once since she'd made the choice to pack her life into the car, thoughts of her parents returned. Had her father known about Aiden's business? He had worked for that family for as long as she could remember. Her soft-handed, soft-hearted father, could he have known? She would never find those answers, and that added to the confusing mess inside his head.

Letting the camera drop and hang on the cord around her neck she swatted at the bugs buzzing in front of her nose.

Not everything here was beautiful, these mosquitoes were the size of moths, and it didn't seem to matter how much spray she put on, they just kept coming. "Mean and determined, aren't you?" She fished around in her bag for the spray and pulled it out. Instead of spraying her face again, because if she digested much more of this she was going to be sick, she blasted the swarm of insects in front of her. Frowning as she lowered the bottle to see that had helped for only a few short seconds. "It's time to find some sunlight and leave you nasty things behind." Rayne turned around in a circle, picking which way to go.

This had, at one time, been a well-traveled path, but now was overgrown with very little clear direction to follow. There were still remnants of last fall's leaves with the new growth bursting through them. It was quite something to see the old and decaying mixed with the bright new green growth. Rayne had only ever seen moss and ferns like this in the movies, and it added to the mystical appearance with so much of it around her.

Taking slow and measured steps as she picked up the camera again, she held her breath. A large red-tailed squirrel paused in the path a few feet in front of her. Readying the viewfinder quickly, Rayne managed to take two pictures before it disappeared into the ferns and practically flew up the side of a thickly barked tree.

Life goes on Rayne thought as she headed down the incline of the trail. The new trees were pushing up towards the light, they'd have to fight to survive with so many larger trees hogging all the sunshine above them. The old trees that had their time, now lay on the overgrown ground, recycling back into the earth. She took several pictures of a huge rock that seemed so out of place among the trees, it looked like it had been here since time began, and the trees were new.

She headed towards the light in the trees, her thoughts went back to Devin. She knew she shouldn't think about him. *Don't you have enough complications in your life right now? Wasn't it because of a male that you're hiding in this place?* At some point, Rayne needed to figure out what she was going to do about Aiden, or at least figure out what she was going to do without Aiden, and find a life of her own again. A life of her own choosing; there was something she'd never had. Pausing beside a few plants, that she didn't know the names of, she photographed them from several angles. If she was going to do this whole life-of-her-own thing, waiting for a man to kiss her again probably wasn't what she should be focusing on. She exhaled long and noisily. "No men." Hearing it out loud made her chuckle, not that she had them lined up, as the one she was near clearly didn't want a lot to do with her. Putting the camera back up to her face, she turned around and focused in on the path that led back into the darkened area.

Chapter Fifteen

As Devin cleaned his paintbrushes, he looked around the landscape. Coming out and painting in the fresh air had been a good idea. It had been a long time since he'd painted anywhere except in the studio. His mind wasn't co-operating completely by thinking only of painting. It was bouncing from past to present with a constant annoying pace.

Devin's past was one of trials, heartache, and things he didn't want to relive. Before coming here to work, he refused to believe he was hiding, he had come dangerously close to giving away the only part of himself he held sacred. His heritage. Devin may not be ready to step to the head of the line, but he was in no way ashamed of his family or his kind. He had been one breath from telling Leeann who and what he was when he'd found her with another man—after that he lost his temper and control of his wolf, leaving no need to tell her. She had been repulsed and scared at the same time.

Stopping, he looked down at his hands. A normal pair of man's hands holding a paintbrush. At least there was no shaking when he thought about Leeann, that was progress.

Without warning his mind skipped right back to thinking about Rayne. He could still taste her, and as hard as he tried not to think about kissing her, it was as if she was now burning inside of him. *What am I going to do about the appealing woman that invades my every thought? What if my father is right and she is my mate?* Devin rolled his eyes at his own denial. He knew she was his mate. He wasn't sure how exactly, he just felt it. *What if I do get too close to her and I lose control of my wolf again?* With all the if's he was feeling, he knew one thing for sure, he wasn't ready to find out what would happen.

Inhaling deeply, Devin froze and began to look around. He could smell citronella and knew there was nothing on his land with that particular scent. At least he'd *had* nothing on his land that didn't have two sexy legs with that scent. Rayne was nearby. *What is she doing this far from the camp? Was she trying to get lost or hurt?* Slowly turning, he inhaled trying to pinpoint where she was. Stopping, he looked down the far trail at the bottom of the hill. She'd been in the densest part of the bush. He tensed every muscle in his body, forcing himself to stand there and not go rushing to find her. Surely, she had some sense of direction. He scanned the trees, trying to find her.

Devin took one step forward, then paused when he spotted her wandering along without even looking where she was walking. He thought for a moment, trying to recall if there were any ditches along that area. His heart thudded when she tumbled right from his sight. He gave her to the count of ten to reappear before he took off to find her. He heard her laughing. The sound of it tickled along his skin and he had no choice but to shake his head while he smiled. She popped back up again, walking out of the long grass and brushing off her jeans. She fiddled with her camera for a few seconds. It must have been all right because she lifted it to her face again and aimed it up towards where he stood. She stopped moving and lowered it slowly, still looking in his direction. Devin fought to stay where he was and not go down to her. Just seeing her standing there pulled at him in ways he couldn't identify. His heart sped up as he clenched his jaw to focus and control his body from taking that first step towards her. She took two steps in his direction and then stopped and lowered her head for a few seconds. When she lifted it once again and looked squarely at him, he was sure she was going to come to him. Instead, she turned and moved quickly into the long grass she had come from.

Frowning, Devin watched where she had gone for a few heartbeats. It was good she hadn't come over, that saved him from trying to decide what to do if she had, yet it bothered him that she'd just walked away. He looked back to where she had last stood for several moments before he went back over to where he'd been painting. Studying the canvas, he sighed, any notion of painting now was completely gone.

Chapter Sixteen

Surprisingly she had calmed down from seeing Devin. She wasn't sure why she had started to go to him. *Hadn't I just decided to avoid him?* Even though her heart had been dancing inside her chest when she'd spotted him, she noticed he wasn't too quick to come in her direction or wave or— anything. That was a good thing, right? It removed the possible complications of her staying on his property, for the time being.

As the pictures uploaded to the laptop, she closed her eyes and lifted her face towards the sun. Rayne was in no hurry to leave. So, she wasn't a professional camper and the night still scared her half out of her skin, but she loved the peacefulness the surrounded her. Leaning down, she picked up the container of nuts beside the chair. Tomorrow she would try cooking on that camp stove, for now though, she could live on nibbling and snacking all through the day. She popped an almond into her mouth and looked to the path that led to the lake.

Every muscle in her body stiffened, she swallowed the almond almost whole, grimacing as it scratched her throat on the way down. A wolf, a very large wolf was standing in the path looking right at her. She didn't want to look away and was afraid to move. It was no more than ten feet away and she knew there was no way she could make it to the little cabin that was more than ten feet away. Now what? Her heart was sitting at the bottom of her throat, and she was fairly certain the almond was stuck there too, as she attempted to swallow it again.

Rayne took short shallow breaths trying not to move any part of her body. Were all wolves that large and if so, how big would a bear possibly be? The furry raccoon that had invaded her clothes didn't seem so bad right now. It looked—worried? Not even sure where the thought came from as she moved one hand slowly towards the armrest of the chair. The animals' ears moved forward. *Was that a bad thing? Why didn't you buy some animal books?* She'd only bought plant ones, clearly that had been an error in judgement as the plants weren't likely to eat her.

Devin stood there looking at her. In this form, he could do that as much or as little as he pleased. Much pleased him. He could sense her fear and smell the sweat it was causing her. *Why had I come here again? Did I want to scare her away?* As he pulled his lip up to growl at her, he met her eyes again and stopped. There was something about those eyes that affected him, he didn't know what, but he knew he didn't want to frighten her into trying to bolt and possibly hurting herself. With slow movements, he sat down and continued to watch her.

Her eyes widened as she pulled her hand back into her lap. She swallowed and he couldn't help but to let his eyes watch her pale throat move.

"I suppose I'm in *your* space too," she whispered in an unsteady voice.

She was going to sit there and talk to a wild animal? This might be entertaining to draw out a bit. He lowered down to lie there watching her.

"You may not know it but *you're* in Devin's space and he's not entirely a friendly sort." She spoke softly to him now. Her voice was soothing.

Not entirely a friendly sort? Okay, she was right. He could still smell her fear, but she seemed determined not to do anything to give it away to him.

"If I share my snack, do you promise to not be rude and bite me?"

He tilted his head and looked at her.

"I'm afraid I don't have any meat, I'm a vegetarian you see, but I have some nuts—if you eat that sort of thing." She moved slowly and took a nut out of the container on her lap and held it between two fingers. "If I toss this to you are you going to feel threatened?"

She bit her bottom lip and looked at him with those alluring eyes of hers. Afraid she might stop talking to him, he lowered his head, resting his chin on his paws. *It doesn't get any more submissive than this, lady.* She took a shallow breath and leaned forward a bit and tossed the nut so it landed a few inches in front of his nose. He stretched slowly and sniffed it, but had no intentions of eating it.

"Not to your taste, is it?" She bit her lip again and sat there looking at him.

He could sense she was forcing herself to stay calm.

"You're very large, aren't you?" She pursed her lips together and studied him for a moment more. "I'm hoping you're a him, because honestly I don't think my heart would survive if you were a tiny female and I ran into a full-grown male."

Devin had to wonder for a moment if he looked feminine in any way and then she smirked at him.

"Definitely male, you have that very alpha aura to you."

She straightened a bit in her chair and he thought she was going to try to run to the cabin, but she cleared her throat and continued to talk.

"I'm Rayne, by the way. Rayne Andrews..." she smirked again, "I guess I'll have to pick a name for you because I doubt you're going to introduce yourself."

He lifted his head, but remained lying down so he didn't

frighten her.

"I'm going to call you..."

She bit that lip again and he had to curb the sudden inkling to go over and lick that lip she held trapped beneath her teeth.

Rayne huffed out a breath. "I can't think of a name that would do you any justice, you really are beautiful."

Beautiful?

She reached over and picked up her camera from the small table. "Will you let me take a picture I wonder?" Slowly she raised the camera up towards her face.

Devin debated on leaving, but decided he wouldn't mind seeing what he looked like in this form, so he stayed still. After she took three pictures, he stood up slowly and took a few steps closer to her. She tensed up again, watching him warily with her large eyes. The idea of upsetting her bothered him more than he could handle, so he turned and ran off in the opposite direction.

Chapter Seventeen

Maybe the fact that she survived a wolf encounter and felt braver than she had ever felt before is why she found herself standing on the shore of the lake looking at the canoe. Rayne hugged the container she'd sealed her camera in, mostly because she treasured it and drowning it would upset her more than drowning herself. *Do I want to try canoeing? Yes, mostly.* She set the camera down and walked over to the canoe. Taking a deep breath, she flipped it over, finding out it was much heavier than it had looked. The paddle was on the ground, having been hidden underneath. Picking it up, she frowned at it. It was almost as tall as she was. Rayne looked at the water and then back to the canoe, there was no way around it, some of her was going to get wet. She knew she didn't have the strength to climb in on shore and shove it out into the water. She placed the paddle in and then her shoes, carefully setting the camera on top.

Grabbing the handle as she'd seen Devin do, she yanked on it only to discover that it was going to be a challenge just getting it to the water, never mind getting in it once it was there. *Would pushing it be easier? Doubtful.* Rayne grabbed the handle again with both hands and backed towards the lake, one inch at a time. This gave her a new-found respect for early settlers that used to carry their canoes over their heads when they hit a spot without water. Obviously modern life made people soft and weak, well, at least it had her.

During the back-straining event of getting the canoe to the water thinking that would be the hardest part, and she was wrong. Rayne stood in the water up to her knees holding the canoe and trying to figure out the best way to get inside it without tipping right out the other side only to land on her face with a splash. She wasn't going to make the mistake again of thinking any part of this was going to be easy. Balancing on one foot, she lifted the other one to rest inside, longer legs probably would have made this simpler, but, she didn't have any of those handy. Rayne stretched so her foot was close to the middle and then slowly shifted her weight to swing the other foot in. Her yoga instructor would have been proud of her technique and flexibility when she finally had both feet inside.

As she started to straighten the canoe started rocking from side to side and the more she tried to counter balance the worse it rocked. Her camera rolled around making her wonder if she was even in enough water to flip it. Not having any other choice, she plopped down onto her knees and held the sides until the rocking stopped. The expression 'don't rock the boat' took on a whole new meaning that she completely understood now. Making sure she made small movements she wiggled around until she was comfortable. She'd seen how people used the narrow seats at either end, but there was no way she was going to try to move to try to get to them. She felt less like she was going to fall out by sitting in the middle.

Looking around, she decided she'd just paddle a bit along the shore and see how this worked before she left the safety of a few feet of water to the deeper, darker water in the middle of the lake. *How hard could this be?* Rayne took the paddle and slid it in her hands a few times trying to figure out at which length she should hold it. Small movements worked for her and hopefully she could control things.

It took less than twenty practice strokes to figure out that she had to paddle a bit on each side or she didn't go straight forward. The third try she ended up with the front of the canoe beached on the shore, and she knew if she was going to accomplish anything, she'd have to go out deeper where she couldn't ground herself so easily. As the bottom of the lake started to get harder to see, she looked back at the shore and was surprised how far out she'd travelled. She'd never win any races, but she was managing to go straight and hadn't fallen out, yet. A win for her.

Rayne could see why people liked this as she rested the paddle in front of her and coasted through the water, it was peaceful. One more thing that made her want to stay longer.

She pushed herself along a few more times and then just sat there, thinking. Aside from taking pictures, what had she decided to do? Nothing, but that was okay, it had only been a few days. Rayne laughed out loud, thinking what a few days it had been. She was no longer engaged, employed, or had a place to live. She was hiding out in the wilderness with no real clue to what she was doing. Then again, she'd also survived a near miss with a racoon and a social visit with a wolf, not to mention she was coasting in a canoe on a serene lake right at this moment. Maybe the good didn't outweigh the bad, but she'd take what she could get.

Figuring she was close to the middle of the lake, she put the paddle down, inside the canoe so she wouldn't knock it in the water. Making tiny movements, she stretched until she could grasp the camera and took it out of its waterproof container. Rayne felt a little overwhelmed, not sure what she should take a picture of first, but then realized there was really no rush, was there?

Rayne spent several minutes trying to capture a picture of a fish, at least she really hoped it was a fish, as it skimmed the surface and caused ripples to spread out. The problem with that was she didn't know where to look other than where it had been last, and she suspected they kept moving and didn't hit the same place more than once.

She looked everywhere, taking pictures of everything within her sight, she would always want to remember this, and the more pictures she had the more she could conjure the same feeling as the moment she took the picture. Everything was so natural and beautiful. The trees surrounding the lake weren't perfectly balanced, they just grew where they wanted to. The water, so many shades of blue but colorless at the same time, even the sky...

She lowered the camera and moved her eyes to the sky. There were some very dark, foreboding clouds heading her way, fast.

After experiencing a few storms of this area, she didn't need to think twice about putting her camera back into the container and heading to the shore. She did not want to be in the middle of a body of water when that darkness reached here. How long did she have?

Rayne turned the canoe without any problems and made the call that carefree paddling was out of the question, however going fast seemed to rock her around too much, and she didn't want to tip over, so she found a pace that wasn't meandering and didn't tip her over, and hoped it would get her there in time.

There had been no wind to speak of two seconds ago, but a gust of wind caught her and started to turn her away from the shore. Rayne had no idea what to do other than to keep paddling and trying to get closer. Glancing towards the trees, she caught sight of several birds heading for cover, she didn't need to be an outdoorsman to know that wasn't a good sign at all. The wind continued to pick up causing the calm water to become choppy. What kind of storm was she in for?

She was trying not to panic when she noticed she wasn't lined up with where she'd been heading, the wind was forcing the canoe away from the small building on the shore. Rayne glanced behind her and panicked when she realized she was closer to the other side than to Devin's shore line. Did she turn and head for the closest land or keep trying? As the first few drops of rain hit her face she found the decision much easier to make. Any land was better than blowing around a lake during a storm. A loud crack of thunder sounded in the distance sent a warning chill down her spine.

Rayne's heart was racing faster than she was moving when the rain began to fall with stinging force against her skin. *Just let me reach a shore, soon.* She prayed as she pushed the paddle through the water to bring the shore closer to her. She was able to steer in the very general direction of some taller trees, hoping when she got there she'd be able to get the canoe out of the water and find somewhere reasonably sheltered to sit the storm out. The weather in this part of the world was pure craziness. She'd just been worrying about getting sunburned one moment and then the next the sky washes black and she's soaked to the skin.

This time when the thunder echoed across the water a bright jagged bolt of lightning lit up half the sky in the dark clouds. The shore was still at least a hundred feet away as she leaned and took longer strokes through the water, believing she was reaching it in record time. The rain pelted her in the strong wind and she had half a mind to let the wind blow her to the nearest ground, but that held no guarantee, so she got up on her knees and kept her head low and fought to keep the canoe heading to the trees.

The bottom of the canoe dragged across something and she cried out in relief knowing she was close now. Rayne didn't wait to see if she was strong enough to push it further in, she dropped the paddle and scrambled out the second she could see the bottom beneath the murky water. The canoe was stuck on a log so she jumped in the water and didn't even pause when it was up to her hips, grabbing the edge, she worked her way to the front and grasped the handle. She ignored the roughened lake bed that hurt her feet and used the adrenalin to find the strength, pulling the canoe further onto the shore. A rock blocked her from pulling it completely onto land, but with most of it out of the water, she figured it wasn't going to go too far. Another bolt of lightning flashed overhead and she stumbled towards the trees.

Rayne knew nothing of safety in the wilderness during a storm, but logic told her to find the tightest grouping of trees so she would be safe from anything falling on her. She just prayed she was right. Spotting a group of larger trunks, she didn't stop until she was between them. *Let these be big strong trees that will hide me safely.* She looked up. The rain was coming down so hard that the thick foliage on the tops wasn't able to stop her from getting wet, but at least she was on land and safer.

Limbs creaked as the wind howled through them. Rayne dropped down to lean against the largest tree and wrapped her arms around her knees. She didn't know if she was shivering from fear or was cold, but wasn't able to stop. Wind she was used to, but never had she heard wind like this. All around her trees were swaying in the force of the gusts that seemed to go in more than one direction. She didn't want to think what would have happened to her out there in the open if she hadn't seen the clouds in time, or barely in time. She was a strong swimmer, but Mother Nature was much stronger. She hoped Mother Nature would get this out of her system quickly and move along to somewhere she wasn't.

A terrifying snap cracked through the air and she jumped up looking around. No more than thirty feet from her, the top of a large tree was speared into the ground. Rayne looked up at the trees she was using as her sanctuary and wondered if they were stronger than the tree that had plummeted to its death. She was really, really starting to not like thunder storms. Sliding back down, she sat on the large root at the bottom of the tree. There was nothing she could do but wait this out.

Rayne wondered for a moment how she was going to get the water out of the canoe, but decided that wasn't important right this second. Turning, she looked through the trees towards the lake. Just seeing the water rising up in choppy waves made her more thankful she'd reached the shore when she did. Through the pelting rain, she glanced to where she'd left the canoe, it wasn't there. Had she run straight into the trees or weaved through them? She stood up and leaned around the tree more, looking along the edge of the lake as far as she could from there. She did not see the canoe. Maybe the wind had blown it away. Wiping the water off her face she squinted through the rain trying to see if the canoe was out in the lake when a something whipped up against her face.

Holding her stinging cheek, she lowered herself back down to sit on the root again. A canoe search and rescue was going to have to wait, she was not giving up this shelter for anything until the storm was gone.

She had no idea how long she'd stayed hidden amongst the trees. It was one of those times that felt like hours but, in reality, could only be a few minutes. Peeking around the tree once more, she noticed the puddles on the ground in the open area between the shore and where she hid, she was pretty sure it was more than a few minutes. Her muscles hurt, she was cold and now that the adrenalin had ebbed, she was scared. All the wrong thoughts were whizzing around in her brain. What if the canoe was gone, how would she get back? Could she even find her way back by going all the way around the lake? What if the storm didn't end before it got dark? Was she going to last the night here alone? Unless Devin noticed the canoe missing, there wasn't another soul on earth that would even know she was missing. She didn't want to turn into one of those horror stories of people lost in wilderness and never found again. She really didn't.

Rolling her shoulders Rayne tried to relax, but with her shivering and fear wouldn't allow that to happen. She rubbed her hands up and down her arms and tried to warm up. Her feet were throbbing and she finally allowed herself to examine them and see how much damage she'd done by running over the rough ground. Picking up her right foot, she turned it to look at the bottom, it had a few scratches and was dirty, but she didn't see anything wrong with it. Her left foot, however, wasn't in great shape. There was a long gash covered with bits of nature and blood. She brushed it off as best as she could, gritting her teeth as she pulled a piece of twig out. If she had to walk back, she was sure it would be the longest walk of her life.

Her bare legs hadn't faired all that well either. They were covered in scratches that were likely going to attract every mosquito on the planet when the wind and rain stopped. She was going to be an insect smorgasbord. Rayne looked deeper into the trees and scanned the area around her, if the bugs were the only thing she had to worry about, she'd consider herself very lucky.

Unable to distract herself from the noise of the storm any longer, she covered her ears, just wanting a few seconds of silence. How long could a storm like this last? Didn't they scream themselves out quickly when they were this intense? She had no idea, but was starting to think that she should begin coming up with a plan to get out of here. She couldn't leave her survival to a man that may not even know she was missing.

She was so cold now, her body started to ache. Uncovering her ears, she leaned around the tree and looked for the canoe again. If she could drag it ashore further she might be able to flip it over and hide under it out of the rain. Of course, that plan would only work if she could find where she had left it, and that she was brave enough to go look. She stood up on stiff legs and stepped away from the comfort of the trees and back into the wind.

Her foot objected to touching the ground, but she ignored it and moved in the direction she thought she'd come from. If she couldn't move the canoe, she could at least get her shoes and camera. *I can't believe I left my camera.* Not that she'd had any time, the only thing she'd been concerned with at that moment was to get off the water.

The closer she got to the water, the stronger the wind was. The rain, although it hurt, didn't really matter. There was no getting any wetter than she was. Rayne crouched down and held onto a fallen tree to catch her breath and look along the shore. She saw the log that had stopped her being able to pull the canoe all the way in, but she did not see the canoe. It wasn't there. She looked along the shore for as far as she could see and it wasn't there. Squinting, she looked out onto the lake and her heart sunk as the blurry image of the canoe spinning about, out in the deep water, registered. She was stranded. Would Devin see it? Would he come looking for her now?

A small branch smacked up against her arm and snapped her back into action. The only choice she had was to go back to find a better spot to wait this out. Her wet hair whipped around and stuck to her face as she stepped carefully away from the shore, so discouraged she didn't even bother to move it away from her face. Something blew right past her and she straightened to follow it with her eyes. It looked like a piece of plastic. Plastic was waterproof. Rayne held her breath and watched as it snagged in a branch and flapped chaotically in the wind. She looked back at the trees she'd been hiding in, memorizing what they looked like so she could head back and turned to work her way to capture the snapping piece of plastic.

She hissed with each step, the gash on her foot burned now, but she kept going, determined to get that plastic. When she was a few feet from it, it jerked in the wind like it was trying to free itself. Rayne lunged and grabbed just as the wind jerked it free from the branch. Quickly, she hugged it tight before the wind claimed it again. She had to use both hands as she jogged, well, limped back towards the shelter of the trees.

As she slid back against the large tree, she discovered the plastic wasn't as large as it had looked, there were a few tears, but it would still cover part of her and give her a short respite from the rain. Carefully, she opened one of the tears further and pulled it over her head. She didn't know what the bag had been used for, but at this point it didn't matter. Wiggling it down over her wet shoulders, she was more than happy that it covered her almost to the waist. Even though she was wet and cold, the plastic hugged her and brought a small amount of comfort with it.

Now she just had to wait for the wind to go away. She didn't care if the rain stopped or not, it was the wind that scared her and prevented her from going anywhere. Had the thunder lessened? She hadn't even noticed, but hoped she was right and this onslaught was almost over.

She just had to wait.

Chapter Eighteen

He lowered the binoculars and cursed again. The rain was so hard he couldn't see clearly. *Why didn't I go out and warn her? I knew an hour before it hit.* Devin realized now she wouldn't have had any way to know. It was doubtful she had a radio, or one that could pick up any broadcasts in this region. And she didn't have his animal instinct when the weather was going to shift.

He'd watched her play around by the shore for a few minutes, figuring she'd be there for hours trying to discover how to steer the canoe, but when he came back a short while later she was out in the middle of the lake. It wasn't often he was surprised, yet more than once since she'd brought her scent into his world he'd been just that. He found himself watching her with amusement and oddly, pride, as she paddled away with smooth, even strokes.

If he hadn't gotten wrapped up searching through the archives his father had emailed, he would have had more time to warn her when the sky began to darken. *Did she see the little shelter on the far end of the lake? Was that where she was?* He'd already gone out and tried to see that far, but the wind was too much for him to cope with.

Pacing back to the other window, he lifted the binoculars

and searched the shore line for the canoe. It wasn't there. *Where is she?* Clenching his jaw, he exhaled slowly through his nose trying to find calm, Devin was not used to worrying about someone, and he wasn't sure if he even could do anything to stop it.

Of course, in light of what his research had told him, he had a reason to be worried. The partial outline of the archives from his father told him that Rayne, his Rayne, was most likely the child of Nicolas and Sarah Andrews. They had moved from Canada to the states more than twenty years ago, and had never returned. They were also true bloods and of his clan. So, in fact he had more than substantial reason to be worrying, he'd pretty much confirmed that Rayne was indeed one of his own, and without a doubt the mate that destiny had selected for him. And he had no idea where she was—all while every fiber of his body was screaming at him to find and protect her.

All of this did not mean he had made the choice to be the next to head the clan and Alliance, it merely meant that one of his own was in trouble and he felt unable to do anything about it. At least this is what he kept telling himself as he constantly scanned the lake looking for her.

As soon as the wind died down he was going to make sure she was all right. He would need his wolf to find her, which meant he'd either have to stay wolfed out, or walk around naked once he did. Naked wasn't a problem for him, but he guessed it might be for her. He didn't even know where the pack was that he used to carry his clothes, it had been a long time since he'd had to worry about people. He looked out the window once more to check the sky, this was not going to be a quick storm. He couldn't just stand here for much longer, patience had never been one of his strong points.

If he could make it through the wind to the shower building by the lake, he may be able to see where she was. With that goal in mind he turned and jogged to his room, he had to find that pack and a blanket small enough to fit in it.

The windows vibrated from the force of the thunder, spurring his worry close to panic as he tore things from the closet looking for that stupid pack. He'd have to use his wolf form to get through the wind and rain down to the shore and didn't want to stand there naked with the rain beating off parts of his body that he'd prefer it not to.

Devin found the pack and striped off his clothes, jamming them into the bag. He had to find her before dark, he wasn't the only animal in this area and he needed to protect her. Securing the pack across his shoulder, he swung open the door and stepped out into the storm. Before the door was latched closed he was on the ground, paws working quickly to get him to the lake. The wind yanked at his fur and burned as it pulled at him, but he kept going. Short of being blown away he was going to get down there to find Rayne.

Devin had fifty feet of open space to cover before he would be able to reach the building, and the wind wasn't going to make it easy. With each step he took a strong gust pushed him sideways, twice he had to stop and crouch down closer to the ground to balance himself again. The closer to the shore he got, the harder it was to keep going. He was pushing right into the wind and the rain was hitting with bruising force. Crawling, determined he was going to be able to do it, the wind grabbed hold of the pack and lifted the front end of his body right off the ground. For a few seconds he panicked, doubting whether he'd make it at all. Snarling at the storm, he hunkered down and crept towards the building. It was going to be painful when he shifted back to skin to open the door, but it was something he had to do. Rayne was out there somewhere and Devin wasn't stopping until he knew she was okay.

It felt like an hour passed as he struggled against the weather to reach the door, but finally he managed, shifting with lightning speed and darting inside the building. He stood there leaning on the door and trying to catch his breath. Water dripped from his hair into his eyes as he swatted at it to keep it off his face.

He unclipped the pack and dropped it to the floor as he went to the small window to see if he could spot the canoe. He couldn't see anything; the rain ran down the window so hard it was like trying to look through a waterfall. He was just going to have to wait it out. Devin didn't like it, but he wasn't presented any other options. As he'd barely made it this far, he knew he wouldn't be able to scout along the shore and look for her in any form.

Pulling his jeans on, he stood in front of the window and waited. Was there a chance she had made it back and was sitting this out in her car? Again, he'd have to wait until the wind died down to check out that possibility, but for now he was going to try to convince himself of that so his heart would get out of his throat and stay in his chest where it belonged.

He listened to the pounding rain on the roof and tried to hear if it was letting up at all. Closing his eyes, he focused on listening, the wind wasn't howling as loudly, at least that's what he heard. He opened his eyes again to look out the window. It might sound like it was easing up, but it didn't look like it. Something caught the corner of his vision and he pressed his face almost against the glass. Devin couldn't decide what he was seeing through the streaked window.

Moving back to the door in two strides, he whipped the door open and held himself steady by holding onto the frame. His eyes strained to make out the movement out in the lake, his heart stopped when he realized it was the canoe. From where he was standing he couldn't see if anyone was in the canoe. *Was she lying in the bottom of it? Can I get out there to it?*

Taking two steps, he stopped. Drowning as he tried to reach it wasn't going to help. Backing up until he was inside the building he stood without taking his eyes off the canoe that the wind was slapping around. She had to be all right, he wasn't going to accept anything else.

It felt like an eternity had passed while he stood there watching. As soon as it was closer he was going out, wind be damned. If she was still in it, he wasn't going to leave her there until the storm burned itself out.

He tried to occupy his mind. How was he going to find out if Rayne knew about her heritage? He knew she hadn't had her first shift, or he'd smell it. Females didn't shift as early on as the males. Males shifted at the onset of puberty and then the rough lessons of learning to cope with shifting began. Woman didn't usually begin shifting until they were closer to their first estrous—or, simply put, were ready to breed. Which meant that if Rayne hadn't reached that point, she might not even be aware of what she was. She had to be close, which would make her somewhere in her twenties.

Why hadn't her parents registered her in the archives? That question brought another, where were her parents and why was she here alone? Did he bring the Alliance in to see if they could find her parents? What bothered him the most was how, or why, she had driven all the way from Illinois, according to her license plate, to here? Was it some sort of test she had to pass before reaching her first shift, sending her out into the middle of the wilderness? He'd heard of some odd rituals of that sort in some packs, but had never known anyone to go through it personally. Did someone from her pack know she was here, or was it fate's way of getting his attention? He needed to speak to his father again, but regardless of answers, he still had to find her.

The canoe now floated fifty feet from the shore. His patience gone, Devin stepped out into the vicious wind and started for the water. His wolf may be able to fight the wind and repel the rain, but his man was a stronger swimmer and had hands to grab the canoe. He ploughed right into the lake, not hesitating. The wind pushed back against him to stop him from going out to the canoe, Devin leaned forward, trudging through the water. At the speed the wind was pushing in the canoe, he'd only have to swim a short distance when the bottom beneath his feet dropped away. Swim, walk, run he didn't care how he reached it, just as long as he did.

The strength of the wind choked him, he had to put a

hand over his mouth to take in a breath. Another ten feet and he'd have to swim. His muscles clenched in anticipation as he gauged where he was in the lake and how much further he could go before the bottom dropped off. The water splashed up against his chest as he tried to balance his footing as long as possible. The canoe was getting closer as the wind shoved at it. Then, taking a deep breath, Devin pushed out with as much strength as he could find and began to swim through the choppy water in the direction of the canoe. His mouth filled with water more than once as he fought the waves to reach the boat.

Devin had just a few more feet to go when a strong gust of wind spun the canoe and he had to go under to avoid being blindsided by the spinning canoe. When he surfaced again, he gasped for a breath and spit the water out. The canoe had gone right over his head and was heading towards the shore without him. He dove under in an attempt to close the distance and resurfaced close enough to reach up and grab the side, careful not tip it. If Rayne was in it, he didn't want to flip her out into the water, she'd have had enough of the water right now. Walking his hands back along the side, he moved behind it and started swimming with determined kicks towards the shore. She had to be all right.

He couldn't see how close he was to the shore, so when the bottom of the canoe dragged into dirt he was able to stand again and see inside it. Gasping for air, he struggled to his feet and leaned over the canoe, it was empty. The paddle was there, her shoes and her camera, but she wasn't. Devin held the edge and spun back towards the water, had she fallen out? His heart was beating in his throat, making breathing hurt. Shoving the morbid thought aside, he tried to focus on possibilities. If she'd fallen out, wouldn't the paddle have gone with her? He looked to see it floating in the water that covered the bottom of the canoe. Walking to the front, he grabbed the handle and pulled it almost to the building. Grabbing her shoes and camera, he darted back into the building. *Where is she?*

Devin stood beside the open door and looked down at her camera, carefully sealed inside a container. If she'd had the time to stop and seal it up from the rain she would have had the sense to find somewhere to hole up until this passed. He had to hold onto that thought, because the alternative made his chest ache. Setting her shoes and the camera down, he turned back to stand in the open door. The wind had lessened, but after fighting it to swim, it could just be wishful thinking.

He wanted to scream and beat something into pieces. He felt utterly useless. Rayne was out there, somewhere, and he was being forced to hide in a shed and wait on the weather. Devin looked out at the lake, his eyes constantly moving, hoping to see her or anything that could tell him where she was. Another hour and dusk would arrive as his chances of finding her lessened, and he was having a hard time thinking that he may not be able to find her until morning. *She has to be okay. Let her be okay.*

He watched the wind send some small branches flying around the shore and snarled. Even if he tied the canoe to his body and started to walk along the shore of the lake, heading towards the small shelter at the other side, there was no way he would get there before dark. Then he remembered there was no way he could walk the whole distance because of the places that were not manageable on foot, and would have to get in the canoe and paddle around them. Devin may have a little added strength, thanks to his shifter abilities, but he wasn't superman by any terms. Did he dare try? He debated with himself as he continued to look out over the lake.

If he was going to be stupid enough to do it, he'd better be prepared which meant another trip outside and back to the house. He wasn't going without rope, his cell phone, and some sort of provisions in case he had to take cover. Should he check her camp area first? He didn't see her making it to the shore and back there, leaving her camera in the canoe. But, then again, the way the storm hit, he supposed it might be possible. A small part of him hoped he was freaking out in vain and she was at her camp, safe.

Cursing, he stripped the heavy wet jeans from his body and bolted out the door. As a wolf, he could get through the bush to her camp without having to fight the storm with each step.

He stumbled twice as the wind banged into his ribs. With quick moves, he braced his paws to prevent from toppling right over. Of course, he had to get to the bush first, before quick movement was possible. He was thinking he didn't love summer storms quite as much as he had thought, as he pushed himself to the limits trying to reach the haven of the trees.

Devin arrived at the camp area in one piece and stood at the edge, hidden in the trees for several moments. He hadn't stopped to consider what he was going to do when he did get here. He couldn't see in the cabin in this form, and if she was inside a naked man standing at the window may not be what she'd want to see. There was no movement in her car, no sign of anyone being in it. The tent, which miraculously was still staked to the ground and in one piece, flapped against the wind and not even he would sit inside it in weather like this. He looked towards the small cabin and wondered again how he was going to see inside. Creeping out of the bush on all fours, he went slowly towards the cabin and naked or not, decided he had to find out if she was in there.

He looked up at the window for a few seconds and then shifted with as much speed as he could. Crouching below the window, he moved off to the side and then stood up. Making sure he was as far to the edge of it as he could be, Devin glanced inside quickly and then leaned back against the wet wood. She wasn't there. Not even pausing longer than that, he shifted back to wolf and ran as fast as he could through the trees heading to his house.

As the house came into sight he reached the decision to call his father and tell him what he was about to do so someone would know if he was missing. How long would it take him in this storm to circle the lake, on two feet? He'd done it in the past, but never in a storm that he would have to outwit with each step. By dawn if they didn't hear back from him, his father would know to alert someone. Devin had a few moments of guilt at putting him through that, but at this point he didn't have a choice.

Chapter Nineteen

Devin dropped the bag beside Rayne's shoes and shifted back. He dropped down to the floor. He was tired already and hadn't even begun searching. He didn't want to wait any longer than needed, but if he didn't stop for a few and take in some food he wouldn't make it. Shifting was hard on his man and the more he shifted back and forth, the more energy he consumed. Opening the bag, he pulled out some awful vanilla flavored nutritional supplement bars and ripped open the packaging. He'd prefer a large steak at this point, but didn't have time for that, and he couldn't very well find Rayne and offer her meat. She'd told his wolf she was a vegetarian, which at the time had been too ironic for thought, but he'd remembered at the last moment when he was packing a few supplies.

Devin stood up and dressed between bites. He hoped the nylon straps he'd brought would be long enough to tie to the canoe and hook over his shoulder, but wasn't sure. Whether they were or not wouldn't matter, between the lake and the rain, he was going to be soaked. Securing everything else back into the water-resistant bag, he looked once more down at her camera and stepped out the door into the rushing wind.

His shoulders hurt, back ached and he'd never been so wet in his life. Even the thought of a hot shower repulsed him right now. He'd made it almost to the shelter in roughly an hour. The wind was finally letting up, but the rain continued. His jeans were so wet, they were a few pounds heavier and he didn't want to think about what would be chafed in the morning. He hadn't thought to bring a flashlight, not that he needed one in the dark, but it would have allowed him to look further in the direction he was heading. If she wasn't at the shelter, he wasn't sure whether he was going to continue to drag the canoe along the shore or get in to paddle over each inch of the lake.

With the wind now lessened, he tried to pick up Rayne's scent. The heavy rain made that hard. Each tree and plant seemed to ooze their own fragrance and it was dizzying trying to sort through them to find a trace of her. He trudged on, his shoes slipping every few steps. His thoughts kept shoving too many what ifs forward as he became wearier, but he managed to shake them off. She was going to be okay, maybe wet and scared, but otherwise fine. He had to keep positive or he'd lose it completely, and then he'd be no help to anyone.

Twenty more feet and he'd be there. Devin paused and stood there, suddenly aware that the rain had ended. He listened just to be sure. It was over, finally.

Devin hurried to the shelter, taking the strap from across his chest and flipping it over his head as he went. He wrapped it around a tree and ran the last few feet to the shelter. Pushing the door open, he half expected a greeting but was met with an empty silence. He stood in the small door and looked at the vacant space, she wasn't here. Closing his eyes, he dropped his head down and tried to curb the anxiety that was choking him. *Where do I look now?*

He turned and walked back towards the canoe. When he reached it, he stared without a clue of where to look next. He would not think the worst, not until he'd searched each inch of the land around the lake. She was going to be just fine, he was going to find her. He looked out across the lake and scowled. When he'd spotted the canoe blowing adrift he had thought she was safe.

Turning back, he pulled the strap from the tree and a thought hit him. He spun back to the lake and looked over to the other end. He'd been in the shower building when he'd spotted it and the wind was blowing East over the lake, maybe more North-East. He turned and looked back towards the shore near the building, the wind had been pretty consistently gusting in the same direction, so that meant the canoe possibly came from the North-East side of the lake. He could be completely wrong, but it was the best idea of where to head to next. Tossing the strap into the canoe he stepped in and sat down.

The whole lake and area around it was silent now, only crickets could be heard, which increased his chances of finding her. When he was close enough to the shore line he could call her and if there were things such as the fates, they would make her hear him and answer.

Devin paused every few strokes and let the canoe coast silently through the water, while listening for any sign of something or someone not normally in the bush surrounding the lake. Limbs were cracking as things settled after the storm, making it hard to single out any particular sound. How long had she been out here? He tried to do the math to distract his mind as he paddled. He'd watched her play around near the shore for only a few minutes and then he'd gone back to the archives. Two cold cups of coffee later he looked out to see the clouds. Two hours, maybe and then two of pacing around the house like a lunatic. Five hours? Closer to six that she'd been out here alone, he guesstimated. Which would be about four hours longer than she'd be able to cope with, or was that him that couldn't cope with it?

Devin sliced the paddle through the water with as much strength as he could find and headed towards the clearest area on the shoreline. "Rayne!" He bellowed and listened to it echo in the night. Pausing with the paddle in the air, he listened and looked. Nothing. He paddled several more feet and then called out again. He heard the sound of branches breaking, he didn't know if it was something falling from the tree tops or something moving on the ground, but it was the first inkling of hope he'd felt, so he paddled with a new-found speed until he was running adrift up the shore.

Grabbing the strap, he snagged it on a log near the water's edge and splashed with wide strides onto the shore. "Rayne?" He called out and then held his breath, waiting. More branches snapped almost straight ahead of him. He took a few cautious steps in that direction, allowing his wolf instincts to the surface just in case it wasn't something he wanted to find.

Every muscle in his body tensed and he stopped. He'd heard...

"Here."

He heard it again and wildlife didn't gasp out words. Devin stumbled through some small bushes towards the one word whispered to the night. "Rayne? Stay where you are and talk to me so I can find you." He wanted to charge through the trees to find her, but without sure direction he'd only be wasting his time. The wet smells of nature after the storm didn't allow for him to pick up her scent.

"Here. I'm here."

He heard more movement.

"Please."

He headed towards the sounds of movement, having heard them better than the voice. Just as he was about to stop and call out to her again he saw a movement in the corner of his eye. He spun around and then stopped short. She was leaning against a large tree, with her head resting on her arm. He ran to her, almost sliding into her on the wet soil. "Are you all right?"

She leaned into his chest without speaking. Devin wrapped his arms around her cold, shivering form and tried to slow his heart enough so he could speak. "Are you hurt?"

She clung to his wet shirt. "Foot," she breathed.

Without waiting for any further explanation, he scooped her up into his arms and walked back towards the canoe. Every muscle in her body was rigid and cold.

"Sorry," she croaked in a voice that was raw.

"Shh, we'll get you back to the house and fixed up." He tucked her head under his chin as he trudged back into the water to set her in the canoe. Setting her in the middle of it, he yanked on the strap until it came free and tossed it into the canoe. Climbing in, he sat behind her on the bottom of the canoe and pulled her back into his arms, and then he remembered the blanket. Reaching around her, he pulled the bag closer, pulled the plastic bag from her shoulders and wrapped the blanket around her.

He had intended to wrap her in it and then get up on the seat to paddle, but as soon as he secured it around her shoulders she leaned into him again and he found he wasn't able to move even that short distance away from her. He needed to be close to her right now as much as she needed to be close to him. Shifting without moving her more than he needed to, Devin knelt on the bottom and reached for the paddle. His legs wouldn't like this, but if this is what she needed to make her feel better, then he had no choice.

She still hadn't moved when he was half way across the lake, so he paused long enough to check on her. "How are you doing?" She rubbed her face into his chest but didn't speak. At least her shivering had eased up a little bit. "I'll have you in a warm bath shortly, hun. Just hang on." Determined that he was telling her the truth, he forced his aching arms to guide the canoe towards the shore with as much speed as possible.

Chapter Twenty

As her brain slowly registered consciousness Rayne wondered if she was getting better at this outdoors stuff or maybe just used to the air mattress. She didn't recall it being this soft though...

Her eyes popped open and she looked up, not having the slightest idea of where she was. She ached, everywhere. Squeezing her eyes shut again, Rayne struggled through the fog for some answers and then it all came back to her, the lake, the canoe, the storm and—Devin. She jerked her body up onto her elbows and looked all around to see where she was.

It was a huge room that was not her tent or little cabin. A hospital was out of the question, unless she'd become royal. Turning her stiff neck, she was startled to see Devin slumped in a chair sleeping. She was in Devin's house.

Just seeing him forced her mind to fill in all the blanks. He'd found her, just when she'd almost given up him even noticing she was missing. He'd brought her back in the very same canoe that had left her stranded and held onto her in the hot shower, clothes and all until her arms had feeling again and then he'd tended each of her scratches with some sort of silky ointment. Rayne looked down and noticed she was wrapped in a big fuzzy navy robe that she didn't remember *anything* about.

She started to climb out of the warm blankets but the slightest movement of her foot made her drop back against the pillow and try not to moan out loud. She'd forgotten about her foot too. Lifting the cover, she grit her teeth and bent her leg up so she could see her foot. A white bandage was wrapped around it covering the bottom. Sitting up carefully, Rayne assessed the rest of her body for further injury and pain, there wasn't anything more serious than a few muscle aches. She decided she was very lucky and continued to attempt getting out of bed.

The loud shrill of a phone startled Rayne and her foot hit the floor sending jarring pains all the way up her leg. Who in their right mind in this day of ringer choices would opt for that racket? Lifting the foot quickly she turned to see Devin had bolted from the chair and was reaching for the phone.

"Hello? Hang on." He tilted his head and looked at her as he held the phone against his chest. "Don't try to get up yet. I'll be right back."

He turned and strode from the room so quickly that she had to admire his coordination after a startling wake up. Rayne didn't pause on that thought very long. Why shouldn't she try to get up yet? Was there more wrong with her than she knew? Flipping the covers completely off, she pulled the robe up so to see her legs. Other than a few scratches and digs there didn't seem to be anything wrong with them. She peeked into the top of the robe and wasn't shocked by anything new there either. She flexed the foot that wasn't wrapped up and other than it being a little tender, it seemed fine. Maybe he was just one of those paranoid people.

Swinging her legs off the bed again she slowly lowered them towards the floor. It wasn't pleasant, and burned more than she wanted to admit, but still didn't see why she shouldn't be able to get up and move around. The alternative to getting up and moving was to stay in a strange man's bed in a house she wasn't welcome in, and that didn't seem like something she wanted to do today. Rayne managed to get onto both feet and mostly upright when he came back into the room.

"No, just a little banged up, nothing serious."

She stopped and held onto the table beside the bed and looked at him. She may not know the first thing about the man, but the look he was sending her was very displeased and she concluded it was because she was doing what he'd said not to.

Now, he stood in the door way with one hand on his hip, his eyes moving over her slowly. "I'll call you later, thanks, Dad." He lowered the phone. "Well, you didn't land on your face as I suspected you might." As he moved towards her he tossed the phone on the bed. "I couldn't get you to eat or drink anything last night, so dehydration has been a concern..."

Rayne snorted. "I had more than my share of water, thank you."

"I can relate." He stopped in front of her and smirked. "The hot shower was for my benefit to return all the circulation to the right spots."

She hadn't thought of what he'd gone through to find her, he'd seemed so invincible. "I'm sorry, I didn't mean to come across as snarky and unappreciative."

Reaching, he held out his hand. "You weren't. I'd be downright miserable if I went through what you did." He flexed his hand. "Let me help and we'll go hunt down some coffee."

The magic words. Rayne reached a shaky hand out to his. "Coffee is just what the doctor ordered." She didn't realize it until she grasped his hand how weak she really was. The startling awakening had worn off and reality was setting in. She took a few limping steps towards him before he reached around her and hugged her waist.

"I can carry you."

There was such concern in his voice Rayne had to stop and look up at him. He looked as tired as she was suddenly feeling. "I'd like to at least try to get there on my own feet."

His expression went blank, but he nodded and stood there with his arm around her.

Rayne took a few more steps and bit her lip so she wouldn't hiss out loud. He made a sound that almost sounded like a growl, but she continued to move because if she stopped there wouldn't be starting again. The throbbing in her foot radiated up into her ankle and even though he was keeping most of her weight from hitting the floor it still brought tears to her eyes.

"Sorry," he said abruptly and then she was swung up into his arms. He shrugged his head to one side and started walking. "I'm a wimp, I can't deal with seeing anyone in pain."

She clung to his neck, her head felt dizzy from the fast movement. Somehow, she doubted he was a wimp of any kind, but was silently grateful as the pain in her foot lessened. "How bad is my foot?" Rayne looked in the direction they were going and tried not to notice the musky smell of him.

He grunted a noncommittal sort of noise. "Not bad. It's not deep, just inconveniently located. It should be fine in a few days."

She didn't know what to say. Was she supposed to stay here for a few days or could she manage back at her little cabin? She avoided having to answer for now, as he stepped into his kitchen and set her gently on a chair. He tenderly grasped the injured foot and pulled out another chair and rested it there.

"You should eat something too."

Rayne rubbed a hand over her face and then looked back at him. "Coffee first and foremost, please."

He gave her another one of those lopsided smirks causing her heart to slam against her ribs. "Strong and mean or diluted?"

She had no choice but to grin at that. "Strong and mean, please."

Devin nodded and turned to the counter. She watched

him as he moved around and started the coffee maker. His movements were fluid and that told her he had survived without being damaged like she was. "Devin, thank you, for coming to find me."

Flicking the machine on, he turned and rested one hip against the counter. "No problem." He seemed very nonchalant about it.

"Rescue a lot of damsels in distress?"

His eye brows shot up for a second and then he shook his head. "No. You would be the first and if I'm lucky, the last." His grey eyes burned into hers for a moment with such emotion. "I didn't think I was going to find you." Pain moved through his eyes.

"Well you did and that's all that matters to me." She continued to look into his eyes and wasn't sure if she was just tired and groggy or he was, but the way he was looking at her was like a caress. Rayne sighed quietly. *I really need that coffee, and soon.*

Jolting ramrod straight, he quickly turned to face the cupboards and opened one, taking two mugs out. "I'm sorry if I came across as a bit of a jerk when you first got here."

She grinned at his back. "Don't worry about that, I more or less invaded your space." She glanced out the window. "Other than the horrible habit of it storming here, I don't blame you for protecting your territory, it's beautiful here."

He kept his back to her and was silent for too long for her to feel comfortable. "I, uh, I'm a little too used to having my own space."

"I came to find some space of my own." Rayne watched him pour the amazing smelling coffee into the mugs. "I can go..."

"No. That's not necessary." He turned and set the mugs on the table before turning back to the counter. Opening another cupboard, he pulled out two bowls. "It's a big space, I'll share."

Rayne didn't know why, but it felt like she'd just been

granted something that didn't happen often. She suspected this man in front of her didn't voluntarily share his space or time with many. "Thank you."

Devin moved back over to the table with cereal and the bowls and set them down before turning towards the fridge. "On one condition."

She paused in taking a sip.

"You stop thanking me and apologizing."

She lowered the cup and watched him walk over with the milk. His eyes held amusement. "I can do that," she said quietly before taking a sip of the coffee.

"Good." He sat down and picked up his own mug. "Can I ask why you did come here?"

Rayne lowered the cup again and looked down into the steaming dark liquid. "To get away. To start over." She couldn't talk to this man, a stranger about why, she couldn't even think about it completely just yet. She chanced a glance at him through her lowered eyelashes.

He sat there watching her. "Fair enough." That was all he said and then lifted his own cup and took a drink.

Thank you was on the tip of her tongue, but she swallowed it down with another drink of the bold brew.

Several moments went by as they sat there silently just looking at each other and drinking. Rayne put her mug on the table and cupped it between my hands. "Was that your father that called? He knew?"

Devin nodded in thought for a second. "I called him before I went out to find you, just in case something happened."

"Oh." She was surprised, but not. Of course, he knew more about things like that and would think to call someone beforehand. She had no one to call, Rayne remembered. She flicked her eyes down to look at the floor, so he wouldn't be able to see what she was feeling. Lost and alone, it was as if it was sinking in just now. *I have no one anymore.* Rayne cleared her throat and pushed the cup further onto the table. She turned in the chair and was pulling her sore foot off the other when she heard him shove his back from the table. "Which way is the bathroom?" She couldn't sit here in front of this man and fall apart.

"I can take you." He was on his feet in front of her before she could object.

"I'd like to try on my own." She shifted and braced a hand on the table and pushed herself to her feet. Rayne couldn't help the sharp intake of breath when she put her weight onto her throbbing foot.

Grabbing her other hand, he gently squeezed it. "Just—wait, I'll be right back."

Rayne watched him dart out of the room, not sure what to do. She didn't have a choice but to wait, she had no idea where the bathroom was. He was back before she figured out what to do with a wooden cane in his hand.

"I carved it a few years ago, seemed like something new to do."

She sent him a puzzled look, but accepted it. "It's lovely." And it was. It was smooth across the handle with chips carved out of it in an organized pattern down the length of it. Rayne lowered it to the floor and moved to take another step. The cane was a bit tall, but then again, she was a bit short. After another step, she figured it out. Her foot still objected, but it was slightly more bearable now. "Thank you, it's much better."

He sent her an annoyed look, probably because she'd thanked him, again. "The bathroom is the second door on the left." He pointed.

Nodding to him so she wouldn't say thank you aloud, she slowly moved toward the door, not stopping even to look around. She just wanted to get there without wobbling awkwardly as she tried to focus on using the cane. It took synchronization to use one, and with the way she was feeling, a lot of concentration.

When she reached the bathroom, Rayne quickly went in and closed the door. Resting her head against it she shut her eyes and let out a sigh of relief. She knew she couldn't hide in here forever, she would have to go back out there, she just needed a few minutes alone to shake the pitiful-me feeling before she faced him again.

She slid down to the floor right where she'd been leaning. Rayne didn't need any soul searching or to take stock of her life. She knew her situation, what she didn't know was why it was bothering her more now than it had yesterday. She shook her head and looked down at her foot, blaming it on being tired and sore wasn't good enough for her. She picked at the robe that covered her legs thinking that she should ask for some clothes. Not that it wasn't a nice robe, she just wasn't sure she should be wearing a stranger's clothes. Lifting the collar Rayne buried her nose in it and inhaled. It smelled of Devin's deep musky scent, which made sense as it was his. Straightening up she frowned at the wall, what possessed her to sniff his clothes she couldn't know.

The peculiar idea of telling Devin everything popped into her head. *How would I even begin? Where would I begin? Tell him about my parents dying and how the head of some sort of criminal ring took me in, only I didn't know? Explain to him how I took money and my ex's car and drove as far as I could to get away from him and now I was hiding?* She let out a wistful breath, he'd probably tell her to leave then. Rayne glanced back down at her foot, not that she could drive until this was healed.

"Rayne? Are you all right?"

She slid away from the door. "Yes. Be out in a minute." She listened to make sure he moved away from the door. Hearing a few movements, but couldn't be sure, he moved very quietly for a man, she waited a little longer. Aiden wasn't as tall as Devin, but you could hear him coming from three rooms away. Rayne squeezed my eyes closed. She was not going to compare them. There was nothing to compare, nothing similar other than they both were male. She attempted to convince herself, but knew she was only fooling herself.

She stood up slowly, trying to stretch her sore muscles

without putting too much weight on her foot. When she turned and looked in the mirror she almost shrieked. Her hair was all over the place, sticking out and clumped together. *Well, what did you expect when you hang out in a storm?* She shuffled over to the mirror and leaned in to take a closer look. Around her eyes the skin was shadowed, a long scratch covered one cheek. No wonder the man didn't want her to move, she looked like she was a zombie from some d-list movie.

Turning away from the mirror, she stared at the tub, a bath would feel wonderful, but the idea of having one while he stood outside the door felt all wrong. Sighing loudly, she decided to go back out.

Chapter Twenty-One

Devin wasn't hovering outside the door as she'd imagined. In fact, she didn't see or hear him, anywhere. She got as far as the open area at the end of the hall and knew she needed to stop and rest. A large couch in the sitting area called to her, so she elected to try for that instead of attempting to reach the kitchen.

Rayne had just managed to reach the couch and sit down when he appeared in the doorway carrying a tray.

Tilting his head, he gave her a once over. "Feel a bit like you just ran a mile?" She nodded, not trusting her voice. "I didn't think you'd sprint any time soon."

Rayne hoped the tray carried coffee, because she really needed the shot of caffeine. He came over and set it on the table, she'd been half right, it had the coffee, toast and juice.

"You really need to eat something in or you're not going to feel any better."

"I know." She let him lift her legs and swing her around on the couch, while she trying not to notice the warmth of his hands on her skin. Rayne took the cup of juice he offered her and somehow knew she'd have to drink it to get the coffee back. She took a sip and watched him sit on the table. "You could have warned me that I looked like night of the dead.”

He chuckled. “I thought it was better that you looked for yourself.”

She grimaced, he was right.

Shrugging, he leaned down onto his knees, his eyes wandering all over her face. “I was going to go check and make sure your tent and things were still there, get you some clothes...”

Rayne dropped her head back and closed her eyes, she hadn’t even thought of that. “Yes, please.” Opening them slowly she looked back at him. “I know I’m not supposed to thank you, but I am, again. This...” she waved a hand around in the air, “...is a whole new world for me, and in case I have been faking too well, I really have no clue.” She turned her head to avoid looking at him and noticed her camera sitting on the table. She straightened up. “You found my camera.” It came out in a mumbled way.

“It was still in the canoe when I swam out to it...”

Rayne snapped her head back around to look at him. “You swam out to it?” *Is he insane?*

“I didn’t have to go far, the wind was pushing it in faster than I could ever swim.”

She knew her eyes bulged open as she looked at him. “Are you crazy? To swim in that? I may not be Miss Wilderness here, but that—*that* was not something anyone should have attempted.”

His brow creased as he watched her. “I thought you were still in the canoe and I wasn’t going to leave you bobbing around the lake in the middle of a storm.”

“Oh.” She looked at his arms and over the rest of his body slowly. “What else did you have to go through to find me?” Pains of guilt flashed through her. *Not crazy, just heroic.*

Devin shrugged. “I pulled the canoe along the shore, hoping you’d made it to the shelter.” Her eyebrows shot up, not knowing what shelter he was referring to. “You were blown in the other direction I’m guessing.” He rubbed a hand over his chest. “I have a bit of chafing from the strap, and got really, *really* wet but it's nothing."

Rayne set the juice down and sat up. "Chafing?" She knew what chafing was, mostly but she didn't know what he meant.

He exhaled slowly and straightened up and lifted his t-shirt up. There was a red bruise running across his chest.

She swung her good foot off the couch and leaned closer. "You *tied* the canoe to you?" He looked from her to his chest and started to lower the shirt. Rayne stopped him and gently ran her hand beside the mark.

"Yeah," he sucked in a breath as her fingers carefully caressed it.

"You need to put something on this." She rested her hand against his warm skin and looked back to his face. "Get me some ointment and I'll put it on." Rayne completely felt awful now that he'd gone through this because of her.

He leaned back, causing her hand to drop away. "I did." He pulled his shirt back down quickly and sat up straight, his hands on his knees. The guilt must have been visible on her face because he sighed loudly. "I'm fine, it doesn't even hurt."

She bit her lip and studied him for a moment. She was going to apologize again, and as if he knew what was coming, he jumped up.

"I'll go check on your stuff." He stood looking down at her. "Eat the toast and I'll be back shortly."

She nodded without saying a word and watched as he almost ran from the room. Rayne waited until she heard the door close and dropped her head back onto the couch. She wasn't hungry, she was just plain tired. Guilt over what Devin had done again flooded through her. Begrudgingly she looked over at the tray with the toast on it. She'd eat the toast, just so she didn't burden him any longer than needed.

Chapter Twenty-Two

Feeling like a coward for running from her, Devin walked briskly through the trees. One innocent touch from her and his body went berserk. Her hand on his bare skin had brought him close to swallowing his own tongue, her touch was so soft, so warm. This was going to be harder than he thought. He needed to keep his distance to learn more about her, and doing that when she was under his roof and lying on his couch—in *his* robe, was just a little too tempting. He didn't want to send her back to her camp, not until she healed. His stomach tightened in an odd way. Devin stopped and rested his forehead against the rough bark of the closest tree while he thought this through. *Do I want to send her back at all?* His stomach clenched once more, *no I don't.* What was he going to do? He had no idea. All he did know was that he wanted her in his house close by.

Exhaling loudly, he turned and quickly closed the distance to her camp site. Did this happen to all the males that found their mates? That might be the reason many avoided being mated.

Walking through the door, Devin quickly bee lined to the sitting area, only to find she wasn't there. A few scraps of the toast were left on the plate sitting beside the empty juice glass, the pain killers he'd left on the tray were also gone. He turned and glanced into the kitchen, she wasn't there either. In long strides, he went towards the bedroom and stopped suddenly when he noticed the studio door was open.

Stepping through the doorway he stopped and just stood there. Her back was towards him, he had to smile when he noticed how big the robe was on her, coming close to touching the floor. She stood without moving as she studied the five paintings along the one wall, they were all various storms he'd painted. Devin thought they were quite good, but he may be a little biased. He held his breath when she turned and hobbled with the cane towards the one that had her image in it. She was never meant to see that one.

He cleared his throat, so he wouldn't startle her and felt he should offer an explanation. "I'm not a stalker." Her spine stiffened. "Painting you was a nice change, I seem to be in a rut."

She laughed softly. "I don't think I'd describe your work as a rut." The cane clicked across the wooden floor as she moved back to the first painting. "When I first stepped in here I thought I'd just discovered a brilliant artist." She smirked over her shoulder at him. "Then I read the signature." She turned to face me completely. "You're D. Addison."

He jammed his hands into his pockets and nodded, not sure why her tone made him feel like a chastised child.

"I've always liked your flare for enhancing the tiny details, most painters will just blur the small stuff and make the main focal point something larger."

Devin was shocked, she knew his work. Not that he was an unknown, he lived off the commissions from his painting. He was just surprised that she knew his paintings. "I see things differently I suppose."

Rayne jerked her head towards the painting with herself in it. "Do I have any say with that one? I'd prefer not to be hung over someone's mantel."

"I think I'll keep it all to myself."

"Good. Thank you." She turned back to the paintings once more and wobbled a little.

He reached her in three strides. "You should be resting." He placed a hand gently on her arm, afraid she was going to tip right over.

"I know, I thought this door might lead to the outside so I could sit in the sun." She sighed. "I still feel cold." She moved to head back out of the room. "Thank you for not being a temperamental artist and throwing a fit when you caught me snooping." She teetered again, sidestepping a few steps, and then hissing out a breath when she stepped on her injured foot.

Devin didn't ask, he just scooped her up into his arms and started for the door. "I am very temperamental, but I can't rant at someone that isn't up to full strength."

"I'm glad I'm feeble at this moment, then."

Her smile hit him and went right through his chest. He tried not to feel like he was falling into her eyes, but it wasn't working. Just looking into her eyes gave him a sense of completion, and made him experience physical urges that were not nearly as mellowing. "I'm sure you'll be up to one of my offended artist rants in no time." He went over to the couch and set her down. "I'll give you a hand getting some of the tangles out of your hair and then you can soak in the tub and see if you can get some warmth back into your bones." She nodded and offered him a tired smile, which made him worry that there, might be something really wrong. Maybe her foot was infected. Should he take her to a doctor so they can check her out? He'd reassess that later once she'd rested further.

Going over, he picked up her brush. He'd been thankful it was in plain sight when he stepped into her cabin, rifling through her things was not a task he was prepared to resort to. He debated on how to go about brushing her hair while she was leaning back on it. He could kneel at the end of the couch and do it that way, but he wanted to be closer to her.

Yes, he remembered the whole internal discussion on the way to her camp site, but he had never thought of himself as smart. Leaning down, he helped her to sit upright, then slid behind her to cradle her between his thighs. She willingly leaned further away so he could work between their bodies.

Devin started at the bottom, figuring if he worked his way up it would hurt less. "I'm afraid I'm out of practise, I haven't brushed someone else's hair since my sister was young." He grinned at the memory. "She had long hair then, and got tangled in some burrs, mother threatened to cut it off..." Leaning her head to the side to rest on the couch, she seemed completely relaxed with his touch.

"You have a sister? That must be nice."

He worked carefully, hoping it wasn't pulling too much. "You don't have any brothers or sisters?"

"No. I always wanted at least one, but mama said it wasn't in the cards."

No siblings. "I'm sure you kept your parents busy."

"Are you insinuating I was a handful?"

It was hard not to notice how silky her hair was as it slid through his fingers, he had to focus to keep from lifting it to his nose to take in her unique scent. "No. Were you?"

She shook her head slightly. "I don't think so. We moved a lot though, so maybe I was a bit pouty from time to time."

"Your parent's jobs move you around?"

"I don't think so, I don't remember much about the places when I was young. When they finally settled in Chicago, I was more than happy to find one place to call home." She exhaled slowly. "I still miss them. The last five years haven't been easy."

"Didn't you have any relatives nearby?" Her parents had both passed, was that why she didn't know who she was? She leaned back, making it a little more difficult to work on her long hair, but he wasn't about to tell her to move.

"No. Well, I'm sure I have some somewhere, but I've never met them. Mama always said that someday they'd take me home so I could meet our family but…"

"Do you know where home is?" She shook her head gently. "You've been on your own all this time?" He still hadn't pegged her age, and he was experienced enough to know not to ask.

Her shoulders stiffened, pulling her back away from him. "A family, the one my father worked for took me in."

Instinct told him to ask questions and find out why that upset her, but she sighed and leaned back against him again. He closed his eyes, enjoying the warmth of her body against his.

"I'm too tired to talk about all of that right now."

Not talking worked out fine for him too, as he tried not to inhale her scent each time he took a breath, but he was failing. The heat from her against him made his body grow hard inside the jeans. Devin shifted a little to not be pressed right into her, even though every single cell in his body wanted to press into her. Remembering the brush in his hand, he began to gently work on the top of her head, not even sure if he'd already done that area.

She made a quiet sound of contentment and leaned her back against his chest. He dropped the hand that held the brush and rested his chin on the top of her head.

"Devin?"

His groin responded to his name by pushing against the denim. "Yes," he barely managed to whisper.

"I don't think I'm going to be able to stay awake for the bath part. Those pills have kicked in and I feel so wonderfully relaxed suddenly."

Devin let the brush slide to the floor and lightly ran his hand down over her shoulder and arm. "Just rest, the tub will be there later." His brain told him to help her into the bedroom. His body didn't want her to move from where she was so he sat there, breathing shallowly, and trying to keep her scent from enveloping him further. It wasn't working.

After some long moments of internal torment, she stirred in his arms. He was ready to get up when she turned on her side and snuggled into his chest. Her hip rested against the throbbing hard-on in his pants, and he could barely control the drive to give into his urges. When he looked down and noticed the robe gaped and one creamy breast was visible, he quickly pulled the robe closed. Forcing his eyes away from her breast, they traveled back up to her face to see her eyelids flutter open before she looked up at him. *Does she have any idea how sexy she looked right now half asleep? I'm sick, I know this now, she is exhausted, injured and medicated and all I want to do is rub my naked body against hers.* Her eyes fluttered again and her lips curved into a small smile. Did she know what he was thinking?

"You're so warm, it's nice."

Warm? That's an understatement, I'm on fire from the inside out.

"Do you want me to move?" She whispered breathlessly, causing his heart and other parts of anatomy to respond.

Did I? "No," he said quickly before she did. "Just rest." He slid their combined weight down a bit further so she would be more comfortable. The movement shifted her hip so it rubbed over the bulge he was trying to ignore. He may not make it with his sanity intact having her close, but she needed to rest.

Devin placed his hands on her back, concentrating on not moving them over her body. She sighed again and turned her face into him, her warm lips brushed over his throat as she placed a sweet kiss against it. He squeezed his eyes shut and forced his body to go rigid so he wouldn't grab her.

Her warm body squirmed around while she got more comfortable. "Stretch out, you can rest too," she mumbled.

Does she know what she was asking of me? Could he lie with her, on this suddenly very small piece of furniture, and *just* rest without touching her? He hadn't even decided what to do when he realized his body was doing just that. Careful to not jar her foot, he flipped them both on their sides, so they were facing each other.

"Much better," she whispered against his throat.

Devin swallowed and counted to ten inside his head. "Rayne?" She made a noise that caused her lips to vibrate against his throat, spurring flames that engulfed his guts. "I can't resist you. I'm going to..."

"Then don't," she sighed and leaned into him more.

He lay there feeling the heat from the length of her body against him, trying to decide if he'd heard her correctly. Her warm breath against his throat was driving him crazy, he had to get up, now.

"Devin, kiss me. Then rest," she mumbled as she leaned her head back.

He'd get up in a minute. *One kiss, how can I say no to that?* He couldn't resist a small taste of her, at least this was his reasoning as he lowered his mouth to hers. Devin hesitated close enough to taste her breath, and before he could decide if he should her arm snaked up around his neck and pulled his head towards hers.

He only meant a mere touching of lips, just a small taste, but the second her soft lips brushed over his, he completely forgot. Her warm mouth opened to him and he grasped that opportunity to plunge his tongue into the wet cavity of her mouth. She tasted of home and sin, and he didn't know how he was going to stop.

Devin ran his hand down her back, pulling her tight against him. Flames shot through his groin, tightening with anticipation. She gasped into his mouth and the last threads of logical thought flew from his mind. He wanted her in a way he'd never wanted another woman in his life, and here she was in his arms, against his body. Rising onto one arm he leaned over her, without taking his mouth from her eager one, then he pinned her to the cushions with his whole body, revelling in the feel of her beneath him.

Her small hand grabbed his hair and pulled so he couldn't move away, not that he had any plans to. He was drinking her in, as he worked out how to manage this on the couch. Devin wasn't small and he didn't want to hurt her any more than she already was. Then he realized the last thoughts, and if someone had poured ice water over their heads, he didn't think he would have come back to reality faster.

Wrenching his mouth from hers, he buried his face in her neck and tried to remember how to breathe as he dug for the will to move away from her. Her fingers continued to move through his hair as she hugged his head to her. "Before I forget you're..." Her mouth moved against his ear and lust surged again. "You need rest, I can't do this." Devin moved back and his lower body slid off the couch. Coming to his knees, he looked down at her glazed eyes and had to clench his jaw to stop from climbing right back up there with her. "You need sleep, hun."

He pulled her into his arms and walked with stiff legs towards the bedroom. This was where he found out how strong he really was, he thought as he lowered her to the bed. *Now, walk away.* Devin stood there looking down at her, with her golden hair spread across *his* pillow and felt his resolve fading quickly. Before it was completely gone, he took a step back. "You rest."

She gave him a sleepy smile and his heart skipped several beats. "Okay," she rolled onto her side and closed her eyes.

He continued to stand there, his eyes roving over her, his heart softening even as his body still throbbed. Devin hadn't even realized he was moving back towards her until the bed bumped against his leg. Rubbing a hand over his face, he turned to get out of there, stumbling over his own feet as he did.

Chapter Twenty-Three

Devin was pacing around the yard when he caught a whiff of exhaust fumes. He felt every nerve in his body tightening, ready to face an intruder, when the black cruiser appeared through the trees coming towards the house. He curbed the need to growl at the Sergeant as he got closer, Devin didn't want anyone near Rayne. In some areas of life, he was willing to compromise, sort of, but not this one. An odd realization to have hit him with the car only a few feet away now.

The car stopped and the man inside opened the window. "Hey, Devin."

"Mark." He'd known him years before he's ever worn a badge. Devin hadn't liked him then either. "What brings you out this far?"

He shrugged. "Just checking into a stolen car and I thought I'd drop in and see if you'd seen anything."

"A car?"

He nodded.

Devin made an exaggerated motion of looking around the driveway.

Mark laughed. "I didn't mean one that pulled right up to your door, I wondered if you'd been out painting or whatever and seen anything."

"Haven't gone far lately. What am I looking for if I do?" Devin was relieved he was staying in his car, with his blood still running a little hot, he didn't want to take a chance on doing something stupid like he'd almost done inside a short while ago.

"It crossed the border a few days back, it's a white Cabriolet, one of those little tiny boxy cars..."

"I know what one looks like, Mark." He needed to leave and he needed to do it now. "I'll keep an eye out."

"Appreciate it." He nodded once and then put the window back up.

Devin stood without moving and watched until he couldn't see his car. A white Cabriolet? It wasn't a coincidence that Rayne drove the same thing. He shook his head and then looked back to the house. He may have been out of touch with the rest of the population on the planet, but he knew Rayne wasn't a car thief. Devin could sense a lie and smell scents that went with them, and he knew she hadn't lied so far.

Frowning, he started towards her campsite. Devin didn't want to snoop around in her things, but he couldn't just pretend this hadn't happened. What could happen that would make her steal a car and hide this far from where she'd been?

He was almost to the site before he decided that he was going to have to move down another level to find out who the car belonged to. Devin had to know and if he asked her, or told her about the police looking for her, she might run and he *knew* he couldn't live with that. There had to be a damn good reason why Rayne had taken a car and drove this far to hide.

He glanced at the car as he went into the cabin. If he could find her keys then look at the registration and not have to search further. Pausing inside, he surveyed the room. Everything was neat and in order, so he would have to be careful to not move anything out of place. Devin walked to what looked like a purse, the most logical place to start but stopped when he saw it was behind another bag that looked like a purse. Regardless of reason, no male wanted to put his hand into a purse. He cursed under his breath and turned to see what was on the other side first, a glint of caught his eye and he found himself looking at a ring of keys hanging under the window. He struggled with a moment of disappointment, having found them so easily. He had to admit, then, that he'd wanted to go through her things to see what else he could find out. In the last few days a few kinks in his personality had been shown to him, and he wasn't happy with the revelations.

Devin paced along the path a third time, his mind too scattered to make the call. He looked down at the phone in his hand and then back to the front door of his house. He couldn't take a chance of calling his father in the house, in case Rayne woke up. Sometimes finding out your gut instincts are right isn't a good thing, and of course this was one of those times. Devin's mind was lost right now, the thousand scenarios bouncing around weren't helping. He didn't even know where to begin.

Confirming, from an old photo, that Rayne was indeed Nicholas and Sarah Andrews' daughter had been the highlight of his search. He hadn't searched through *everything*, just the one case sitting on passenger's seat of her car. He'd stopped after that, not needing anything else. That was the good part. The rest fell somewhere between anger and jealousy, and all the degrees of annoyance from one to the other. Rayne's car was not *her* car it was registered to a man. A man, if he wasn't mistaken that she sure as hell *shouldn't* have ever been anywhere near, yet her driver's license had the same address as the car registration. If that was *the* family that had taken her in when her parents died, the one her father had worked for, then the beginning of something ugly was here.

Devin let out a ragged breath. Aiden Tomas, the son of Alberto was one of the families, and he used that term in a non-blood-relative-very-criminal way, that the Alliance was trying to erase, diplomatically of course. That *family* had been known to blackmail and entrap shifters into unlawful and dangerous employment for more years that he could remember. What was Rayne doing with them? How had she gotten this far out of their grasp? It was no wonder she didn't know her own heritage, her parents probably hid it to protect her. He didn't want to dwell on how they had died, he knew it wasn't by any natural means. Did Rayne know this? Was that why she was here? Too many questions and not enough answers. He had to remedy that.

Devin took a deep breath as he dialled the phone. His mother answered. "Hello, Mom. I need to speak to Dad," he closed my eyes and reached for some patience, "It's Alliance business." Surprised when she relinquished the phone immediately to his father. Well, perhaps that was the key to getting around her? He could hear his father walking somewhere, probably private.

"Devin?"

"Yeah." Everything he'd just learned flooded to his mind at the same moment and Devin didn't know where to start in trying to explain it all to him.

"Is everything okay, son? Is *she* all right?"

The mention of Rayne grounded him, helped find his focus. "Yes and no. She'll be fine in a day or two from her boat trip, but there's a lot more going on than a few scrapes."

"Is there anything I can do?"

"Actually, there's a lot. I need you to look into a few things in the Alliance archives."

"Oh?"

His tone was suddenly harsher, that soft voice from seconds before gone. "I had a visit from the police, inquiring about a stolen car..."

"A car?" His confusion was more than clear.

"Just bear with me as I try to get all this vocalized. Dad, it's a mess."

"I'm listening."

"The car is the one Rayne was driving."

"Her name is Rayne?"

Devin had to ignore the warm feeling from hearing someone say her name. "Yes, and she *is* the daughter of Nicholas and Sarah."

"You've found them? Do I need to send the Alliance? Are they in trouble?"

"They're dead. I don't know how or when, I just know both of her parents are gone." He rubbed a hand over his jaw, trying to focus. He had his father's attention and he'd was on the way to getting answers. "The car Rayne is driving is registered to Aiden Tomas..."

"What?" Devin heard a door close loudly as he no doubt was ensuring he had complete privacy. "Was she running from him?"

"I don't know. I do know it had to be pretty serious, stealing a vehicle and driving from Chicago to here, is not something Rayne would do on a whim."

"I suppose not." He sighed loudly. "They're going to come after her."

"I know." Devin's chest felt tight.

"You can't let her out of your sight, Devin. If they find her, you won't see her again."

A pain went through his heart because he knew his Alpha was right. Some part of him had known that when he'd read the name on the registration. His father confirming it didn't make him feel any better. "I don't know how to keep her here, indefinitely."

He snorted in a way that wasn't from entertainment. "She's your mate, Devin. You'll find a way."

"She doesn't know her own heritage. She mentioned her mother wanting to take her home, but she has no idea about any of it..."

"If Aiden Tomas gets his hands on her, she'll find out in a very unhealthy way. The last informant we managed to get inside, before he vanished, was able to find out that they're trying to set up their own breeding program so they can raise their own. They mean to rent them out like hired guns..."

"I remember you discussing it with Calum's dad. I haven't thought much of it since, I thought you'd have dealt with it by now."

"We haven't. We've managed to get a few out, but that's made it worse for those that are still trapped inside."

"Dammit!" Devin wanted to beat or tear something apart. He took a breath and waited for a few seconds, giving them both a bit of time. "What do you suggest?"

"You have to find a way to tell her what she is, what you are..."

"I'm working up to it, slowly. I can't just shift in front of her, as far as I know she doesn't even know we exist." Devin swallowed the knot in his throat. "She's close to her first estrus." He hoped his father caught where he was going with that, because a part of his wolf understood it, but his human side was still trying to catch up.

His father sighed. He could hear his heels clicking along the wooden floor. "I was planning to send some of our pack that way, but not if she's close and yet—unclaimed."

He said the word as a challenge to Devin, and he knew it, just didn't have time for that right now to rise to it.

"I'm sending Calum. He's cat and shouldn't make you feel threatened in that way and he has a vested interested in making sure nothing happens to you and your mate."

Devin wanted to say no. It was right on the tip of his tongue, he wasn't sure if being cat was less of a threat than being male, but he did need backup and Calum and he had a fairly good understanding of one another. "Tell him to keep his distance, for now."

"I will. I'm going to see if I can find out what the Tomas family are doing about their missing... car."

"Keep me up-to-date. If they're heading this way I want as much notice as I can get."

"You'll get it." He cleared his throat. "Be careful, Devin. This is not going to be easy, mating issues, most especially when she isn't even aware and protecting her…"

He didn't need to add the explanation, Devin had already arrived at the same conclusion, the moment he'd tasted her and read the registration. "I'll call if I find out anything else."

"Do that." He hung up.

Chapter Twenty-Four

Rayne's mouth felt like she'd dipped her tongue in paste, and was so dry she could barely swallow. She would never take pills again without finding out exactly what they were. She was sure she'd never been that looped before from medication, but with everything she'd been through in the last day it wasn't completely shocking. Rolling over, she pushed back the covers, suddenly feeling too warm, which would have been welcome after constantly feeling cold since her storm experience, but this wasn't a toasty warm feeling. What she felt was hot and groggy, that same way you feel when you wake up with the flu, but haven't had any symptoms yet.

"Rayne?"

She opened her eyes, they seemed heavy or larger she wasn't sure, and tried to focus in on the man at the end of her—his bed. Rayne tried to swallow again. "Drink," she croaked. Devin moved with a startling speed and was beside her. He placed a cool hand on her forehead and she relished the feel of it for the few seconds he left it there. He cursed under his breath and moved away.

"I'll be right back."

She didn't watch him leave, her eyes fogged right over so

she just closed them and would wait until he came back. She wanted to go back to sleep, but felt so odd she wasn't sure it would be the best plan.

The mattress beside her moved. "Can you sit up?"

Rayne wanted to answer, or shake her head but she couldn't find the energy. The bed shifted some just before she felt him slide his arm under her shoulders. Everything spun as he lifted her head from the pillow.

"You need to drink. I think I underestimated your size when I left you those pills."

Rayne wanted to quip something sarcastic, but her vocal skills weren't up to the task. She felt the cool glass against her lips and was able to at least part them. As long as it washed this awful taste from her mouth and the fog from her body, she was willing to try. After three small sips, she was as least able to move her mouth. It took a few more sips for it to register on her taste buds that it wasn't water she was drinking, not that she was going to stop, it tasted okay and seemed to be washing the paste from her tongue. Rayne swallowed again and then tilted her head to the side.

"I'll get you some more shortly, you need to get upright and try to talk to me for a bit before you sleep it off."

She felt his warm lips against her forehead.

"I'm going to get a cool cloth for you."

As Rayne felt him move away she blinked a few times and tried to get her eyes working again. Her mouth felt better and she could swallow again, but her brain was still heavy under a fog blanket. When she tried to pull herself up, she had no strength in her arms. After three attempts, she should have been almost sitting up, but had only managed to move up on the pillow.

"Let me help." Devin's arm slid under her and pulled her into a sitting position so quickly her head floated for several heartbeats.

"What's wrong with me?" She was almost certain she had said it out loud.

"I'm not a doctor, but I think it's a combination of you

catching a chill last night and my underestimating your body size, giving you too much painkiller." He tucked the blanket around her waist and she felt him straightening the robe on her upper body, but didn't really care what it looked like.

"How's your foot?"

She felt the bed move and finally opened her eyes as wide as she could manage to see where he was. He was sitting by her side and fuzzy brain or not she could tell he was worried. Rayne thought about her foot and then rolled her eyes slowly back to him. "I don't have any feet right now," her speech was slow, even to her.

His grey eyes lit up and he smirked at her. "Definitely too much medication." He placed a wet cloth on her forehead and it felt amazing, she wanted to hold it but her arms were presently detached from the rest of her.

"I don't take drugs, normally." She had to focus to form each word and knew that should bother her but it wasn't. "My body doesn't react well to most drugs."

He sighed. "Now you tell me."

Rayne found her eyes wandering back to his lips. She remembered asking him to kiss me. "I'm sorry for before."

He moved the cloth over her eyes and down to the side of her neck. "For what?"

"Telling you to kiss me."

He chuckled, "You may not have noticed but persuasion wasn't really required, I was a willing participant."

Rayne grinned, at least she tried to. "I like the way you kiss. I shouldn't... even be thinking of stuff like that right now, but I can't help it."

He was grinning at her.

"I'm serious. Tell me no next time, for my own good." She watched him study her as she fought to stay focused and keep her eyes opened.

"Why shouldn't you?"

Rayne didn't want to talk about that with him but she opened her mouth and did anyways. "I don't usually throw myself into men's arms."

He snorted quietly. "Good to know."

"I don't. I can't get into a relationship right now." He moved the cloth from her face and she missed it as soon as he did.

"And why is that?" He just sat there looking at me.

"I just broke off an engagement." Rayne leaned her head to the side, it felt too heavy to keep upright. "I want to lie down again."

He still didn't speak, but gently helped her back down into the bed. She kept her eyes open as long as she could while he sat there looking at her. Rayne was just going to close her eyes for a few minutes until this groggy feeling went away and then she'd work on getting back to her campsite.

Chapter Twenty-Five

Looking into the room Devin checked on Rayne. As far
as mates went he wasn't doing a great job of keeping her safe.
He'd let her get lost in a storm, cut and then he over-
medicated her. Feeling inadequate wasn't something he had
ever experienced. Shaking his head, he forced himself to
leave her alone to rest, and went back to his small office. He
had to figure this out. If what she said meant what he
thought, then things were worse then he'd first imagined.
Rayne had not only taken Tomas's car, but she'd broken off
her engagement to him. Rage rushed through Devin's veins
at the thought of her being with a man like that, but he forced
it aside and looked back at the archive information on the
screen.

Nicholas hadn't been Sarah's true mate, but they had
been in love. After a challenge for Sarah by her mate they
had fled Canada and gone to the States. What the archive
wasn't going to tell him was how Nicholas had ended up in
servitude with the Tomas family.

The phone rang, he grabbed it so it wouldn't wake
Rayne. "Hello?"

"Devin. It's Calum."

He hadn't thought hearing from anyone would ease the

tension in his body, but Calum did that. "You've talked to father?"

"Briefly. I'm heading in that direction now, thought you could fill in some blanks."

Rubbing a hand over his eyes Devin opened them again and looked at the screen. "I have a lot of blanks myself."

He chortled, "That doesn't surprise me." He paused for a few seconds. "Look, after I got over my shock of your dad calling me to back you up, I realized you'd agreed and I have to tell you I never thought I'd see that day and it worries me."

"I know. How much do you know?"

"Well, you have a mate. Were you planning on sharing that sometime soon?"

Devin closed his eyes and exhaled loudly. "I've only had a few days to come to terms with it myself. I never imagined..."

Calum laughed, "We all know there's that one for us out there, and yet each time we're surprised. I was more referring to letting me in on it, I am your first and what affects you is going to affect both Gage and myself at some point."

He hadn't thought of that either, then again, it's not like he knew he had a mate before this week. If Devin took his place in the pack and Alliance, Calum was his first and Gage his second and the three of them would continue along that path until they passed it on to their sons. It was, regardless of his position, their responsibility to watch his back. Until this week, he'd never had the need for either one.

"Are you still there?"

"Yeah. Sorry my mind is all over the place right now."

"With good reason."

Devin got up and wandered over to the window. "Okay, quick summary. My mate doesn't even know what she is or anything about her own heritage, as far as I can tell. She's the daughter of Nicholas and Sarah Andrews, they're dead and he worked for the Tomas family in Chicago..."

"Shit! It's as bad as I imagined it was going to be."

"I'm not done yet." He took a deep breath and tried not

to focus on the jealousy that wanted to surface as he thought of the next part. "Rayne was engaged to Aiden Tomas, I don't know the details yet, but as far as I can figure she took one of his cars and took off and ended up here..."

"Jesus, Devin, we're going to be ass deep in it now." He sighed. "Couldn't you just have an impending challenge to your place in the pack or something?"

Devin ran a hand through his hair and tried to relax a bit. "I know."

"You should be high-tailing it back to your pack, where you have a lot more back up than myself."

"It's complicated. Rayne doesn't know anything." He glanced towards the door and debated on going to check on her.

"Anything? Are you saying she has no clue about Tomas? She had to know what her parents were."

"I don't think she did."

"Cripes, you had to do it all the hard way. So, what's the plan?"

"I'm waiting to see how bad her foot is and then head for higher ground. I just have to figure out how to tell her..."

"Wait. Her foot? You lost me. She's hurt?"

Devin went back over to the window and leaned against it. "She got caught in the storm last night, it took me hours to find her..."

"What the hell was she doing out in a storm? Is there something else I need to know?"

He pictured the expression on his friend and protectors face. Annoyed and confused unless Devin missed his guess. "It's a long story, Calum." He opened the window and let the breeze bring all the scents from outside in. Nothing seemed out of place. "How soon can you be here? Have you talked to Gage?" He may not be ready to be king, but he knew when he was outnumbered.

He made a noise that sounded like a cross between a growl and a laugh. "Gage is tail deep in his own mate issues right now."

Devin felt sympathy for him. "Kelsey's back?"

"Any day now, and he's barely hanging on."

He could hear the sounds in the background as Calum drove, he was still in the city. "I am so very thankful I haven't had to cool my heels for years knowing who my mate is, but not being able to touch her." He growled. "Besides if Gage knew that the Tomas's were involved, I don't think he'd be very cool-headed, it was never confirmed, but all directions pointed to them being the cause of Kelsey's parents' death."

Devin clenched his jaw. "I remember. If you're talking to him, tell him we're only a call away if he needs us."

"I did. Look, keep me informed, I'll be there tonight."

He still didn't like the idea of someone else around Rayne right now, but knew he didn't have any other option. "Let me know when you're here. I'm hoping by then I'll have found some way to tell Rayne what's going on."

"Good luck with that." He hung up before Devin could add anything further.

Had things just gotten better or worse? He didn't know, but none of it was going to be easy and he had to get started. Glancing again at the computer screen, Devin focused in on Nicholas's family line, someone needed to add Rayne to that. Flicking the screen off, he headed back towards the bedroom. He was out of time where letting her find out on her own was concerned.

Chapter Twenty-Six

After waking her up three times, she finally opened her eyes and they weren't glazed over. The medication had finally worked its way through her system. When she smiled at him so sleepily, Devin's stern resolutions faltered. "Hey, we need to get you up and moving and some food into you." He watched her stretch and felt his body take notice of her every movement.

"Is there coffee in there somewhere?"

He tried not to smile at her playful tone, but failed. "If that's what you'd like, there can be."

She smiled again. "I'd like." Pulling the robe tightly around her, she wiggled her way up on the bed. A frown appeared on her beautiful face. "I have good news." She flipped the covers back and moved her legs slowly towards the side. "I think the painkiller has worn off, my foot is really throbbing."

Devin knelt beside the bed and gently took her foot in his hands. She hissed when he pulled the gauze from it. It took all his willpower to keep his hands and eyes on only her foot. *Yep, I am some kind of sick puppy.*

"Is it bad?" Her voice squeaked in pain.

He studied it. It wasn't pretty, but it didn't look like

there was any infection around it. "It's not infected, just as I said before, inconveniently located." The inconvenience part being that he needed her mobile and ready to move and she wasn't going to be for a few days, at least.

"I suppose it could be worse then." Rayne bent her knee and pulled her leg up to take a look for herself. She made a female sound that told him she was annoyed with herself. "I will never go in a boat again without my shoes on."

He didn't bother to tell her that hadn't been the lesson she should have learned, but that could wait until later. "I'm going to wrap it again lightly, so you don't get any dirt in it and then we'll go find some food." She nodded and kept looking at her foot.

"Bring back my clothes, please. I'd like to get dressed."

Devin curbed any comment his mind came up with, because no matter what he attempted to say his brain locked in on her changing and wasn't going to budge from there.

He waited for her to wash up and change and waited through two cups of coffee and a light lunch. Devin waited while she went through the pictures on her camera, constantly having to stick to light conversation was wearing his patience down. He had no idea how to begin to work any of this into a conversation. Unless she outright said 'hey, I think I'm a wolf', there was no way to lead into this. Setting the juice on the table, he took the chair opposite her and sat down. "Rayne, I didn't get a chance to tell you about your camp site."

Her head popped up and she grimaced. "Is it bad? Did everything blow away?"

He shook his head quickly. "No, surprisingly enough it didn't." He clasped his hands together on the table, trying to look relaxed. "A few branches scuffed up your car, but nothing a little touch up won't fix."

"Oh." She started to fidget with the camera in her hand. "That's okay, if it's nothing serious it doesn't really matter."

Devin watched her sit there and knew she was avoiding

talking about the car. "Are you sure? I can have someone come and take a look at it."

Her head popped back up and she looked at him, eyes huge, panic obvious. "No." She cleared her throat, "it's fine."

Leaning back in the chair he made sure to keep eye contact with her. "What aren't you telling me, Rayne?" He knew already, but wanted this talk to start with her.

She bit her bottom lip and looked down at the camera a few times. Finally, she set it down and flicked her eyes from it to him. "It's technically not *my* car."

He waited.

"It was bought for me, but isn't mine."

"Who does it belong to?"

Several emotions crossed her face and he wasn't sure how much longer he could just sit here and pretend to know none of it.

"I told you..." She dropped her head down for a few seconds and then looked back up at him, the pain evident on her face. "I told you I was engaged."

Devin nodded.

"I found out some things that I couldn't live with and I..." she lifted her hands in hesitant gesture. "I left."

"What things?" He had to clench his teeth together to stop from blurting that he knew everything, or at least nearly everything.

"Um, my fiancé wasn't the man I thought him to be."

He leaned back and crossed his arms, showing her he had all the time in the world for her to explain, they didn't, but she didn't need to know that just yet.

"He—I think, well, know, he did some things that are..." she took a shaky breath. "When my parents died so suddenly, I was on my own and too young to really be on my own..." She rolled her eyes. "Maybe not in age, but my parents had kept me very sheltered and although I was almost twenty, I didn't know much about living..." She rubbed twitching fingers over her eyes and cheeks before she looked back at him. "Mister Tomas took me in, it was his son I was engaged to..." she swallowed slowly, the emotions so plain in her eyes. Fear and hurt and it were those emotions that broke his silence.

"Alberto Tomas?"

Her eyes widened with surprise. "You knew him?"

Devin shook his head and hoped the distain for the man mentioned wasn't completely obvious. "Not personally, of him and his family *business*, yes."

She opened her mouth and then closed it again, frowning. "How?"

"He was not a nice man, Rayne..."

"I know that, now." The vulnerability was plain on her face.

He leaned forward slowly and watched her reaction. "Did Alberto or his son hurt you?"

She shook her head quickly. "No, never." Looking down, she began to wring her fingers together. "I think I always knew something wasn't right, but I didn't know what until five days ago..." she hugged herself tightly. "I went to the office, I can't even remember why exactly, to see Aiden and I overheard..." Her eyes looked down at the camera and then back to him. "I overheard things that I couldn't possibly misconstrue the meaning of." She swallowed again. "I left, went home and packed and started driving."

"Until you ended up here." He wasn't sure how long they sat there in the silence just looking at each other. She was working out the fact that he knew the people she was hiding from and Devin was still completely puzzled as to how he was going to tell her everything without her thinking he was insane. "Let's go sit somewhere comfortable, I need to tell you some things."

She didn't move, the confusion showing clearly on her face. "About Aiden and his father?"

Devin nodded slowly. "That's part of it." She started to stand up and then remembered the cane. He moved over quickly and took her arm to help steady her. "We'll go sit outside."

He helped her walk to the deck around the back of the house, it overlooked the hills and was the most peaceful view a person could ask for. He'd need the serenity on his side in a few minutes' time, when he took everything Rayne had ever thought she knew and tossed it aside, only to replace it with shifters, hierarchy and villains.

He let her sit there for a few minutes and take in the hills, trees and fluffy summer clouds, not sure exactly how he should begin. Devin sighed loudly and she turned to look at him, curiosity in her eyes. He offered a tentative smile. "I'm not sure where to begin," he shrugged. "I could dive right in and have you think I'm a lunatic or start slow and let you fit the pieces together."

"I've had a lot of shock to deal with recently, so I'd appreciate a bit of tact, for now."

Devin closed his eyes long enough to find the words to begin and when he opened them he watched her closely. "I know people that knew your parents, Rayne, my father being one of them."

She opened her mouth.

"I'll get to those details in a few."

She sat back and although she appeared to be exercising patience, but he could see the questions in her eyes.

"My father is the leader in an Alliance, a group that protects people like you and I..."

"A law enforcement agency?"

Devin tossed that around inside his head. He supposed it could be called that, with a special purpose. "Sort of. Anyways they've been aware of the Tomas family for twenty years now, they blackmail or take those indebted to them and force repayment by servitude. I don't know what you overheard, but believe me, it's definitely worse than you can imagine." He studied her eyes and waited for questions that didn't come. "Your parents were two of those indebted to Alberto Tomas, or very likely your father was. They left Canada and the protection of the Alliance before you were born, when you were barely conceived and I don't know the details, we may never know them, but they ended up in the clutches of Alberto." This part she seemed to be digesting without too much difficulty, so he pushed further. "Do you know anything about your parent's families or heritage?"

She shook her head and then looked a little lost and forlorn. "Nothing really. Mom always wanted me to meet her family, but it seemed like each time we planned it something happened."

Devin was pretty sure he knew what happened, but wasn't cruel enough to say it out loud. He'd let her love for her parents and the memories stay untarnished, for now. "Now, for the part you may have trouble swallowing."

She raised an eyebrow.

Unable to just sit there and play like he was relaxed and cool with all of this, he got up and paced across the deck. He looked out over the trees in every shade of green and tried to find the right words to begin. Turning, he leaned back against the railing. "You and I are not like everyone else, Rayne." Both eyebrows rose as she looked at him. "I know this is going to sound ridiculous but your parents, you and I are not just normal people."

She hissed out a breath and then scowled at him. "My parents were quite normal, thank you very much!"

"I wasn't trying to insult them, honestly. I just have no idea how to explain this. It's not something I've told many people and I never thought I'd have to tell someone else they were like me, most know already."

She sat back and crossed her arms over her chest, and not in a nonchalant way, her patience was at the end. "What are you trying to say, Devin? I'd prefer complete honesty, please."

Devin let out a slow breath and debated for two seconds on shifting in front of her, but then realized that the second he started striping off his clothes she was going to leave and he might get injured. "I can shift into another form." He thought momentarily he'd found a tactful way to say it, until she laughed.

"I think the painkillers have affected my mind." She laughed quietly for a few more seconds and then looked back at him. "I thought you said you could shift into something." She tried to stop laughing and ended up gasping quietly and holding her hand over her mouth.

For any other reason, he would have enjoyed seeing her laugh to the point of her eyes tearing up, not over this though. "I did." Devin grasped the railing beside him and squeezed it, trying not to feel offended that she was laughing at him.

"Oh, really? And what other form can you take?" She snorted, trying to not laugh again.

"A wolf."

This time she didn't try to laugh quietly, she leaned back in her chair and laughed so hard she was gasping to catch her breath.

Crossing his arms, he stood there and waited until she got herself under control again. He'd tried to tell her, the least shocking way he could think of, and she was *laughing*. "I'm going to get a drink. Do you want anything?"

She gasped a few times and tried to stop laughing to answer. Between the breaths she took, she managed to say water.

Chapter Twenty-Seven

With long strides Devin stomped off the deck and back into the house. She wanted complete honesty, she was damn well going to get it. He went into the kitchen and grabbed a bottle of water from the fridge. Turning, he stripped off his shirt and kicked off his shoes as he headed back towards the deck. He only paused long enough to figure out how he was going to take pants and the water back out with him.

Shifting when you're angry or upset doesn't give you the same rush as when you're doing it because you want to. He felt robbed of that and it made his mood even blacker. Devin didn't take the time to stop and consider what he was about to do, he just grabbed the cuff of his jeans and flung them over his shoulders and then with the top of the bottle between his teeth he trotted back though the open door out to where Rayne was sitting.

He stood behind her long enough to hear that she had managed to regain some of her composure while he'd been gone, but she still chuckled quietly. Lowering his head, he backed up so the jeans would drop to the deck and then went around the chair without any hesitation and dropped the bottle of water in her lap. Devin could never have anticipated what happened next. Rayne shrieked so loud he thought his sensitive ear drums would be pierced right through. She dropped the cane and then reached down for it with one hand as she threw the bottle of water at him with the other, hitting him right between the eyes. He hadn't even seen that coming. Devin forgot about taunting her in his wolf form and shifted back to skin, as he rubbed the spot between his eyes he went over and picked up his jeans, keeping his back to her as he pulled them on.

When Devin turned again she had both hands over her mouth, her eyes couldn't have been any wider and her chest heaved as she hyperventilated, and now he felt like slime having been the cause. He squatted down a few feet away from her and rubbed a hand over the throbbing target on his forehead. "I'm sorry," he managed to whisper. Leaning his head into hand, he let out a slow breath and hoped she'd look calmer when he finally managed to look at her.

She didn't. The shock was still there, but there was something else now, anger.

"I didn't know how to show you without startling you..."

"Startling?" she squeaked. "I think that's an understatement!"

He took a long-ragged breath. "I know. I'm sorry..."

She held up a hand to silence him. Now looking at him like he'd grown two heads, and his heart fell deeper into his chest. He'd seen that look before. Words like freak and monster usually came with that expression. She opened her mouth and then closed it, frowning at him for a second or two more.

"Are you saying my parents could do that?" Her voice shook, but there wasn't fear behind it. She sounded hurt.

Devin looked right into her eyes and hoped she'd see the truth in his own. "Yes."

She stared so intently in his eyes, he was afraid to blink. "And you think I can? I'm pretty sure I'd know if I could."

He didn't move from where he was, still not sure if she'd bolt and hurt herself or throw something else at him. "Both of your parents could and you will be able to. Males can shift at the onset of puberty and females a few years after that."

She frowned, but continued to look at him. "I am well past puberty and I'd know if I could grow a tail by now."

Devin was so out of his depth in this discussion he didn't know where to go with it. "You're not going to just suddenly grow a tail, it's a gradual thing."

"I'm gradually going to turn into a wolf?"

He shook his head. "No, once you can shift, and have a few times, you should be able to change almost instantly, but leading up to it there will be gradual changes..."

"Because turning all furry isn't enough, there's more?"

Devin struggled to figure out how to explain this better, but he didn't know. He'd grown up knowing, everyone knew in his clan grew up knowing. "I don't know how to explain this and we're running out of time..."

"What?" She sat forward and gave him an annoyed look.

"I have more to tell you, Rayne." He took a chance and stood up slowly. His ego wouldn't let him go right over to her or sit next to her, so he went back to the railing and stood there. "Aiden Tomas isn't going to just let you drive away."

She closed her eyes and took a shaky breath. "I know, he's going to be so..."

"No, you don't know."

Her eyes popped open.

"The people I mentioned that end up indebted to the Tomas family have always been shifters from one clan or another..."

"There's more than one kind?"

Devin nodded, but didn't take the time to explain it. "He knows what you are, what your parents were, and he is not going to let you get away from him that easily."

"Oh." Turning, she looked all around the deck. "I have to go."

She started to stand up and he wasn't about to let her just walk away. Devin went over and knelt in front of her. "No, you have to stay." Her eyes were filled with questions and weariness, reminding him of what she'd been through the day before. "I can protect you here."

"No, if I keep going there's no way he'll..."

"The police have already been notified that the car is stolen."

Her eyes widened. She huffed out a breath and then leaned back and closed her eyes. "I kept hoping he'd just get mad and leave it at that, but if all that you're saying is true, he's not going to, is he?" She opened her eyes and he shook his head. "Why, if I'm what you say, would he even want me?"

Devin knew that tone and he'd felt the shame at times when he was young. "There's nothing wrong with what you are, it makes you extraordinary if you ask me." He winked at her and she rolled her eyes back at him. "To a Tomas, having a half breed with our little extras would make them stronger and their empire better."

"Extras?"

"We're faster, our senses better and we're stronger..." He stood up when she grasped the cane in both hands.

She held up her head and looked offended. "Are you saying Aiden only wanted me so he could get a puppy from me?"

He didn't smirk at the way she worded it, it was far from a funny matter, but her dignified manner pleased him. "More or less."

Sliding to the edge of the wooden chair, she picked up the cane. Devin didn't try to stop her as she got to her feet and took slow shuffling steps towards him. He wanted to hug her for taking things as well as she was, but still wasn't sure if he should attempt to touch her. He'd fallen for women who said what he was worked for them, but they hadn't meant it. She stood only a few inches from away and looked up at him. "You said you could protect me. How and what is the cost of this?"

He didn't blame her for the question, but it still hurt that she had to think like that now. "No one knows this area like I do, it's where I'm the most comfortable and have the advantage." Her eyes remained fixed on his. "My firs-*friend* is on his way to help and my father is working with the Alliance to find out what Tomas is doing." He knew he should explain the rest to her, but if he'd just found out everything she had, there wasn't room for any more just yet, never mind the detail of who he really was to her and the pack.

"I need to think." She looked into his eyes for a second more and then turned. "Please help me get back to my tent."

Devin didn't want her to go back there and be alone. He wanted her right here where he could watch her and make sure she was going to be okay. "Rayne..."

When her eyes met his, he felt the full impact of her sadness.

"Please, Devin."

He grasped the railing to stop from taking her into his arms. She was hurting and although he wasn't the cause, he was still the one that had put that look in her eyes. "Okay."

Chapter Twenty-Eight

Three pairs of shoes later, Rayne finally found a pair of sandals that didn't hurt as much to walk in, not that she was going to be walking far right now—she just couldn't sit still. Her mind was going faster than it was able to process, but yet the first thing she did after testing her footwear was sit down.

If she hadn't seen the wolf turn into Devin with her own eyes she never would have thought something like that was possible. Combine that with the additional information that she was supposed to be doing that sometime in the future?! End result; her brain was a stew of chaos. She looked down at her arms as if they were suddenly going to sprout fur. She honestly didn't know what to do with all this new information. If the last day had been a novel, it would have been an intriguing best seller, but for the real-life parts, this heroine had no idea what to do next.

Rayne's mind ricocheted back to the information about her parents were being the same as Devin. How did things like this exist and no one know? She had lived a very sheltered existence, yes, she admitted that. But people that could change their shape, their entire specie to be out there and not be widely known was a lot to take in. To know that people who looked like everyone else but were far from it were walking around every day, was just crazy. If she I hadn't noticed something about her own parents, she could have come in contact with someone that could change into an animal over the years and never know it.

She had to get up and move, try to work this out with some physical energy. Awkwardly, she managed to get up from the chair and limp over to the car. Trying to balance on the cane and get the door open without tipping over took more skill than she thought, she wobbled a few times. Hopefully she didn't have to be an invalid for long. If what Devin said was right, she was going to have to go through more than she'd anticipated in breaking off from Aiden. Rayne didn't want to dwell on the possibilities that might involve right now, she had more than enough to cope with, worrying about some lethal man coming after her was just too much to take on at this moment.

Dropping down onto the edge of the passenger's seat, she pulled a handful of photos out of the case, photos of her parents. She studied their images, not seeing anything different about them that she hadn't seen her whole life. They didn't look like they were hiding something as huge as being able to shift forms, and yet they were. Devin couldn't have made up that part, at least that's what her inner voice said. The voice that told her it was too bizarre to be wrong, but unbelievable at the same time.

Rayne really wanted to tell herself that Devin was lying, but she'd seen it happen. She'd seen the fur retract and skin cover him. It was like something out of a movie, where you sit there eating your popcorn and watching the screen and your adrenalin kicks up as you watch the fantastic transformation—but there's always been that small part in your brain that's saying 'yeah right, like that could happen!' Now that she knew it could happen she was completely lost. *How could my parents hide something like this from me?* If she was going to do this too, why wouldn't they have told her? She had been well past puberty before they died, and they hadn't warned her that she was going to go through some other change? Sure, puberty had been enough of a change to suffer through. Maybe they meant to tell her, but died before they could.

Hugging the pictures into her chest Rayne closed her eyes and tried to think of anything she could remember that had hinted this was possible. They had moved a lot, lived in rural and urban areas alike, so that didn't tell her a thing. They rarely went out and most definitely never came back naked when they did. If they were what Devin said, they hadn't done anything out of the ordinary that would give her a clue that it was true.

Sighing, she opened her eyes and tucked the pictures back into the pocket on the case. Getting back out of the car, she slammed the door harder than needed but it made her feel better. Turning, she looked at the car, Aiden was going to come for it, for her and she didn't know how she was going to deal with him when he did. Frustration bubbled in her stomach and she had the fleeting thought of pushing his car into the lake.

The reality she now faced was overwhelming. She didn't know where to begin to deal with all of this. Devin knew more about Aiden and his family than she did, and now he was saying she was in danger. Rayne didn't really need to know any more to confirm that, Aiden's words still played through her mind like a recording.

The part of her that should have been heartbroken, discovering he only wanted her for puppies, wasn't. She'd always known there was something going on, she just didn't know what. Everything she had learned today explained all the little things that used to nag at her. Some of the staff that worked for Aiden always seemed a little afraid of him and those that didn't seemed to be the oddest bunch of men.

She stopped and looked over at the trees. The realization that she believed every word Devin had said surprised her. A month ago, she would have laughed, or screamed, and then she would have packed up and left as fast as she could. Rayne now could admit that the way she thought about things had changed recently. She didn't know if it was because of the changes Devin referred to, she only knew that she wasn't the same as before. Of course, she could still hope that she'd wake up at any moment to find out this was a bizarre dream from eating too much sugar before bed, or reading some fantasy story.

Chuckling at her own weirdness, she turned and tried to walk, as normally as she could, to go back to the cabin. The hair on the back of her neck suddenly stood up. Rayne stopped and turned around slowly, half expecting Aiden to be lurking behind her, but he wasn't. The wolf with the familiar eyes stood on the edge of the trees. At least now she knew why the eyes gave her a feeling of recognition. Her heart sped up as her mind replayed watching that same wolf turn into Devin—at least she wasn't going to have to worry about being eaten this time.

"Are you going to skulk around in the trees and watch me all the time, Devin?" She leaned on the cane and waited for him to decide to do next. He took two hesitant steps before slowly walking over to her. When he stopped right in front of her she realized how big he actually was. "Normal wolves aren't as large as you are, are they?" Rayne debated on reaching out and touching him, but grasped the cane with both hands to keep them away from him. "I've only been alone for a few hours you didn't need to check on me."

The grey eyes held hers. Now that she wasn't scared half out of her mind she noticed that in those eyes there was the man. They had the same look of concern and worry that he'd had when he was looking after her. She sighed and glanced away, determined to look at the ground and not at him, but he came closer and rubbed against her leg. His fur was softer than she'd imagined it would be. She looked down to see the large wolf half wrapped around her and the grey eyes watching carefully. "I'm fine. Just a little overwhelmed right now." Without hesitation, Rayne reached down and ran her hand down over his head. He nudged her hand so it would slide back over his fur again. "Did you bring clothes?" She felt a bit odd talking to a wolf that didn't answer. He watched her without moving, something played through his eyes that looked like a smile. Leaning around, he ran his tongue up over the back of her knee and then turned and darted back into the trees.

Rayne was still standing there trying to figure out why she wasn't mad at him showing up after she'd asked to be alone when he stepped out of the trees. He had brought clothes, or at least jeans. His feet were bare as was his chest, the jeans rode low on his hips and it took her a heartbeat to pull her eyes from the hard muscles of his abdomen back up to his face. He held up a small bag.

"I brought your camera and some more bandages, in case you needed them."

The fact that she'd forgotten her camera was shocking, she never went anywhere without it. "Oh."

His lips moved into one of his lopsided smirks. "I thought I'd test the water before I barged in on you, in case you felt like throwing things again."

Her eyes jumped to the red welt on his forehead. "I'd apologize for that, but I think you deserved it."

Devin stopped right in front of her and looked down, regret in his eyes. "I did. I'm sorry, it wasn't the nicest way to show you."

"I don't think any way would have been less shocking..." She stopped when his knuckles glided over the scratch on her cheek. Her heart started beating in her throat when he leaned down slowly and placed a light kiss over it.

"I'm sorry, Rayne."

His deep whisper vibrated through her body and she wanted to wrap her arms around him and lose herself in his warmth. Rayne pulled her head back and looked up at him. "If you're trying to distract me from throwing things at you, it's not necessary."

"That wasn't the reason, but it's good to know." He glanced past her head and she could tell he was trying to decide something. "There's more I need to explain, but I don't..."

Putting a hand on his chest, she shook her head. "If it's not life threatening, I'd prefer not to have more things to wrap my brain around right now. I'm barely hanging on as it is. I'm sure at any moment it's all going to hit me and I'm going to turn into a hysterical woman that's suddenly found herself in a strange new world."

"I think you're handling all of it very well. Other than one shriek and a strong throwing arm, you've been very calm." He ran one finger down her bare arm and she tried not to notice the trail of tingling it caused. "I've never had someone find out and actually touch me afterwards, in wolf or human form."

The wistful note in his voice caused a pain in her heart. He'd been hurt because of what he was, before. That was one emotion she could relate with. "I'm not repulsed by any of it, if that's what you're afraid of, I'm just in such a state of shock I'm not sure what I'm thinking." His eyes caressed her face and she had to force her gaze away or be drawn in by them. Rayne moved her eyes down his throat to his bare chest. The ridiculous notion of leaning towards him and licking his chest shocked her to the point that her eyes widened as they jerked them back to his. His eye were half closed as he watched her. "I..." she took a short breath and tried again. "I have questions." He reached out and ran his hand lightly down over her hair, running his fingers through it. When her nipples hardened just from that simple movement, she took a step back from him and held up her hand. "If you didn't bring more clothes to wear, you can go stand over there while we talk." She pointed to the cabin.

"I'm sorry, I can't help myself. I'm a male, you're beautiful and you don't think I'm a freak..." He grinned and for a moment, it reminded her of the wolf that had stood in front of her.

She put a hand on his chest and pushed lightly. "And I can't think when you're this close to me," she frowned up at him. "Why is that?"

He tilted his head, his eyes filled with humor. "It's bad that you're attracted to me?"

Rayne bit her lip and shook her head. "No, just not in my character to throw myself at a man I don't know." She slid her hand down his chest and that strange urge to taste his skin crept back into her mind. Dropping her hand to the cane, she turned and started back to the chair beside the cabin. "Is it because of what you say I am?"

Taking her arm, he balanced more of her weight than she was. "You still don't completely believe me, do you?" He paused for a moment and then shrugged. "It's partially that. You may not have been through your first estrus yet, but your wolf recognizes mine."

Rayne stopped and blinked up at him. "My first what? Is that what the changing part is called?"

He continued to half carry her back to the chair. She didn't feel like struggling and really wanted to sit right now. "Another woman from our clan explaining this would be better, but that's kind of like puberty all over again, other wolves will scent you during this time..." He paused and helped her sit.

She swallowed when he sat in front of her on the ground and picked up her throbbing foot to place it gently in his lap.

"My wolf recognized you before I understood what was going on."

She'd heard about animals being able to smell other animals nearby, but this was taking it to a whole new level for her. "I suppose that makes sense. So, all of your—clan are attracted to each other?" Rayne wasn't comfortable with the idea of that at all.

"No. Thankfully not." He laughed softly. "That would wreak havoc like you've never seen."

Slightly relieved as she was, Rayne still didn't understand. "So, what is this, animal magnetism?"

He lowered his eyes to her foot as his hands began to lightly massage her ankle. "Something like that." His eyes flicked up to her face briefly before he continued. "You don't think we'd be attracted to each other if we weren't wolf?"

She chewed on her lip and studied him. His sandy hair had fallen down to cover half of his eyes. "Oh, I'm pretty sure you know how appealing you are to women."

He turned the full power of a lustful look on her. "But not you?" His voice had dropped to a whisper.

Rayne felt her cheeks flush. "I'm sure you know the answer to that."

He nodded slowly and then looked back down. "I do. I can smell your desire."

As odd as this whole day had been, that took the prize. The man could actually smell that she was turned on by him. She felt like she'd been exposed and denied at the same time because she couldn't do the same. "I think we need to change the subject."

His eyes flicked back to hers and she knew the look was daring her to continue. A part of her, the normal Rayne won, and she lowered her eyes from his. He still held her foot, but his other hand now moved in achingly slow circles along her thigh. "You've had a hell of a day, Rayne. Just relax and give yourself time to take all of it in. I can still answer questions tomorrow."

She closed her eyes as his fingers danced over her leg. Rayne had so much to try and figure out, so many questions that she wasn't even sure she wanted to know the answers to. Her head ached with them. "You might be right. My mind is soup right now."

His palm rested against her inner thigh, but the movement stopped. "Come back to the house for tonight where you can rest and not have to worry about anything."

Rayne opened her eyes and looked at him. "I don't think that's a good idea."

He shrugged. "It's your choice, but know that I'll have to stay awake all night and skulk around in the trees to watch over you if you don't."

She smirked, "It would serve you right." Glancing over

at the tent. *Do I want to spend a night alone out here right now? Maybe I should be asking was if I should spend the night alone with Devin right now. If I went back with him, I wouldn't have to worry about wild animals...* she hid the smirk from him. Not the scary wild animals at least. Sighing, she lowered her eyes and looked back at him, he sat there without movement watching her. "I don't want to give you the wrong idea..."

He tilted his head and gave her a serious look. "Rayne, just the fact that you're a female from my clan means I'm obligated to protect you with my life if need be, that's the way it works." She sent him a surprised look. "Seriously. Our females are revered and treasured."

What normal society could learn from this other race was something that needed a major overhaul. Women in normal human society were still the underdogs, the servants and, in most cases. the least respected. Maybe all of this wouldn't be bad. She took a deep breath and watched him for a few moments. "I'll stay on the couch."

He laughed as he stood up. "We'll work out the details later. I want to help you back up to the house and then do a sweep of the property and make sure there's no one here that shouldn't be."

Her heart stumbled. "You really think Aiden is coming after me?" Rayne accepted his hand and let him help her stand up.

A serious look filled his eyes. "Yes." He shrugged. "Even if you weren't a shifter of true blood, I sure as hell would come after you, just to grovel."

"I don't see you grovelling for some reason."

He flashed white teeth at her. "There's a first for everything."

Chapter Twenty-Nine

Devin's heart hadn't slowed since she'd touched him while he was on four paws. Never in his adult life had a woman that was not from his own family touched him while he was in wolf form. That small piece that had allowed him to hold onto his restraint had faded quickly after her hand had caressed over his coat. He didn't think it would mean as much to him as it did, added to the fact that he knew she was his mate, and he was in trouble.

Now all he had to do was explain that he was her mate and the position he held within the community and Alliance. Devin planned to tell her, once he was sure she was ready for more.

He watched her out of the corner of his eye as she read over the archives of her family history, still surprised she was taking everything as well as she was. In the back of his mind he was waiting for her to scream and run for her car to escape the weirdness of his world.

She turned and looked at him, his heart stuttered when he noticed the tears running down her cheeks. This was not the reaction he pictured. Devin was on his feet and moving towards her before he realized he'd even stood up.

"I have cousins, aunts and uncles?"

He stopped, startled by the question before nodding slowly. "Yes."

She jumped up and then winced when her foot touched the floor. He reached out to steady her and she looked at him, a beautiful smile on her face. "I have a family."

Devin nodded again, his heart pounding wildly in his chest. He'd had a lifetime of family and too many people in his world. She'd only had her parents. "Once we deal with Tomas, I can take you to meet them."

Opening her mouth, she snapped it closed it again and held her hand over it. A wild look filled her eyes. She nodded. "Yes." Grabbing his hand, cupping it between both her small ones she smiled again. "Yes!" She started laughing and squeezed his hand. "I've never met any relatives, I wasn't even sure if I had any..."

His heart swelled in his chest seeing her happy. "Believe me, you have more than enough."

"So, I just read. Both of my parents had three siblings each, I have ten cousins!" She laughed again and then pulled him towards her.

He was just trying to adjust when she wrapped her arms around him in a tight hug. Devin knew she was just happy, but his body didn't care what the reason, simply she was there causing his blood to kick up the heat. Wrapping his arms around her, he let his hands glide down over her silky hair. At that point he realized he still hadn't put a shirt on as her warm breath brushed over his skin, his body hardening even though he knew she wasn't in his arms for that reason.

With her arms still wrapped around him, she looked up. "Thank you." She sighed. "If it wasn't for you, I would never know." She rested her cheek against his chest, right over his heart. If she'd be still she could feel it pounding.

"I had nothing to do with your heritage."

Laughing she pushed her face into his flesh. "I know. I'm just glad I pointed to a spot on a map and it brought me here."

He blinked down at the top of her head, surprised.

"That's how you chose where you were going?" Maybe it was his creative side, but he'd pictured fate intervening at least a little bit with her showing up here.

"Yes." She smiled, no trace of tears or sadness in her eyes.

Devin stood there smiling back at her, his body throbbing with wanting her. She was so happy he debated briefly whether he wanted to take a chance and possibly change that. He smiled at her again and lowered his face closer to hers. "I'm glad you did too." He brushed his lips lightly over hers, testing her reaction.

A serious look crossed over her face. "Why can't I resist you?"

He knew the answer, but wasn't going to go there right now, not when he wanted a real taste of her sexy mouth. Leaning down again, he ran the tip of his tongue over her lips. She opened her mouth. He cupped the back of her head in one hand and pressed his lips to hers, unable to control the urgency that came over him, Devin plunged his tongue inside her mouth, almost whimpering when she didn't object.

The taste of her filled him, taking his already aroused body and stoking more flames. Her soft mouth moved with his, as the flames engulfed his entire system. Devin wanted her in a way that made him tremble from just a kiss. *Can I be with her and not claim her as my mate?* He would not claim her as his own until she knew and had a choice, but he couldn't stop either. Her hands moved over the skin on his back, urging him on. He needed to feel her pressed against him, so he wrapped an arm around her waist and straightened up, lifting her feet from the floor.

She moaned softly as his lips traveled over the soft flesh of her neck. "I shouldn't..."

Devin nipped the sensitive spot by her shoulder. "Shouldn't what?"

Lifting her head to look at him with lust filled eyes. "Be doing this. Until a few days ago, I was..."

He cut off the word he didn't want to hear by crushing

her mouth with his own. *Mine. No one will ever touch her again.* He knew where the possessive urge came from, but he knew that he couldn't let her know or he would lose this chance. Gentling the kiss, he began to coax her lips with his, softly trying to convince her that she could trust him. When he lifted her higher on his body he expected her to protest the intimacy in the way their bodies connected, but she only wrapped her arms around his neck and held tight to him.

Knowing that only a few pieces of material between their bodies did not hinder the desire he had to feel her rubbing against his body. He pushed his throbbing hard on into her and groaned when she whimpered against his mouth. Devin felt like he was starving for her, unable to continue if he didn't have her. If this was what it felt like to have a mate destined just for you, how did they ever leave each other's sides?

Running his hands down over her ass, he grasped the backs of her thighs, lifting her so he could rock his body between her legs. Her knees clamped against his hips, holding her body open to him. Growling, he tore his mouth from hers and looked into her passion heavy eyes. Her breathing was as ragged as his, he knew he could carry her into the bedroom right now and have her.

Even as his brain fought through the need coursing inside, reminding him that this wasn't the right time, he was lowering his mouth to her throat. Inhaling the scent of gardenias and how much she wanted him. Her skin was soft and warm and it sent more erotic thoughts through his mind.

Devin turned and headed towards the bedroom, afraid she'd change her mind if he lingered too long. He'd only gone three steps when her teeth nipped along his throat. Heat surged through his groin letting him know that if he didn't get these jeans off soon they were going to rip open. He grasped the back of her head, taking a handful of hair, and pulled her mouth from his neck, if she touched him again with that mouth he was going to take her right here on the floor.

With his teeth and tongue he teased the soft skin of her throat. She ground herself into him making him want to race for his bed. His sharp senses were going insane being able to smell how wet she was. With another long stride his legs hit the bed. He wasted no time in lowering their entangled bodies to the mattress. She sucked in a breath when his weight pinned her to the bed and to his ears it was one of the most erotic noises he'd ever heard.

Devin didn't want to release her as feelings of desperation gnawed at his guts when he lifted slightly away from the heat of her warm curves, but his brain reminded his engorged body that things wouldn't go very far fully clothed. Assaulting her mouth with his, Devin drank in her taste once more before he raised up on his arms to look down at her.

If she still had doubts they didn't show in her eyes, they contained the most sensual look of yes he'd ever witnessed. Moving up to kneel between her legs, he pulled her shirt up slowly and as hard as he tried to look only at her eyes, he couldn't. Her body was absolute perfection, from the pale flawless skin of her small waist up to her small firm breasts with the hard nipples begging for his mouth. She lay there and let him pull the shirt over her head, leaving her arms over her head as the material moved from her arms. Devin didn't think she realized what her submissive behavior did to him, making the animal inside him scream with victory.

Leaning down, he reached under her shoulders and lifted her body upright until he was kneeling with her resting in his lap. The heat of her bare skin against his took the heightened level of his arousal to its peak, the game of slow exploration was shakily nearing an end. Grasping her waist, Devin lifted her to taste her ripe breasts, she moaned and squeezed his shoulders tightly as he suckled on a taut nipple.

Reaching between their heated flesh, he ripped the button on her shorts open and then dropped both of them back to the bed. Growling with a firm nipple still in his mouth, he yanked at the waist of her shorts to get them off, she lifted her hips and let the material slide down her legs. He didn't wait to remove them before he ran his hand up her thigh to cradle between her legs.

He stroked his fingers over her wet heat and had to struggle for control when she opened her legs wider, completely surrendering. Grasping his hair, she pulled his face back up to her mouth. Her hands moved down his back as they traveled to the waist of his jeans. She undid them and started to shove them down, Devin shifted his weight to help her and then froze when her small hand wrapped around his hard length and squeezed. Dropping his head back down, he dragged his teeth across her shoulder, every instinct inside him that wasn't man told him to flip her over and place his mark on her, to claim her.

Devin grabbed her wrist and pulled her hand up above her head and held it there. Moving to her other arm he did the same until she was stretched out beneath him like an offering. Holding her hands firmly with one hand, he reached under her hips with his other as he lowered between her thighs. She froze and for a half a breath he thought she was having second thoughts until she lifted her hips so her wet heat was rubbing against him.

He inhaled as he lowered his mouth to her shoulder and when his teeth gently grasped the flesh there he realized how close he was to marking her, one way or the other. Moving away from the temptation quickly, he crushed her mouth as he lifted her hips and shoved into her wet folds.

She groaned into his mouth when he pushed deep and connected their bodies. A haze covered his eyes, blinding him at the feeling of completion when surrounded by her tight flesh. Devin fought to keep his control as his instincts screamed at him to claim her.

Holding still, he lifted his mouth away from hers and looked down. He wasn't sure if he could form words, but had to make sure before continuing. "Is this..." She lifted her head up and bit his bottom lip, struggling against his hold on her hands and lifting her hips tighter into him. Devin took that as a yes, growling against her mouth as he pulled out slowly until only the tip was still inside her. She tried to pull her hands free again until he slammed into her and she moaned loudly.

Chapter Thirty

Not sure whether it was just Devin or everything that had happened to her recently, Rayne knew she'd never wanted what she did right now. She didn't want to make love, she wanted to be taken. Never before had she felt this kind of heat, a need that bordered on desperation. She bit his tongue when he slid it into her mouth, hoping it would encourage him to do what he wanted, what he felt. As if he could read her mind, he pounded into her again. The feeling sent more heat coursing through her, but she still wanted more. Pulling her mouth free, she ran her lips down his throat until she was almost at his shoulder and didn't know why she did it but bit into the soft skin there and held it between her teeth.

He growled and released her hands. She reached out to grab at any part of his body she could touch when he pushed up on his arms and looked down at her as he thrust again. Each time he did he came close to hitting the end of her, but Rayne still wanted more, she was reaching for something she'd never felt before. Lifting, she rubbed against him when his body touched hers again.

He hissed out a breath between his teeth and lifted his body up onto his knees, pulling her hips up with him.

Grasping the back of her thighs in his big hands, he held her body open to him, so she was unable to move. Squeezing her ass, he pulled her towards him as he thrust his hips between her legs. The angle he held her as their bodies collided sent waves of need all the way up to her head.

Rayne opened her eyes and glanced up at him, the way he was looking at her sent another burst of heat through her. He pulled her onto him again and she sucked in a breath as the lust consumed her. His eyes flicked from her face to her breasts that slapped back and forth each time he plunged.

Her entire body felt like it was on fire and each time he pulled out she wanted to whimper so he would move faster. As he stared at her breasts the nipples ached for his mouth, but Rayne didn't want him to stop. She'd never touched herself during sex, but she wanted to see the look in his eyes as she did. Moving her hands from the bed she slid them up her waist and cupped a breast in each hand. He slammed into her harder. She squeezed them until the nipples were crushed between her thumb and finger, he hissed out a breath and grasped her ass harder, moving faster in and out of her.

Rayne was so close to exploding she didn't know if she could focus enough to play with her own nipples as his thrusts sent her rocking on the bed. Her muscles were clenching around him, so close to orgasm that she almost ached. He moved harder and faster until she was gasping and then screamed as her orgasm crashed through her, electrifying her whole body.

Dropping her hands to the mattress, she squirmed as her muscles continued to convulse around him, squeezing him inside her. He let her hips go and she felt herself being shoved higher in the bed and then she was sitting in his lap in one movement. Opening her eyes, she looked at his sweat covered chest and if she'd had the strength would have liked to lick it.

His mouth suddenly sucked a sensitive nipple into it and he sucked it hard as he trust into her again. Rayne didn't think she could take much more but still wasn't able to breathe enough to tell him. He slammed into her over and over until she screamed as her body went up in flames with another violent orgasm that took her by surprise.

Devin thrust into her through it and then growled as his body pulsed inside of her and she felt the heat of his liquid shooting deep inside.

Rayne couldn't open her eyes or move any part of her body. She felt him move her back to lay flat on the bed and could feel him still deep inside, but the limpness of her every part hindered her from helping to adjust their positions. She could hear his heavy breathing beside her ear and knew her own wasn't any better.

He moved his hips and aftershocks shot through her like lightening. She moaned and tried to remember how to breathe for a few moments. He was still throbbing inside of her and if he didn't pull out soon she didn't think she was going to survive much longer. She realized he was speaking and it took a lot of focus to understand him.

"... never..." he gasped, "...like that..." his hot breath brushed over her neck, "...before."

She wanted to respond, but couldn't form any sort of logical thought yet. "Same." Was the best she could force out.

It was several minutes, or felt like it, before he shifted his weight and pulled out. She felt different when he pulled away, almost like panic and nearly voiced it until he dropped beside her and pulled her tight into his body. She wrapped around him and placed her head near his chest listening to his heart, which was still beating as fast as her own.

He kissed the top of her head. "I'm going to need a few minutes before I can move, then I get us something to drink."

Rayne nodded, still too relaxed to say anything.

"I still have to go look around outside, but I won't be gone long." He lifted her face up towards his and kissed her so softly, she was pretty sure she sighed with utter contentment. He smiled at her as she fought to keep her eyes open.

Chapter Thirty-One

For the first time in longer than he could remember, he didn't want to charge through the trees as fast as his legs could move. He walked along, sniffing the air from time to time as he headed up the hill. If there was anyone here that shouldn't be, he'd be able to scent them from there. For the last few minutes he debated on shifting to get there faster, but he had no plans to be away from Rayne longer than necessary, and if he let his wolf out for a run he'd lose the taste of her he still carried in his mouth, and he wasn't ready to let that go just yet.

What had just happened between them was beyond anything he could explain. He thought at one point his heart was going to explode and it wasn't from what they were doing, but just being with her. Even as he thought it, he knew it made no sense but it was still the truth. Devin had been so close to marking her and that scared him. No one told him control was something he'd have to fight when he found his mate. So many of the odd stories that he'd heard or experienced now about difficulties when two mates met, all seemed more than possible now.

Devin turned and inhaled deeply, taking the time to analyze the scents that came back to him. The hair on the back of his neck stood when it registered there was another animal nearby. He turned slowly, every muscle in his body tense, ready. A soft chuckling came from his left.

"I don't think I've ever been able to sneak up on you, not even when we were kids, Dev."

Devin exhaled with relief and turned to face Calum with a shrug. "I was preoccupied."

Calum gave him one of his knowing looks and then rubbed at the grin he was trying to hide. "I don't have to ask with what, I can smell why."

He walked over closer and Devin was reminded how large he was. Devin wasn't a small man by any means, but Calum made him feel inadequate from time to time. Then again, his size was also one of the reasons he'd agreed he was to be his first if he ever required one.

He wasn't going to give into his prodding. "When did you get here?"

He gave him another nonchalant look. "A while ago. I originally went to the house, but heard you were busy so I thought I'd reacquaint myself with the land." This time he did grin.

Devin laughed. "Thank you."

He shrugged. "I still can't believe you have a mate, but my nose tells me you do indeed. How is the soon to be queen of the Alliance doing?"

Devin looked down at the ground while he answered. "About that..." He glanced at his almost emerald eyes for a second. "Today, Rayne has just found out what she is. I thought I'd wait and tell her the rest when she's had a chance to absorb it all."

His eyes widened. "Which part doesn't she know?"

Devin jammed his hands into pockets and gave him a steady look. "She knows she's a shifter."

Calum's dark eyebrows shot up, making his eyes seem even wider. "She doesn't know who you are—who she'll be?"

He shook his head, it didn't sound good with the tone he

used.

"And you claimed her without telling her everything?"

Running a hand through his hair, Devin rolled his shoulders and wished the usual tension they carried hadn't returned quite so soon. "I didn't mark her." He closed his eyes long enough to picture her and then looked at him again. "I won't until she knows. She has a choice in all of this too."

Calum shook his head and then stood there with his hands on his hips watching Devin, giving him the same glare he used to when we were kids and he was about to do something stupid. "Your scent will be all over her and unless tonight was a onetime thing, it always will be." He rolled his eyes. "That's near enough to marking her as mated. As for her having a choice, do you still believe you could just walk away?"

"Does the lecturing come *with* the protection or is there an additional fee?" *I damn well know what I've done and don't need him to stand here and tell me I shouldn't have. This I already knew.* The problem was he would do it again, and planned to whenever he could. He'd been drawn to her before he touched her and now that he had it was even worse, just being away from her for this short time had him anxious and more than a little irritable. If he had to move to the ends of the earth to stay away from her he would. Devin hadn't even decided whether having her or keeping her was the best for anyone. If she agreed to have him and he claimed her, he was bowing before his clan as their alpha, and his decision on that challenge was still up in the air.

"It's free advice." Calum turned his head and looked around the area, probably trying to decide if he wanted to continue this conversation.

When he turned jacnd looked at Devin, he felt like he could see straight into his soul. *Why do cat eyes do that? I could look at someone for an eternity and never have the weight of his stare.*

"You haven't decided, have you?"

Devin shrugged, knowing anything he said would sound hollow before he finished the words.

Calum blew out a breath. "You better hurry on the decision. You can't just keep her as something casual, it doesn't work that way."

He knew that all too well, by the range of events and emotions in the last few days. For Devin, Rayne was either everything or nothing, there was no in between in his world. Mates could not just be friends. "I know—I'm working it out."

He shook his head in a startled way. "Aside from all of that, how is she doing? Has there been any word on what Tomas is up to?"

Devin sighed with relief that he was going to let it go. "She's taking everything better than I'd imagined she would and no there's no word yet." Crossing his arms over his chest, he studied him for a long moment. "You look a little ragged, Cal, what's going on?"

He ran his hands through his hair and groaned. "I've been trying to chase down some answers on some missing clan and getting nowhere."

"Women?" He hadn't been exaggerating when he'd told Rayne that the females in the clans were looked after. Until they were mated, all clan members looked out for them and even after being mated in most cases, regardless of rank.

"No. That's part of the problem in tracking them, it's the males that seem to disappear without a trace."

The surprise must have shown on Devin's face because Calum nodded abruptly. "Exactly my reaction. I was just home a day from my last dead-end trail when your father called me." He shrugged. "I thought the peacefulness of this place would help me unwind."

Devin cocked his head to the side when he heard a wolf's howl in the distance. A normal wolf, but all the same they should know not to come too close to his land by now. "Once I know Rayne's safety isn't at risk, you're welcome to stay as long as you need."

"I won't impose too long." He smirked. "I'm sure after we deal with Tomas and you tell her the rest of the details that are going to affect *her* life, you'll need a lot of alone time to rectify things"

Devin tucked his hands into his pockets. "She took finding out that she's soon going to change into something furry with four legs better than I ever could have imagined, I'm sure she'll be fine with the rest."

He laughed. "Because finding out you're mated to the prince of all the clans of shifters and will be the queen if he steps into his place isn't a big deal—or that she's the new mama of your pack. No, I'm sure you're right and she'll just giggle when she finds out."

He was right. Devin knew that. All the excuses he told himself while trying to believe she would be fine with it had been pure wishful thinking. If he really believed she'd be okay with it, he would have told her before he'd seduced her. His body tightened at that thought. He looked back at Calum, who was studying him in the silence with his narrowed cat eyes. "I'm going to head back now, try to stay downwind so I can have some warning if someone shows up here."

"I will. I'm going to pitch a tent on top here, and stay clear of the dense areas for a few days."

"Sounds good." He turned and started to walk back the way he'd come. Pausing, Devin glanced at him over his shoulder. "I appreciate the back up."

He gave him a solemn look. "Hey, it's my job to protect your royal ass." Then he laughed softly.

Devin had always hated Calum referring to him in that way and he knew it, yet for as long as he could remember he'd kept on doing it.

He glared at him for a few seconds more and then turned and headed back down the incline. He did feel better having him here. He was a male, but he was an experienced one when it came to knowing how to behave around another man's mate. With him here, Devin hoped, he would be able to focus on Rayne and not have to be running around sniffing out trespassers.

He stood watching her sleep. She looked so much smaller in his large bed. Her golden hair spread out over the navy pillows, making her look almost untouchable. His body hardened making him want her again. She was his mate and she was in his bed, so why was he standing here just looking down at her? His conscience prodded him, reminding him why. He needed to tell her, he just didn't know how.

"Are you planning to watch me all night?"

Her soft voice startled him. "I thought about it." He couldn't help smile down at her.

"Everything's all right?" She rolled over, exposing one bare shoulder.

His throat tightened and he knew it was going to be a long night of aching. He couldn't take a chance of getting too close to her again. Every part of him that was wolf was crying out to take his mate, and he couldn't until she knew and she accepted him. "Everything is fine," Devin whispered back to her. She sighed and then relaxed back into the covers. He knew by her breathing she was asleep before he could walk around to the other side of the bed.

As he settled in under the covers, he waited for her to wake up, half expected her to ask him to sleep on the couch, even though he didn't think she would react that way. A once wounded heart takes a long time to forget.

She made a quiet noise in her sleep and moved back until her warm skin was pressed up against his bare side. Flames licked throughout his body leaving him with no desire but to roll towards her and pull her tight against him, which would then cancel out the not getting too close to her part of the plan.

Devin squeezed his eyes shut and clenched his jaw, forcing his brain to ignore the message his body was sending it. He still had to make sure she was safe from Tomas...

That thought alone allowed him to clamp down on his thoughts and instincts and relax a bit more beside her. That did not mean the rest of the night was going to be any easier.

Chapter Thirty-Two

Rayne stood in the bathroom long after she was showered and dressed. Her mind was lost in a world of thoughts, most of which she didn't know where to begin to sort through. She was almost relieved when she'd awakened and Devin was out of the bed. He was there beside her most of the night, she'd surfaced a few times and found herself right against him. He hadn't pushed the fact that they'd had sex, only draped one arm over her most of the night in a very comfortable way. Of course, her hormones had tried to get her attention more than once, but Rayne had already gone way past the point she'd ever been in her life, so after a few stern lectures she'd been able to thwart any further actions to regret later.

The way she'd been with Devin the night before still shocked her, she didn't do things like that. She didn't have sex with strangers—at least she hadn't up until now. Although, it felt like more than just sex, but Rayne couldn't put a finger on why she thought that. She couldn't figure out what it was about Devin. Normally she was in complete control of her thoughts, and was right up until she was close to him and then not so much. As soon as he touched her, she forgot everything else but him. *Why is that? Why do I want to wrap myself around him and let all these new feelings take me away?* It wasn't just the physical feelings, although they hit her like an explosion, it was all the other ones that were new as well. One of her fears was that she was using him to get through the revelations about Aiden. Rayne didn't think she'd act like that, but wasn't usually at ease with strangers. Yet, here she was entrusting her safety to one, and she believed what he said about everything. *Am I making a big mistake? Another big mistake?*

Rayne looked down at her foot when she realized that almost her full weight was on it and the pain was barely noticeable. She never healed this quickly, ever, so it must not have been as bad as she thought. Her stomach rumbled, reminding her that it had been far too many hours since she'd put food into it. Food... Everything she'd bought was going to waste at her camp site.

Deciding she couldn't hide in the bathroom forever, Rayne opened the door and headed back towards the kitchen. Devin's voice was coming from another room down the hall, he didn't sound happy. She didn't want to listen in, as loud as he was, if she stayed in the house she would be. Turning back Rayne grabbed the cane so she could get down to her campsite without hopping

Rayne turned around, feeling like she was being watched. Devin stood in the hall with the phone against his ear watching her with those grey eyes. Smiling at him, she went out the door.

She congratulated herself as she walked towards the camp, for a moment she thought about driving her car back, but seemed to be managing quite well on foot. Rayne didn't want to baby it too much, she wasn't comfortable with being an invalid. She went around the corner and smiled when to see her tent, still standing where she'd put it up. Okay, where she'd put it up and Devin had fixed it.

As soon as she had started walking she noticed sounds that she had somehow managed to miss since she'd arrived. She could hear the ducks down by the lake, and from the sounds of it momma duck had to issue a few warning squawks to misbehaving little ones. The leaves, having dried out from the endless rain, were rustling gently in the soft breeze that was blowing. Did it always smell this good after storms? She couldn't recall if she'd noticed the smell yesterday. Regardless, she was delighted with how beautiful it all was.

A strange feeling went through her suddenly, like she was being watched. Had Devin followed? Turning slowly, she looked into the trees and then back towards the small cabin. If it was an animal, she'd never make it that far.

"Devin?" She called out quietly, hoping he'd step out of the trees. Two legs or four, she didn't care at this point just as long as it was him. Rayne strained, listening for any sort of movement, although how she'd ever be able to tell the difference between one that should be there and one that shouldn't she didn't know. Unless something not meant to be in the trees wore bells, she was sunk.

"I didn't mean to startle you."

Rayne spun around towards the deep voice. A very large man stood in the shade of the trees. He held up both hands. How had someone that large managed to move through the trees without a sound bothered her, but not as much as not knowing just who exactly he was. She was beginning to regret walking here after all.

"I'm a friend of Dev's."

He stepped out into the light and she had to take a quick breath. He was beautiful, in a dark sort of way. Just the fact that he looked like that made her frown and study him from his bare feet up to his black hair. *Were all, what do I call them…Shifter males so pretty?* She doubted it, actually hoped not, or she might become the ugly duckling, maybe wolfling in this case. "He mentioned someone was coming to help." He flashed teeth at her and she couldn't help but return the smile. "Do you grow a fuzzy tail too?" She had to ask, she wasn't taking anyone's outside appearance as what they were again, or at least for right now.

He chuckled softly. "I wouldn't call it fuzzy." He took a few more steps towards her, but stopped at a comfortable distance away, his eyes roamed towards the trees over her head before he turned the brilliant green eyes back to hers again. He inclined his head slightly. "I'm Calum."

She leaned on the cane. "Rayne." Tilting her head, she looked at him for a long second. "Are you from a different, um, clan?"

A smile went through his eyes, but it didn't reach his lips. "Definitely."

"You don't want to elaborate on that, do you?" He shook his head. "I'm not trying to pry, I'm just figuring things out."

"I understand."

He blinked and for a moment Rayne could have sworn his eyes looked cat like, and not like a cute little Persian kitty type of cat. When he blinked again they were normal once more. "So, is everything okay? No one is lurking that shouldn't be?"

"You don't need to be concerned with that." He shrugged again. "It's my unofficial hobby to watch Dev's back."

Rayne looked at him, her eyes narrowing slightly. "It needs watching that often?"

"Not since we were kids, no."

His eyes moved down over her and stopped at her feet for a few seconds before he turned and glanced back up the path she'd just come down. When his eyes came back to hers, she recognized the male look of concern.

"Are you all right? Should you be walking on that?" He motioned towards her foot.

She looked down at it, having forgotten she was leaning on a cane for a reason. "It's a little tender, but nothing serious." The hair on the back of her neck stood up as a shiver went down her spine. Turning her head, she looked up the path but it was empty.

Calum came over in a few strides and turned towards the

trees. Not a muscle on his body moved as his head turned slowly. She heard him inhale deeply a few times and then his shoulders relaxed as quickly as they'd tensed.

"Devin." He said softly.

Devin stepped out of the dark trees and nodded. "Calum."

Devin's eyes moved slowly over her and she had to suppress the urge to sigh out loud. He came towards her and with each step she literally felt warmer. *What is wrong with me?*

"You made it all the way down here walking?" He glanced down at her foot.

"Yes, it's not too bad today." When he reached her, he gently ran his hand down her arm sending shivers all through her. He smiled and then turned back to his friend. "Anything?"

The large man looked at Devin's hand that still lingered on her arm and then shook his head. "No. I was just out checking the back road, no one has been this way in a few days' time." His eyes flicked to her before they went back to Devin. "I sce... heard movement and thought I'd better check it out, only to find it was Rayne."

Rayne thought that was great news that no one else had been here, but Devin didn't seem to relax at all when he heard it. He stood there tensed and studied his friend.

"I haven't heard back from father yet, but I'll let you know as soon as I do."

Calum nodded abruptly and turned towards her. "A pleasure to meet you, Rayne." He inclined his head again in an almost regal way.

Rayne smiled, not knowing how else to take his gesture. "You too." She thought of asking him to come have coffee, but he was turned and gone into the trees before she could say it. She still stood there looking at the trees when Devin stepped in front of her.

He ran his hand softly down her hair. "You scared me, taking off like that." His voice was as gentle as his touch, but he was still holding himself rigid.

She looked down at her foot and then smirked at him. "I hardly took off with this foot. It feels better but I'm still hobbling." Rayne looked back towards the trees Calum had gone into. "You didn't mention your friend was huge." She smiled up at him. "I don't even think Aiden's men would mess with him."

Devin grinned. "That's the plan." His expression was serious as he glanced around the camp site slowly.

Rayne didn't need to know him much better than she did to know something was bothering him. "What's wrong?"

He looked back at her for a few seconds and then sighed. "I'm sure you over heard me arguing with my agent." She nodded. "I was supposed to go to a showing in a few days."

Her eyebrows shot up. "Supposed to?" She watched his pale eyes for a reaction, but they remained cool and disconnected. "You're still going, aren't you?" She was interfering with his work—her twisted up life was getting in his way.

He shrugged. "It's doubtful." He pushed his hands into his pockets. "I'm not going to leave you here in the middle of nowhere while I go and smile at the art patrons and collectors..."

"The patrons and collectors that *buy* your work and support your painting habit?"

Huffing out a breath, he smiled. "Yes, those."

She placed a hand on his arm and tried not to notice the little zap of energy she felt by touching him. "You have to go. I'm sure I'll be fine here for a few days."

Devin scowled for a moment, not really at her but with deep thought. "I'm not leaving you here alone."

Rayne's eyes widened. "I don't think your enormous friend that's stalking things in the woods right now would be leaving me defenseless. This is your work, you *have* to go."

He shook his head. "No, I don't. That's one of the perks to being an artist, we're moody and unpredictable."

"I think you should go."

He looked down at her hand that still rested on his arm. "You could come with me. Ever been to Toronto?"

Rayne raised both eyebrows and shook her head. "No."

The scowl turned into an irresistible smile, she felt her heart pick up the pace from it. "You'd blend right in." He ran a warm hand down her hair. "While I mingle, you could be spoiled with room service and bubble baths."

She bit her lip, close to being enticed to agreeing. "I could mingle with you, on one condition."

"Name it."

"The painting of me stays here."

He laughed. "That one is only meant for me."

"Okay." She laughed, "and here I thought I wouldn't get a chance to use any of my gowns while camping." Rayne didn't know how far away Toronto was, but she did know she wasn't ready for another long car ride. "When do you have to be there?"

"Tomorrow night."

"Oh. How far is the drive?"

"Too long, that's why we'll be flying." He turned and looked around the small camp site. "Collect up what you need and I'll bring the car back down."

Leaning down, he kissed her cheek so quickly and jogged towards the trees before she could reply. He disappeared into the trees in the same direction Calum had gone. Would Calum be coming with them? Rayne looked around the campsite again and then walked over to the cabin while making a mental list. Gowns, shoes, make-up, accessories... mingling at art events was something she did know.

Tracking Calum wasn't very hard with the waves of anxiety he was giving off, that and the smell of cat helped. He stood on the edge of the trees, where he'd watched Rayne wander a few days earlier. Devin stopped and studied his tense frame. "Did I miss something?"

Calum snorted. "I seriously doubt you did." He turned and glared at him.

Devin could smell the hostility coming off him.

"Your *mate* is very close to the change, in case your brain isn't the body part doing the thinking..."

"I know she's close." And he did, which is why he wasn't going near her right now. Devin threw his hands up in frustration. "I don't even know how to explain what a woman goes through..."

He snorted again. "Then find someone who can." Calum rolled his shoulders making Devin realize he was tenser then he was letting on. "I know she's your mate and it's none of my business, but if I can sense it as strong as I can, then any other shifter will be able to as well." He sighed. "You need to talk to her..."

Devin rubbed his hand across his neck, a headache wasn't far off. "I will." He glanced back into the trees, the constant feeling like he needed to look behind him was starting to get to him. "We're going to Toronto, I can't get out of a show I have to be at."

Calum raised his eyebrows. "You're taking her to your show?" He blew out a slow breath. "Wow, that's..." he shook his head. "Definitely a first."

Devin rolled his eyes at him, making him grin. Calum paced a few feet away and then turned back to him. "I'll call Gage, he's better at the socializing things than I am." He looked back into the trees. "I'll stay here and keep an eye out for Tomas and his crew."

The idea of having to have someone from the Alliance at his show, watching over him didn't sit well, but for Rayne's sake Devin wasn't going to balk about it. "I'll get in touch with my father and see what he knows and fill him in on what's going on."

He nodded. "Maybe you could see if your mother knows anyone that could talk to Rayne..."

Devin huffed out a breath. "Mother doesn't know about Rayne. I'm trying to spare my mate that experience as long as I can."

Calum grinned wide. "Afraid of what Mom will do?"

"You know it."

"I can't say that you're wrong. I think your mother is one of the scariest women I know when she sinks her teeth into something."

He stuffed his hands in his pockets, trying to keep from feeling so jumpy with being away from Rayne again. Hopefully once they were fully mated this constant anxiousness went. "I'll deal with Mother after Rayne knows everything."

Calum sobered as quickly as he'd laughed. "You need to talk to her, Devin." He stared at Devin for a few long seconds. "I'd hate to see anything go wrong."

He didn't know what to say to that, so he chose to say nothing.

"The fact that she has you so unraveled tells me a lot."

Devin scowled. "What do you mean?" *I'm unravelled.*

"I've never seen you like this, her just being near has toned you down or something, I'm not sure what it is, but there is something different and I don't think it's bad."

Devin wasn't sure he understood. "It's been interesting since she turned up here in the middle of a storm, that much I'll admit, but I don't think I'm any different."

"If you say so." He motioned with his head at the trees. "Now run along back to her, I can tell you're barely able to stand still."

He glared at him and then shook his head, knowing he was right. "I'll tell you what I find out after I talk to father."

"I'll be around."

Chapter Thirty-Three

When Devin had said they were flying, Rayne didn't realize he meant on a private jet. He had a private jet at his disposal. They'd driven in his SUV to a small airport of and from there they had loaded up his carefully packed paintings and flown to a much larger airport. How much were his paintings worth? She knew art and knew they were good—but *he had a jet.*

She sat looking out the window, even though he had suggested she get up and wander around. The interior of the jet wasn't overly decorated, but it was nice enough that she knew it was a personal private jet and not one that was rented to the public.

Rayne wasn't feeling quite right, but she didn't want to bother Devin with it though. He was talking to the pilot. She rubbed a hand over her forehead, she felt *really* off today and she hoped it was just from the packing and flying. She didn't want to spend the next few days in bed with the flu or something. Rayne meant it when she'd told him she would mingle at his opening. She had a few moments of panic at the thought of going, afraid of Aiden showing up or finding out she had been there. It had taken a bit of time before she realized that in all the years she'd known Aiden, he'd never gone across the border for any reason that she knew of, so the chances of him coincidentally showing up at a gallery show in Toronto was slim enough to push worry from her mind.

Leaning her head back she closed her eyes. She was coming down with something, her head felt fuzzy and skin felt like it was too tight. This wasn't what she needed right now.

"Are you tired?"

Rayne almost slid out of the seat to the floor when Devin spoke a few inches from her head. She huffed out a breath. "You startled me."

"Sorry, I thought you heard me come back."

"I'm fine." She took a slow breath trying to steady her heart again. "I'm not tired, just not feeling one hundred percent."

He sat down beside her. "Can I do something to help? Was the trip too soon after your ordeal?"

Rayne shrugged. "I don't think so, I just feel... I'm probably coming down with the flu." She rolled her eyes, annoyed that she felt bad enough he'd noticed. "I'm kind of achy and have that numb feeling you get in your head when a virus is setting in. It might just be a girl thing though, one minute I'm cold the next sweaty..."

An odd look crossed his face. "Oh."

It wasn't the kind of oh that was sympathetic, it was more of an 'oh, I know that'. Devin continued to look at her and she started to feel like she was missing an important piece of information. He picked up her hand and held it gently between his.

Rayne tried to think beyond the touch of his skin against hers, but couldn't. She felt like a pet being soothed and distracted and didn't like it. She pulled her hand out of his and cradled it against her chest.

Leaning back in the seat he watched her, many emotions flashing through his eyes. "What you're feeling is normal. I don't know the female version of it, but I know what it feels like." He frowned, not sure what he was saying. He continued in a quiet steady voice. "I'm not sure if being close to one of your own has triggered it to move a little faster or not, but it's possible."

Rayne sat there still hugging her own hand, trying to understand. "What are you saying?" She didn't give him the chance to answer when it hit her. "I'm not getting the flu, am I?"

He shook his head. Rayne knew her eyes widened and her mouth dropped open, but it was the only reaction she could muster. Yes, she believed what he'd told her about his parents and what she would someday be—but she didn't think that day was this close.

"It's okay, Rayne."

She brought him back into focus. "What if I'm not ready?" He gave her a look that said her body was whether she was or not. "I don't mean the physicality of it, I mean the mental aspect."

"I don't think it waits for anything."

Rayne blew out a breath, feeling overwhelmed and a little excited. Then it hit her. She sat up and leaned closer to him. "Will it... I mean I won't... what if..."

Clasping both of her hands in his larger ones, he brought them to his warm lips. "Relax, it's not a magic trick and presto you have four paws." He offered her a gentle smile. "You'll get plenty of warning in the beginning, before you learn how to control it." She must have looked like a frightened rabbit because he bit back a grin. "I'll be with you, I won't let you go through it alone."

Rayne took as much comfort in his words as she could. "How long until I can control it?"

He was silent, as if he was searching for the right words. "It varies, but women seem to learn control a lot faster than men."

That made her feel somewhat better, if anything could make her feel better about turning into a wolf. She had nothing against animals, just wasn't sure she wanted to be one. A little late for that, she thought sarcastically. She closed her eyes and took a deep breath, letting it out slowly before opening them and looking at him again. "So, I just walk around feeling yucky until this happens? How long?"

"I can't say." He kissed her hand again. "If you like I could talk to one of the women and get a few more details for you."

She nodded. This took puberty and everything you went through then and blew it right out of the water. This was serious life-altering stuff. He stood up and pulled on her hand until she was standing too. Rayne let him lead her over to the sofa on the other side of the plane.

"Sometimes," he said in a whispered voice, "being close to another of our kind can help during harder periods." His eyes flashed something she couldn't label. "The animals like the close contact."

She didn't know exactly what he meant. He sat down and then pulled her hand gently until she was sitting between his legs, her back resting against his chest. Rayne took a deep breath and tried to relax a little. She could feel his breath on her cheek and feel the warmth of his body through her clothes, it felt like home.

He ran his hands slowly down her arms and back up, leaving a trail of goose bumps in the wake. "Is this better?"

She let out a slow breath. It was. She didn't know why it was helping, but she felt better. "So, I just have to stay against you and I'll feel semi-normal?"

He chuckled in her ear. "I won't complain if you stay against me."

"I didn't mean in that way."

His lips brushed her cheek lightly. "I know, I'm just teasing."

She wasn't in a teasing mood, she just wanted to turn the few minutes of feeling at ease to let her relax. If she was forced to digest much more of this new-in-my-world stuff, she wasn't sure how she was going to come out of it.

Chapter Thirty-Four

Pacing over to the window for the tenth time in an hour, Rayne looked out over the city, even though being in a city was more familiar, it didn't comfort her. How had she gone from being startled in the wild to yearning for it in such a short time? Devin had asked her to stay inside, and she planned on listening, but that didn't mean she couldn't wish to be somewhere with trees and open spaces. Was this part of the changes he spoke of, or was she a complete wreck over everything because of Aiden? Hugging her arms around her waist as she decided it was probably a bit of both. Any other time she'd chastise herself for feeling so down, but considering how many changes had taken place in such a short time, she was more than entitled to having a woe-is-me moment or two.

Devin's cell phone rang, turning she glanced down at the screen, it said Mom. Did she answer it? What if it was important? Before Rayne could change her mind, she picked it up. "Hello?"

There was a long pause. "I'm sorry I must have..."

"Mrs. Addison? This is Devin's phone."

"Oh. So, is this Rayne?"

For a few seconds, she wanted to deny who she was, but

realized Devin had told his father, so his mother most likely knew. "Yes."

"I'm so pleased you answered dear. Is my son somewhere close by brooding?"

Rayne had to smirk to that. "No. No, he isn't. He had to go to the gallery and make sure they hung his paintings the way he wanted..."

"He dragged you to his showing? I had hoped he'd postponed it—considering everything that's going on." She paused and there was a definite male voice garbled in the background. "I hope you don't mind, dear, but Devin's father explained everything to me,"

Did she mind? It didn't feel like she should. "No, that's fine Mrs..."

"Please call me Irene."

"Okay." She paced back over to the window and looked longingly out it. "Its fine, Irene, and Devin didn't drag me here, I insisted he not ignore his work because of... everything."

"Well, aren't you sweet."

Rayne watched a bird land on the ledge and couldn't help but wish she was out there with it in the open air.

"I'm not sure how well my son has explained things to you, but I want you to know you can ask me any questions, anything at all. I knew your mother, dear, and it would be an honor to guide you through this."

Her attention was no longer on the bird. She'd forgotten that Devin's mother would be like him, like her parents—like *she* was going to be. "Thank you." She swallowed a lump in her throat. "Right now, I'm still trying to take all of this in, it's quite a lot to find out all at once."

Irene made one of those mother noises, the ones that let you know you had her attention and sympathies. "I can't imagine I'd handle it as well as you seem to be, Rayne. I don't want you to worry one second about that Tomas person, you *will* be kept safe."

Her voice seemed harsher with that statement, and it

almost brought tears to her eyes to hear that protective note her own mom used to have with her. "Thank you, very much."

There was more mumbling in the background before she came back on the line. "I'm going to let you go, dear, tell Devin good luck tonight and to call me."

"I will." Rayne turned when she heard the door open, Devin came in and sent her a puzzled look.

"Call me if you need to talk."

"I will, Irene and thank you." Not sure if it was the way Devin's eyebrows shot up or how big his eyes grew when she said his mother's name, but she hung up the phone quickly before she laughed into it.

He looked at the phone before looking back at her. "You were talking to my mother?"

Rayne nodded.

"Why?"

"The phone rang and it said it was mom, so I thought I should just in case it was important."

"Oh, it's always important to my mother, just not to anyone else."

She smirked at his annoyed tone. It was good to know that regardless of the details, like having a tail, that he seemed normal when it his mother was checking up on her son. "Your father told her about...me."

He ran his hands through his hair. "What did she say?"

Rayne wasn't sure why he sounded so hesitant when he said it, but she had nothing too interesting to share on it. "That if I needed to talk to anyone about—everything I've found out or I'm going to find out that I could talk to her."

A surprised look crossed his face. "Oh." He smirked. "That's very out of character for her."

"That's because she's your mother and I'm not her child."

"I suppose." Grinning, he walked over to her. "Now you need to get all fancied up, so we can go out to dinner before this whole-mingle-with-the-art-critics begins."

"We're going out?" She couldn't help smile at the sparkle in his eyes, he was up to something.

He ran a hand gently down her arm and the flames started inside her.

"Yes. I can't possibly face all those people on an empty stomach—and neither can you."

"I'm not a moody artist, I think I can handle them better than you can."

"No, you can't." The look in his eyes became serious. "You need to eat–often, to control what your body is going through." He flashed a not so serious grin. "I need to eat to control the urges to bite one of the patrons that are going to be asking me annoying questions."

Frowning, she took a moment to grasp what he was saying. "Eating regularly helps with control?"

He nodded slowly.

"Okay then, I guess we eat."

When Rayne stepped out of the room Devin almost swallowed his tongue, beautiful didn't come close to describing how she looked. The dress she had on looked like a hundred layers of sheer white cloth that hugged her but didn't at the same time. Each movement she made brought his attention to the curves beneath it. She'd done something with her hair too, that made him want to go over and run my fingers through it.

She stopped and gave me an odd look. "Is this all right?"

He nodded, still not sure if he could speak.

"Then why are you looking at me like that?"

Despite his resolve to keep his hands off her right now, Devin started moving towards her with every intention of ignoring his decision. "I'm not sure I want to take you out of this room now."

"Oh." She laughed and backed up a few feet. "But didn't you just tell me I had to eat to control myself?"

"Ignore me," he whispered as he cornered her. "I'm not

hungry now..."

Placing a hand on his chest she made one of those female sounds that let him know his was not going to get his way.

"Dinner. I don't want to do anything that will embarrass you tonight."

Taking a deep breath, he studied her, trying to find a way around the truth. Knowing he wasn't going to, he kissed her soft lips lightly and took her hand. "With you looking the way you do, it will most likely be me that does something embarrassing."

Devin was rewarded with a smile that made his heart swell inside his chest. How he was going to keep his hands off her, he had no idea.

Chapter Thirty-Five

Normally this was her world, her comfort zone. Art, the people that appreciated it and the pampering that went with it. Tonight, it wasn't. The dinner had been delightful, Devin flirted with her through the whole thing. The food was perfect, a wonderful change from the diet of snacks in the past week.

Rayne just couldn't get into the people tonight, she didn't want to be near them. She didn't know what was wrong, but did know she wasn't going to let Devin down. Devin didn't have to let her stay on his property or come look for her during the storm. Aside from their initial meeting, he had been very kind towards her—and with everything she was going through she needed him. Right now, he needed her, at least that's how she was looking at it. Glancing over to where he was, Rayne could tell by the look on his face this was the last place he wanted to be.

She had tried not to get into any serious conversations with any of the guests, and other than one man that wouldn't stay away, she was succeeding. He seemed to turn up everywhere she wandered to. As Rayne turned to move to the next painting the very same man was working his way towards her, again. Would anyone notice if she went and hid in the bathroom?

"I could stand here and pretend to be your body guard if that would help."

Turning, she came face to chest with a very large man. Looking up slowly Rayne found herself looking into deep blue eyes. She offered a polite smile. "Is it that obvious?"

He grinned wide and she realized he was the third beautiful man she'd encountered recently.

"That the creepy guy in the tacky suit is stalking you? Yes, it is." He extended a large hand. "I'm Gage, a friend of Devin's."

That explained the beautiful part. If this man was a wolf, she'd eat her left shoe and possibly her right. Rayne didn't know why but when she looked at him she sensed some sort of feline. If that wasn't weird enough, she felt safe near him, like she had with Calum. "I take it you're *the* back up because Calum decided to stay at the camp."

"Yes 'mam. That would be me." He took her elbow lightly and steered them away from the man that was determined to be her shadow. "I believe you need to go powder your nose."

Her heart beat sped up. "Is there something wrong?"

Gage shrugged in an easy manner. "That's what I need to find out and it would be easier for me to do if you weren't visible for a few minutes."

She looked around for Devin, suddenly wanting to know where he was.

"I'll find Dev, you just make yourself scarce for five minutes."

Nodding up at him, Rayne turned and head towards the restrooms. That panicky feeling was back, the one that had helped her drive without a plan.

When Gage sauntered towards Devin, it made him wonder, once again, why his clan was chosen to lead. If Calum was considered large, then Gage was a giant. His easy gait showed the cat he was, moving carefully but looking like he didn't have a concern in the world. His adrenalin leapt as soon as Devin noticed the look in his eyes. It did not match his slow stride. Excusing himself from the couple that was more or less talking with him between them, he headed in his direction.

"Gage, what is it?"

Gage grinned. "Great to see you too." He looked around and then walked over to the side of the small group of people.

Devin followed without question.

When Gage stopped, his eyes looked around the room, checking every person there. "I just escorted your lady to the restrooms."

"What? Is she all right? What happened?"

He looked at him briefly before his eyes continued to around the room. "She has a shadow, and I'm not sure about him, my senses say it's not good."

"Shit." Devin turned and watched the door to the bathroom. "Does Rayne know?"

"She knew he wouldn't go away. I stepped in before he could corner her again." For a moment his serious eyes bore into Devin's. "What possessed you to bring her when she was this close?"

Devin exhaled slowly. He should have known Gage, or any other clan member, would know. Calum had told him as much. "I wasn't letting her leave my sight."

He leaned down closer and spoke barely above a whisper. "Calum told me everything— *everything* and I think you need to get your mate the hell out of here and take her back to your wilderness until she is through this and you come to your senses."

He wasn't about to look away from that door to glare at him. "Right and how is Kelsey? Does she know yet?"

Gage growled softly. "She will soon enough, she's coming home for good next month."

Devin flicked a surprised look at him. "And you're going to tell her this time?"

He nodded. "I can't wait any longer, I'm about half out of my mind..."

"Exactly."

He snarled at me.

"I will handle this my way, Gage. And if and when the time comes that there is to be a succession ceremony—you will be informed."

"If there isn't, I'm going to kick your ass." He straightened and jerked his head towards the far corner. "I'm done playing cat and mouse—go get your woman while I go check out this guy. If he's one of Tomas's, I'll know—I'd know that scent anywhere. If I'm right you get the hell out of here."

Devin paused long enough to say one thing. "Thanks."

"Just doing my job, Dev, good luck with Rayne I hope it works out."

Devin didn't reply, just kept moving towards the door Rayne still hadn't come out of. When he was only a few feet away it opened and she came out. He could see the panic in her eyes and smell it on her skin. Without asking, she came to his side and leaned into him as he wrapped my arm around her.

"Your friend Gage told me to stay out of sight."

"I know." Moving slowly towards the nearest exit, he looked around for Gage. Spotting him, he watched him with the man he was talking to. Gage was normally a jovial sort, smiled a lot. He wasn't smiling now and neither was the greasy looking guy he was talking to. Devin needed to know if he was one of Tomas's but there was no way he was taking Rayne anywhere near him.

Pulling his phone out of my pocket he hit Gage's number. His large friend didn't take his eyes off his target as he answered the call. "Is he?"

"Hey, Charlie. Your car is doing what? It could be—the *smell* gives it away."

"Fuck. We're out of here."

"Okay, Charlie, I'm sure you'll make it home, but I'll call

your father and let him know."

"Got it." He made eye contact with him across the room, just long enough to see the lethal look in his eyes that his easy tone didn't give away.

"And, Charlie, don't stop along the way—just in case."

"Thanks, Gage." He tucked Rayne under his arm and hurried towards the door.

"Is he one of Aiden's?"

He could feel her start shaking. "We're not taking a chance, Gage will handle it and call me later."

"What about your show?"

Ushering her towards the door, he glanced over his shoulder at the crowd they were leaving behind. "I'm a moody artist, what can I say?"

Chapter Thirty-Six

It was so warm in the small bedroom on the plane that Rayne woke up soaked in sweat and not sure where she was at first. Sitting up, she wiped a hand across her brow and sighed. All of her felt out of sync, and it was scaring her. At first, she thought it was a nightmare that woke her up, but now she realized it was something else completely. She really didn't feel well, everything ached, her stomach was churning and her temples were pounding all at the same time. Even with the few hangovers she'd had in her life, they had never come close to the way she felt now.

Moving slowly out of the cabin, she squinted against the light and looked for Devin. A movement beside her startled her, making her jump.

"Hey. It's just me." Devin came up beside her and placed a hand on her shoulder.

"Something is wrong."

When she turned to face him, the soft look on his face faded and he frowned. Brushing the hair back from her face, he sighed. "Come on, let's sit down." He wrapped an arm around her and she wanted to cry with relief. Just his touch made the pain lessen and become bearable.

"I don't know what's happening."

Guiding her to the small couch, he sat down and pulled her into his lap. "I do. I can't make it go away, but I can help for now."

"For now?"

He brushed a soft kiss along her jaw. "It's going to happen no matter what anyone does. Just sit back and rest."

Resting wasn't going to be too difficult, she felt completely drained and didn't want to move. Every muscle hurt. She was now feeling muscles in her body that no yoga had ever made her aware of. "How much longer? I want to be outside."

His hand moved in a lazy pattern across her back and shoulders. "Normally, I'd be more than happy to open a window to help with that, but I'm pretty sure that's frowned upon while flying."

She opened her eyes to see him grin, but even then the worry didn't fade from his eyes. Not wanting to seem like a baby, she closed them again. He had grown up with what she was going through, she was taking the crash course and was worried she was failing. Calmness radiated off him, it helped a little, just not enough to slow her heart rate down. Devin's lips brushed over her neck as he spoke in a soft soothing tone. She was so out of it she couldn't even focus enough to understand what he was saying. Her skin was feeling like it was one size too small for her body and all she really wanted to do was whine and wish it away. Swallowing, she tried to keep her voice sounding normal. "Is it like this every time?" Keeping her eyes closed, she tried again to focus on the beating of his heart—which she could hear like a stethoscope was placed over it.

"No. It's just the first time. After a few shifts you will look forward to it—and appreciate it more than you could ever imagine." He stroked a hand lightly down her arm.

She knew he meant it to be soothing, but it just made her skin itch. Not wanting to offend him, she shifted in his hold to stop the contact. "I can't even imagine the first time." She swallowed a moan of discomfort. "I'm scared, Devin," she whispered.

"I've got you, Rayne. I won't let anything happen to you."

His words did make her feel better, to know she wasn't going to be alone. She was still scared and nothing was going to take away that feeling.

"Just close your eyes and try to relax until we land."

Her stomach churning made her decide not to reply. It felt like something was trying to come out through her skin, she didn't want to look and see if it was just a feeling or actually happening, so she closed her eyes again and focused on breathing as evenly as she could manage.

Chapter Thirty-Seven

In all the years he had been making this trip back to the camp, Devin couldn't recall ever making it as quickly. After trying several times to get Rayne to rest, she finally had a short nap on the drive back. During that time, he called his mother to see if there was anything different a female went through with their first change. It took all the patience he had to listen to her—going on like they were about to give birth instead of a first shift. Feeling calmer after that, he called Calum and told him to clear out and find a place where he could watch the entrance to the camp without being on the land. He was thankful he didn't get an 'I told you so' from him. How Devin didn't know she was this close, he still didn't know. Maybe he was too close and that was the reason. Maybe next time, he'd listen when Calum and Gage tried to tell him something... probably not, but he'd consider it more in the future.

Her skin was clammy and she was growing more restless with each minute, even in sleep her muscles twitched preparing for what was to come. For several minutes of the drive Devin wondered if he was strong enough to see her thought this. Immediately following those thoughts, he mentally kicked himself in the ass, knowing he was the only support she had and wasn't going to be anything less than what she needed from him.

He tried to think back and remember what it was like the first time he went through a complete shift. It hadn't been startling and scary for him though, he'd had a life time of education leading up to it. Rayne had only had a few days to adjust to the fact of what she was, never mind the symptoms during the onset of a full shift. Running seemed to be the one thing he craved when he shifted, he sure as hell hoped it was with her too. He knew she'd never forgive herself if the first time it happened she shifted back with animal blood in her mouth. Were there vegetarian shifters? He'd never come across any, so he was clueless when it came to that. Then again, the idea of one being in animal form having a snack of weeds and bark was just too much to try to wrap his brain around.

"Where are we?"

Her voice sounded strained. "A few more minutes and we'll be back on my land, hun. Just stay as relaxed as you can okay?"

Devin didn't take his eyes off the road to look at her, he was already driving faster than he should ever consider going. At least it was a bright night with no clouds so he had a little extra light to help him see.

"Devin?" She shifted so she was sitting up more and he could see her out of the corner of his eye. "After it's over, will I feel better?"

"Oh yeah. Everything will suddenly make more sense, at least it did for me." His brain searched for something to say to her to make her feel better about this. Was that possible? "You may see things differently afterward too. The change doesn't happen over a few days—there could have been things going on with you for a few years that weren't adding up."

She groaned. "There has, but I just kept blaming it on fate and coincidence..." She huffed out a breath, telling him that talking wasn't something she felt much like doing right now.

Reaching over, he squeezed her hand and tried to offer her the least dangerous contact he could afford while driving like a lunatic. "Just a few more minutes."

"Is it going to hurt?"

Digging back as far as my memory went he tried to remember. "Not so much pain as it is a completely unknown." He couldn't lie to her. "It's uncomfortable, mostly because you don't quite know what to expect. The best advice I can give is try to relax through it and just let it happen."

"Kay."

Rayne sat forward in the seat watching out the windshield as the gate to the camp came into sight. He would be lucky if she waited until they stopped before she jumped out. Not that he blamed her, every cell in her body would be telling her to get outside. "Head for the beach when we get there, okay? The sand is going to feel a hell of a lot better than trees and rocks if you lose your balance." He chanced a look to see her nod as she was moving closer to the door.

The truck was barely at the house when her door flew open and she jumped down from it. "Shit." Jamming it into park, Devin bailed out his side and took off after her. This wasn't going to be a slow transition, his guts told him. Not bothering to curse again, he tore his shirt off and tossed it in the air as he ran towards the lake.

Rayne was standing bent over with her hands on her knees making soft moaning noises. He slowed down when he was closer, and took off his shoes flinging them aside. "Take off your clothes, it's a bitch to get hung up in them." He didn't think she heard him until she reached down to untie her shoes.

His brain and his wolf were attempting to battle out why they were here as she stripped down and dropped down onto her knees. He kept his jeans on, unbuttoned and knelt beside her. Gently he rested his hand on her upper back and caressed her skin in what he hoped she found a soothing way. "Just breathe through it and let it happen."

She made a noise that was a mix between a groan and a growl causing his heart and hormones to both pick up. He couldn't help it, this was his mate and the wolf part of him was in sync with every muscle in her body and what was happening. The man part of him wanted to shelter her from this and keep her all to himself. He'd known some females that didn't keep the same personality after their wolf was free and he prayed that wouldn't happen to Rayne.

"Devin." She muttered between clenched teeth.

The panic in her voice brought him back into the mindset to help her. He leaned down near her face and tried to keep his voice as soft as possible. "Just let go, Rayne, I've got you. I will be with you every step of the way."

"I don't... want..." she hissed out a breath, "don't let me—eat anyone." She said quickly before she moaned again.

"I won't. You'll be fine, we'll go for a run and you can test out your new senses and speed—I'll look out for you." Another deeper growl came from her. "Just let it happen." He placed a soft kiss on her temple and leaned back from her. One thing he did know was someone too close could get hurt in the first few moments of a change—he valued all his pieces enough to stay cautious regardless of how close he wanted to be.

The sound of snapping bones would have alarmed any normal person, but to him it signalled one thing. Her body wasn't waiting for her to come to terms with her new knowledge. She yelped and dropped down closer to the ground.

There was a beauty to it that he appreciated, but watching Rayne transform into the blondest she wolf he'd ever set eyes on was the most breathtaking thing he would ever witness. After her silky skin covered over with soft fur, she lay there on the sand panting. "Get up slowly." Opening her eyes, she looked up at him and his heart tripped a few times as he looked into her sultry eyes. "You're gorgeous."

When she started to ease up and stand, his hands flew to his jeans, knowing that once she found her balance she wasn't going to stay put and watch the serene lake beside them. She was going to run and test every single muscle and sense in her new form.

Devin barely managed to change before she took a total of four single steps and then took off towards the trees. Her speed was rare for the first change and left him stunned for a few seconds before his own paws hit the ground and he raced after her.

Chapter Thirty-Eight

Not even being out of breath, Rayne slowed when the building on the beach came into view, her mind wanted her to continue running but her body was feeling a bit shaky. Who would have ever guessed how exhilarating this was? She felt free and completely rejuvenated. She was a wolf and no one was going to control her world again. Rayne stopped almost on the spot she had stripped off her clothes, amazed that she could distinguish her own scent from the sand and smells around her.

Devin came up beside her and licked her ear. She growled playfully at him and nipped at his throat. His response caught her completely off guard as he pushed her sideways and knocked her off balance before he grabbed her neck and tugged at it. Shaking him off, she backed away from him and then found herself sitting on the sand. Her legs were done whether she wanted to continue to be in this form or not. When the first odd twinges started, Devin backed away and sat down.

There was no burning or panic as her body slowly reverted back to skin. Rayne wouldn't say it felt normal, but she wasn't scared senseless as it happened this time. When she could feel the gritty sand against her skin, she opened her eyes and flipped the hair out of her face to see him sitting there naked, watching her with a grin on his face.

"You," he smiled again, "are amazing."

She could smell his excitement and the fact that she could didn't even bother her. Rayne could also smell his sweet smelling sweat and now understood why she'd been having the urge to lick him since they met. The best part was not having to feel weird for having those desires anymore, and she was going to do just that. Taste his skin. Getting up on her hands and knees she began crawling towards him. "Amazing? How so?" A heated look appeared in his eyes as he watched her crawl slowly towards him. It felt like she was stalking him, as an animal would and the feeling exhilarated her further—it turned her on too.

"I could barely keep up with you..." He leaned back on his hands as she got closer to him and she was able to see he was as affected by all of this as she was. "Would you be offended if I told you that even as a wolf you were sexy as hell?"

Rayne shook her head and kept creeping towards him. Never in her life had she done something as bold as she was about to do, but she didn't care. It felt too right to stop. When she crawled over his legs and was close enough to his chest to feel the heat of his skin, she ran her tongue across his shoulder. He hissed out a breath and lifted his face to the sky.

Before her sanity returned she moved closer and tasted the pulse in his neck. Grasping his shoulders, she straddled his legs and straightened up. Following only the uncontrollable urges that filled her, she lowered slowly onto his very stiff organ until he filled her completely. He growled out a breath but didn't move to touch her, just let her do what she wanted.

Gripping his shoulders tighter, Rayne lifted her weight from him, moaning with pleasure. His scent was filling her nostrils and sending heat to her very core. Unable to resist tasting him again, she licked over his shoulder when she impaled herself on him once more. Groaning, she bit down on his muscled neck and was rewarded with a deep moan from him.

His hands grasped her hips and lifted her up so he could thrust hard into her when he pulled her back down. She was lost after that and could no longer control the flames that consumed her.

Rayne continued to slam her body into his as his mouth moved over any flesh he could reach. When his mouth finally got to hers, she couldn't prevent from biting down on his lip. In a single blurred movement, he was on his knees and wrapping her legs around his waist. She held on and let him take over, her whole body was vibrating with a need she'd never felt before. Muscles she didn't know she had were clamping around his slick hardness as he drove into her over and over again.

Devin's mouth crushed hers in a kiss that was as desperate as she was feeling. Gasping, she pulled away and shuddered when the first sign of orgasm radiated through her. Rayne could feel the hard muscles in his legs flexing as her body bounced off them, his hands no longer held her hips but he still thrust into her at a furious speed. As he molded both of her breasts in his hands, another wave of heat flashed through her. His mouth moved over one nipple roughly before he went to the other and bit the flesh causing her to crash violently over the edge. She could hear her voice crying out, but didn't have the focus to control it.

Rayne's head was floating and body convulsing around him when he pulled out of her so quickly she almost fell onto the sand. Before she could catch her breath enough to speak, he had her on hands and knees and was pushing into her from behind. The muscles that were still vibrating were so sensitive in this position she was on the edge again within seconds.

He growled and grasped her hips tighter to hold her still as he slammed into her. She didn't want him to stop either, her body was so hot and close to coming again that all she could do was let him do what he wanted. Lifting her upper body back towards him, he bit into the back of her neck hard enough to make her gasp. With his teeth still holding her as he slid into her hard enough to slap their flesh together Rayne crested in one stroke and was moaning wildly. Growling again, Devin thrust once more before his whole body went rigid and he collapsed against her.

Lowering both of their bodies to lie on the sand, he continued to pulse inside her. She couldn't do anything except try to draw enough air into her body to stay conscious. A few days ago, she would have been shocked by what had just happened, but as hard as she searched, there wasn't one part that felt any remorse for what they'd just done.

Devin kissed the back of her neck gently and she felt the sting. Licking her lips to try to moisten them enough to speak, she tasted an unfamiliar tanginess and knew that he too would have a mark from her teeth. For a reason, she would have to think about later—much later, she liked the idea of that.

"Will I be like that after every time?" she whispered, still without enough air to speak any louder.

"I can only hope so."

Rayne swatted playfully at him.

"We should take a quick swim and get some sand off before we go inside."

A moonlight swim in the lake? Not even that bothered her, when a week ago she would have shrieked and run for the nearest building. "I don't think I can walk yet."

"Good, neither can I." Devin shifted and pulled out of her, rolling her to lie in his arm against his chest. "I have no problem staying right here for a bit longer."

The moonlight shone on his face and she could see the softest look in his eyes she'd ever seen a man have for her. Rayne's heart suddenly felt like it was in her throat. "I'm fine with it too," she managed to say before his mouth moved lovingly over hers.

Chapter Thirty-Nine

Hanging up the phone, Devin moved back over to the window and watched Rayne walk along the water's edge. She had run for cover when his agent had called, feeling responsible for the fast departure. He had expected to be raked over the coals and back when he'd answered the call, only to be shocked beyond words when she had told him that he had sold out. Not one single painting left. What had happened to make that possible he still had no idea, but he'd take it.

Despite the feeling of wonder that had him flying high since last night, the guilt kept over-powering them and leaving him feeling like a heel. He had marked her. She had claimed him. They were a mated pair and she was none the wiser. His instinct and body had taken over when she'd climbed on him and sunk her teeth into him, unknowingly accepting him as hers, but still he had let it happen and now had to face the truth and tell her—everything. What Devin had to figure out now was *how* to tell her. It had to be today, he couldn't let it go any longer, not after last night.

His cell phone cut off thoughts off. Without taking his eyes off the sunbathed woman he answered it.

"A car just headed towards the gate."

Calum's news brought his whole body on alert. "Plates?"

"Way out of towners."

"Fuck!"

"I'm on my way—save some for me."

Snapping the phone shut, he jammed it into his pocket and headed to the front door. His only thought was to reach Rayne before someone else did, but he'd have to stay in skin form until he saw who it was first. As Devin rounded the corner of the house, he looked down to where Rayne was, she wasn't there. His heart slammed to a stop. She had just been there. Inhaling deeply, he sought her scent and almost collapsed in relief when he didn't smell anyone but her. She must have wandered down the path towards her tent.

Jogging in that direction, he focused on listening for the car coming closer. He could hear branches snapping and moving as Calum moved with cat-like speed through the bush from the other direction. When Devin cleared the trees near the small cabin Rayne was using, every muscle in his body came to an abrupt halt. Two large men were with her, and she looked scared shitless.

Tomas had found her.

Branches to his right cracked signaling Calum had arrived. A faint low growl meant for his hearing only told Devin he saw what he was looking at. Moving forward slowly, he gauged the size of the men and knew neither were Tomas himself. Just as he was shifter, so too were the goons that had his mate sandwiched between them.

"Aiden said to bring you back. He doesn't give a damn about the car." The dark-haired man said to Rayne with a smile.

Rayne glared at him. "All he's getting back *is* the damn car. I am *not* going anywhere. You can tell him I want nothing to do with him. Ever."

That was his girl. Devin was trying to stay out of their line of sight until he knew Calum had checked out the entire area.

"You can tell him yourself." The other man grabbed her arm and started to drag her along with him.

He cleared the trees and stood in the path. "I suggest you let go of her. *Now.*" Devin felt Calum move up beside him.

The one holding Rayne snorted at him. "I don't know who the hell you are, but you better mind your own business."

He watched the fear appear in Rayne's eyes and had to clamp down on his temper. "Devin Addison."

Calum emitted a low warning growl.

The shock was clear to see as a look passed between the two strangers. They knew exactly who he was. Rayne was pushed in front of them, the cowards were practically hiding behind his mate.

"We uh..." one of them mumbled.

"Didn't know. We thought she was unclaimed and it wouldn't..."

He no longer looked at either of them as both bent down into what could have loosely been termed a submissive pose. He watched Rayne's face as he uttered the next words. "She *is* marked and if you wish to leave here, you will back away from her slowly." They hunched down further and moved in opposite directions away from her. The confusion was so clear on Rayne's face Devin wanted to drop to his knees and tell her he didn't want it this way.

Calum hunkered down beside him for a second and then moved over to stand with her. He knew the first priority was to get her out of here, as if he'd spoken out loud he circled around her and pushed her gently towards the cabin.

She glanced down at the cat and then at him for a moment before moving quickly to the cabin and going inside. Calum stood outside the door and looked at the cowards almost kneeling on the ground.

Devin had to finish this before he could go to her. "You tell Aiden Tomas who I am—to you and the others that he's trapped into service for him and we'll see if he's man enough to come for her then." They nodded in unison and lifted their heads. "When you're ready to be free, the Alliance will help you." A look of hope appeared in their eyes as they straightened.

"We'll do that. T-thank you." Turning they headed back in the other direction.

Calum chuffed as he went by him to follow them. "Disappointed you didn't get to bite them?" Devin whispered knowing he would hear. He only glanced over his shoulder and then trotted along after Tomas's shifters.

Devin stood there watching, procrastinating before explaining what Rayne needed to know. When the cabin door opened, he waited one heartbeat before turning to face her. Her face carried a hurt expression, and to know he was the reason it was there would be something he would never forget.

"Rayne..."

She shook her head. "I'm marked? What does that mean?" There was a note of anger in her voice.

"I didn't intend to do it. It happened before I could..."

"What happened?"

Letting out a deep breath, he grasped at how to tell her this in the easiest way possible. There was no easy way. "Last night, when we—the mark on your neck, it won't ever leave."

Her eyes widened and flew to his neck before she looked back to his eyes.

"Neither will mine." He took a deep breath. "We're mates. A mated pair—now."

Devin wasn't sure if the look was a scowl or something else. Either way it wasn't a good look.

"And you knew this before last night?"

He tried for the words to explain, but only was able to nod.

"Were you going to tell me?"

"Yes. Yes, I was going to tell you. I just wanted to give you time to adjust to everything else..." He was losing ground and knew it when she crossed her arms over her chest. "I was trying to stay away from you so it wouldn't happen." Devin thought he'd won a few inches when her face relaxed a small bit. She looked in the direction Calum had gone in.

"Who are you, Devin?" She motioned towards the men that had left. "Who are you to them? Why did those idiots of Aiden's almost drop to their knees when you told them your name?"

For one brief moment, he'd hoped she hadn't caught any of that. This part wasn't going to go as well, instinct told him. "My father is the King of the Alliance—the head of all the clans... all shifters."

She pursed her lips and was silent for too long. "So, you're a Prince then?"

He opened his mouth and then snapped it shut and nodded as a reply again.

"I see." Her eyes moved slowly over him. "And I'm your mate? Is that like a wife or something?"

Devin shrugged in a way he never thought he'd ever done. "Sort of, we do have actual weddings though as well..."

"You've made me a Princess of *all* the clans—without my knowledge?'

His mind flew through answers trying to find anything that would make it seem okay, he failed. "Yes."

"Is this—leadership an election sort of position or a monarchy?"

He realized suddenly, that she was far too intelligent for his own good. Glancing at the sky fleetingly, he looked for a storm and prayed lightening would strike him before he had to answer. "My family is the monarchy."

"I would someday be the queen?" Her voice squeaked and he winced.

There was only one more thing to tell her now. "*If* I take the place of my father."

"If? Do you have an older sibling?"

He shook his head and stood perfectly still as she paced a few feet away from him and then spun around and glared at him.

"Is there anything else I should know?"

Where was that lightening? "I would be leader of the Alliance and the alpha of the wolf clan."

"Oh, is that all? A King of two countries—more or less." She huffed out a breath and turned away from him and looked at the trees. "I ran away from endless lies and deceit and you're not any different than what I fled from."

Devin's heart was stuck in his throat, making breathing harder with each breath. "Rayne—I didn't expect..."

She spun and if he'd been a young cub he might have dropped to the ground to hide from the look she was giving him. "You didn't expect me. I understand that part. But you knew who you were and I'm pretty sure you knew we were mates *long* before I did." She looked down at the ground. "*That* I had a right to know."

Calum stepped out of the trees. He had stopped somewhere along the way and dressed. "They're gone." He said solemnly to neither in particular as he looked from one to the other.

Rayne cleared her throat. "Thank you."

She turned from him and looked back at Devin, the pain in her expression almost undid him.

"Devin, I'd like some time alone please."

He could feel Calum's stare boring into him, but didn't meet it. He wanted to drop to his knees and beg forgiveness, but knew enough by the way she held herself she was done listening to him for the day. "I'll be at the house."

He glanced briefly at Calum and knew he wasn't going to let anything happen to her. Turning, Devin started back along the path. With each step his legs trembled as he prayed he hadn't just lost her for good.

Chapter Forty

Losing track of how long he stood under the water, Devin went over every second that had passed since he'd met Rayne. Had there been opportunities to tell her everything? Yes. Would he have done it differently if he could do it again? Probably not.

Turning the now cold water off, he continued to stand there in thought. It was killing him to stay here and give her the time she wanted. He should be with her, talking to her—explaining about everything not standing here thinking about it. Devin kept hoping enough time had passed, but in truth it had only been an hour. He didn't know her all that well, but she had a kind heart and had been very forgiving up to this point...

Stepping out, he grabbed a towel and wrapped it around his waist as he headed to the kitchen. If he were a drinking man, now would have been the time, but as it was he didn't even have a beer in the fridge to distract his heart. Grabbing the coffee pot, he went over to the sink to fill it. The only thing he knew would take his mind off things was to paint, and he'd be at it for a while and would need a lot of caffeine to paint these emotions away.

When he finished in the kitchen he headed to grab some

track pants, as he passed the front window spotted Calum standing down on the beach. How was he keeping an eye on Rayne if he was on the beach? Devin looked around for any sign of her, seeing none, he went to the other window to see if she had gone for a walk and he was keeping his distance. He didn't see her there either.

As soon as he threw the window open, Calum turned and shook his head. Devin didn't understand. As he started walking towards him, Devin bolted to grab his jeans.

By the time he got out on the deck Calum was already there. "Where is she?"

In all the years he had never seen the look Calum was giving him. It was one of hesitance.

"She's gone."

Devin's heart slammed into his ribs. "Gone? Where?" How could he be so stupid as to let her leave? He was sure those goons were long gone and wouldn't be coming back but he still shouldn't have let her leave.

"She'll be safe. I sent her to the one place no one is going to bother her. Actually, she asked to go..."

"She asked to go where?" Devin was trying not to yell at him, but his slow manner in telling him wasn't helping the situation at all.

"To see your mother."

If Devin lived another hundred years, he didn't think he'd ever be as shocked as he was now. He hadn't seen that coming. "You sent her to *my* parents?" Wasn't Calum supposed to be on his side of things?

He shrugged. "Anywhere else and I'd be obligated to follow her and I didn't think you'd go for that."

He was right, but still his mother? "When is she coming back?"

Stuffing his hands in his pockets he looked down at the wood under their feet. "I don't know if she is. She's pretty upset, Dev."

His chest hurt suddenly. The phone shrilled inside the house, and he knew who was going to be on the other end of it. Devin hoped he could explain to his mother the events of the last few days a hell of a lot better than he had Rayne. At least his parents he knew were on his side or he hoped they were.

229

Chapter Forty-One

Glancing around, Rayne couldn't help thinking of the last time she had driven here. She'd been scared, heartbroken and had no clue which direction to go. Her future had been vague and riddled with so many questions she was sure she would never have any answers.

Now, today she had answers. She was no longer scared. In fact, she had a confidence that she'd never had. Her breath was steadier than it had ever been, and she finally had a sense of belonging.

The last few weeks had opened her eyes to a whole world she could never have imagined existed. Strangers that now felt like family she'd known her whole life, had come and offered her patience and knowledge to help get her through the heart-wrenching moments.

Rayne was still processing the history she was told of the shifter world and the Alliance. How could an entire race live with such violence and so many threats over their heads? How could they overcome them to thrive as they were? She felt humbled and honored when many of the elders she'd met asked for her to be the Princess to rule by Devin's side. Her parents, and their parents she was told were highly respected members of the pack and many still mourned their loss. She was overwhelmed to think that if Devin and she did stay together as a mated pair, their children would be Princes and Princesses and revered above all. That was a lot to digest in such a short time.

Having met her relatives, she couldn't believe the love and closeness of them. She had family, in blood and spirit. This alone was the hardest and best thing to grasp. Rayne wasn't alone in the world anymore and never would be again.

The problems that waited were what to do with Devin... She had been carefully schooled in the rituals and ceremonies of the pack—fast lane lessons but still ones she welcomed. Now all she had to do was decide what to do with all the knowledge.

Her heart ached for Devin the entire time they were separated. Her body craved him, inside and out—even just his touch would ease her discomforts and stress she'd been told. She'd had many moments where she didn't think she was going to last another second without him, but the new strength she'd discovered kept her steady enough to stay where she was and think things through.

The moment Rayne realized she was going to go back to see Devin, his parents had gotten quiet, the elders thoughtful. Everyone was leaving it up to her to bring their Prince to his senses. In truth, she wasn't even sure if she wielded the power they thought she did.

Did she want to bring to their Prince home? Yes, but for the entire shifter world, not just her. He held strength and she knew after watching his father for the last few weeks that he hid more away. Did Devin know he was so similar to the man that had sired him? She doubted it, but he was just the same. She knew he thought his mother was a hard person, but had he ever stepped back and watched the interaction between his parents? Probably not. They functioned as one most of the time, always sure of the other and what they were doing.

Rayne wanted that. She wanted oneness with someone that would carry her through anything life wanted to toss at her. Could she have that? She wasn't sure.

Part of her wanted to crawl back to Devin and ask him to shelter her from life once more—that small part was the only part that remained of her prior self. The part that still thought she was a vulnerable, shy woman.

Most of the time now Rayne knew she wasn't that any longer. She had strength that many would only dream of. She'd been told by the women that coached her through the last few weeks that she held a strength that was rare to the females in their pack. Giddiness still flushed through her when she thought of it in those terms.

Glancing around, she realized she was almost out of time. She would be there soon and she couldn't go back and fail. She knew she didn't want to give up the family she'd just discovered or the togetherness that was so new to her.

When she pulled the car into the drive, she stopped and opened the window. The scents filled her and her heart said she was home. Immediately a faint smell riddled through her nose, her wolf sensed her mate and she cried for him.

Taking a deep breath, she parked the car right there, inside the gate and decided she needed to walk the rest of the way. Rayne needed to gather the strength from the nature surrounding her and go to Devin at a new stronger level than she had the first time they'd met.

The breeze blew softly over her skin, sending her hair back away from her face and she even felt, at that moment, that nature was welcoming her home. Rayne was thankful it was blowing her scent away from the house—and was surprised to realize she thought of things like that now. With its help to keep her presence hidden, it also brought the scent that was only Devin and her heart skipped a few times.

Her mind may still have questions and doubts, but her heart knew what she wanted and what she was going to do.

Calum was still here, she could tell his scent now as well. Rayne wouldn't be standing before him this time feeling small and insignificant, she'd be what he seemed to believe she was the last time they spoke face to face.

She was going to be the alpha female, even if she was shaking in her shoes and trying to remember to breathe.

Chapter Forty-Two

The image staring back at him in the mirror was a pitiful sight. His hair hadn't been combed in days and it looked like it. Unshaven and starting to resemble the wolf form he usually had to change to be.

Shaking his head, he moved away to wander back into the studio. Maybe inspiration would strike before he got there.

His parents were on his side, at least partially. Devin phoned once a day to see if Rayne was doing okay, he hadn't been brave enough to ask to speak to her. He assumed if she really wanted to talk to him she would have by now. His mother's answers were short and to the point, she was clearly very annoyed for finding his true mate and screwing it all up. He couldn't say she was wrong. and wasn't sure if he expected sympathy from her. That alone told him his head was a mess, to think his mother was suddenly going to be a soft-hearted woman.

Devin's father was much more sympathetic to his situation, talking to him longer and trying to assure him it would work out the way it was meant to be. The part that drove him insane; he didn't know what the fates planned.

Calum was still here, even though Devin tried to get rid

of him time and time again. He blamed having to stay on him when he'd invited Tomas's men to send Tomas here himself. Both of them knew the chances of him coming after Devin without his animal sidekicks was less than a point of one percent, but he still stayed. For a few fleeting seconds, Devin wondered if his parents had him staying here to keep an eye on him. If it were anyone but Calum he would believe it. Calum didn't answer to anyone, he was his own cat. The only reason he stayed loyal to Devin was their strong connection forged during their childhood. When his mother had vanished, they had spent a lot of time together. His mother was never found. The Alliance suspected she'd been taken for breeding purposes and both knew this, but it was just something they didn't discuss—ever.

He stared at the blank canvas and had been for quite a while now. In the time since Rayne had gone Devin hadn't been able to paint, well at least anything that was worth painting. Calum had come in and seen the last 'work of art' and his comment was similar to 'you're a mess'. He couldn't even generate some temperamental artist angst over that, he was right. His painting had been dark violent colors and a culmination of ill matched brush strokes and blended lines that could be interpreted as a mix of abstract and preschool.

Tossing the clean dry brush onto the tray, he turned to go sit out on the deck. Of course, each time he did, he would go over the memory of shifting and scaring the hell out of Rayne. In hindsight, he was lucky she didn't throw more at him for doing that.

The landscape that usually brought him peace was not bringing him a damn thing today.

"Have you looked in a mirror recently?"

Was he that out of it that a cat could come up behind him without sensing it? The answer wasn't something Devin had to search for. He was out of it—completely scattered without her. "I glanced in one briefly."

"Did it crack?" Calum's voice was the usual calm monotone, but Devin still knew he was trying to lighten the mood.

"I didn't look in it long enough to notice."

Calum moved to where he could see him and leaned his large frame against the railing. He crossed his huge arms over his chest and studied him. The expression was blank, but Devin knew what was coming. "You know you don't have to stay here..."

"Yeah, but I am."

Leaning back, Devin groaned. "I'm safe, no one is going to come after me and I'm not planning on any self-sacrifice rituals."

"I know."

Just once Devin wished he could read what was on his mind. "Then why are you still here? I want to be left alone right now." That wasn't entirely the truth, he didn't want to be alone. He wanted Rayne.

He barely shrugged his shoulders. "Doing my job."

Groaning again he rubbed his hands over his face in frustration. "I haven't agreed..."

"You claimed her."

"I didn't mean to..." Devin's voice sounded whiny even to his own ears.

"Doesn't matter. Unless you formally declare you are stepping aside, you have accepted your place and are the next to rule." Calum smirked, "and if you do step aside, I might kick your ass for being stupid."

He wondered for a few seconds if this was how everyone was looking at this. How many in his world knew he was now mated? How far had the news traveled in the last few weeks. Devin shook my head. "It doesn't matter, Rayne left. I have no mate to stand beside me now... so technically..."

"Do you think she left for good?" His eyes bored into mine. "If she did, I wouldn't blame her. You hid some pretty serious shit from her, Dev."

Devin growled, "I know what I did!"

"Do you?" A very feminine voice asked.

Jumping out of the chair, Devin spun around and looked

at Rayne standing in the doorway. His eyes drank her in, she was more beautiful than the image in the painting that had haunted him each second since she'd left.

Calum stepped over beside him and nodded to her. "You got the drop on both of us. I was so caught up in this one's pity party I didn't even sense you were here."

She gave him an amused look. "I've learned a lot since I was here." Her eyes moved back to Devin and went dark, cold. "We have some things to discuss. Actually, I have some things to say and you're going to stand there and listen."

Devin felt Calum back away and then his heart stopped when she pointed at him. "You. Stay. If I'm inclined to smack him, I may get you to do it for me."

He didn't need to turn to know that a rare smirk would be on his face. Calum moved by him and he would never forget watching him drop to one knee in front of her and lowering his head. Right in front of Devin he acknowledged her as an alpha and ruler. Devin expected a surprised look on Rayne's face, but she only gave him an affectionate look and placed her hand on top of his head for a few seconds. Jealously flared inside him.

When she lifted her hand away from Calum, he stood up and went to stand a few feet away. Rayne moved towards Devin, gracefully and looking more breathtaking than any woman had ever been. His blood was calling for her and it took every ounce of strength for him to stand where he was and wait.

"You look like hell, Devin." Her voice had a hard note in it. "That makes me feel better."

His heart was stuck in my throat. "Rayne..." She held a hand up and gave him a look that let Devin know there would be no soft apologies in this discussion.

"The last few weeks have been both difficult and enlightening for me. Your parents, by the way are wonderful—as are the rest of the members of your pack. They filled in all the blanks and taught me what I needed to know."

The rest of the pack? Devin swallowed and looked over at Calum. He was grinning, standing there with his arms folded over his chest. The bastard had known what was going on.

Rayne glanced at Calum and then back to Devin. "At first I will admit I was hurt and scared. I understand your reservations with taking on the responsibility of what lies ahead. It's an enormous task."

Devin relaxed a little bit, thankful that she did understand.

"But." She lifted her chin and looked at him, her soft eyes appearing to be more steel than anything. "It's also an enormous honor to be offered something like this." She paced over to the railing and then spun back to glare at him. "I have spent my entire life being sheltered and afraid. I had no one except my parents, and then when they were taken from me I was completely alone in this world." She waved a hand towards Calum and then him. "You have an entire race beside you, to support you and be there when you need them to be—and you turn your back on them." The last few words came out clipped, laced with anger.

Devin stepped over towards her, his mind swimming, not sure of anything. "I didn't turn my back on them."

She shook her head and flipped her golden hair away from her face. "You did. Your pack needs to know they have an alpha—the Alliance is still relatively new and it needs to know that it has a leader and you come here and hide away from everything, everyone that needs to know your there for them. Including your family."

When she took brisk steps towards him, Devin froze not sure what to expect. "Do you want to claim me, Devin? With me knowing what's going on?" She added quietly.

"Yes." His voice was barely more than a gasp.

Her blue eyes softened and moved over his face, he wanted it to be her hands, he needed her touch.

"I won't accept you and then be an outcast from the pack—from *my* people."

Devin tried to swallow the lump in his throat.

"If I take you and let you officially claim me as your mate you *will* be the King—you *will* be the alpha and I will stand beside you always."

Devin hesitated, not accepting what his brain had heard. She wasn't walking away from him. She was his. Not knowing what to say or what to do next, he dropped down on both knees and lowered his head. He may be the king, but she would always rule over him. When her warm hands touched his hair, he reached out and pulled her against him, burying his face in the warmth of her chest. She held him tight and Devin realized as long as she was beside him he could live up to any expectations.

Calum cleared his throat. "I will just..."

Rayne's hold loosened on Devin's head, but she didn't let go. "You will go and start cleaning out all the cabins. The rest of the pack and the leaders from the Alliance will be here in two days–for the official ceremony."

Devin lifted his head and looked up at her, astonished. "They will... how did you know?"

"That you'd agree with my terms?"

He nodded.

"In everything I had to learn about, I discovered the interesting fact—as far as claimed mates go, the female rules."

Devin stood quickly and pulled her into his body. He heard Calum laughing as he moved away from them and didn't even bother to glance in his direction. His heart was pounding as hot blood raced through his veins. She stood there smiling up at him and he couldn't wait another breath to taste her again. Her arms wound around his neck and pulled his head down towards hers. The moment their lips touched, his body hardened and demanded its mate.

Leaning back, she broke the kiss. "You need to go get cleaned up, I feel like I'm kissing a stranger."

Chapter Forty-Three

Devin stood at the end of the bed with a towel wrapped loosely around his waist as she walked into the room. His hair was still dripping and rolling down over his broad shoulders and sculpted chest. Rayne thought she would be nervous, knowing now what this would mean, but she wasn't feeling any hesitation. Her body responded as soon as she looked at him, heat coiling through her. Rayne's wolf knew this was her mate standing before her and she didn't have one moment's hesitation either.

He was tense and she knew a part of him still wasn't sure that she really did intend to accept him and be claimed. Rayne loved the power this gave her. Never having been in control of anything in her life, the thrill of knowing she alone was choosing her future left her exhilarated.

She undid the buttons on her blouse as she walked towards him, feeling sexy with each step. His chest rose and fell deeply as his eyes followed the movement of her hands. Rayne slipped her shirt off and dropped it onto the floor while moving closer to him.

The towel didn't hide how aroused he was and just knowing what lie beneath it caused her heart to speed up. Stopping a few feet from him she undid her slacks and slowly slid them over her hips, letting them drop to the floor. She hadn't bothered with underwear. When she had decided to come back today, Rayne knew what she was coming for and made the task as easy as possible to accomplish.

He rubbed a hand over the growing bulge barely hidden by the towel. She watched his face as she moved to stand right in front of him, he had to work hard to not touch her if the clenching of his jaw was any indication. Leaning over, she ran her tongue over his chest and caught her breath as he shivered from the touch. "I just want to make sure I do this right," she licked him again and glanced down at his hands that were clenched into fists as his side. "You're not allowed to touch me in any way until I put my mark on you... is that right?" She lightly bit one nipple.

"Yes," he whispered with a shaky voice.

Rayne feed on the knowledge of her power, feeling dominant for the first time in her life. She knew she was playing with fire, and loved it. Pulling the towel, she let it drop to the floor and moved her body into the heat of his. As she ran her hands up over his chest he shuddered. Wrapping her arms around him she nuzzled her face into his neck. "And it goes right here?" She licked the taught muscle where his shoulder and neck met.

"Yes," he growled.

Dropping her arms, she gently shoved against his chest until he backed up to the bed. As he sat down she smiled down at him and ran her hands through his hair. Lowering her mouth to his, she glanced down to see him gripping the edge of the bed. Rayne kissed him tenderly and almost lost her nerve as he drank at her mouth like a starving man would. "Lie down," she whispered against his lips.

As he slid his body up on the bed, she crawled up it after him until she was straddling his legs. He laid there, fire blazing in his eyes and she knew exactly what was going to happen once she placed her mark on him. Moving slowly, Rayne lowered her mouth to his legs and kissed her way up one of them as she crawled higher on his body. His breathing was ragged by the time she reached his hip. Looking up at him, she ran her tongue over the tip of his hot erection, he groaned and grabbed at the bed with both hands, fighting every instinct to touch her.

Smiling, she moved up on her knees until she was over his hips and lowered herself just enough that she could feel his body resting against the wet core of hers. He clenched his jaw and he watched her with eyes that held a promise of retaliation. Rayne ran her hands up his chest and leaned down to bite gently at one nipple. She could feel his shoulders tighten as he fought to keep from touching her.

Lifting her hips, she lowered onto him, slowly taking him into her body. She'd never felt anything so good. His whole body was tense, but pleasure filled his eyes this time. Sitting up, she smiled at him and ran her hands down over her breasts that were aching for his touch. He jerked his hips, almost squirming beneath her. Rayne knew the moment she relented she wouldn't be able to control the pace, so she lifted her body up and lowered it slowly onto him again. She was barely able to maintain the sensual movement because she was so turned on with wanting him that her legs were shaking already.

Leaning down Rayne continued to slide his body into hers. She licked over his throat and was rewarded with a growl. "I accept you, Devin," she gasped against his skin. There was no hesitation as she opened her mouth against his neck and felt her teeth lengthen just enough to bite into him. She tasted blood in her mouth and heard him gasp loudly.

Before she could lift her mouth again he grasped her hips and slammed her down onto him with another growl. It was her turn to moan as his fingers dug into her flesh while he lifted her over and over again thrusting up as he brought their bodies together.

Rayne cried when the orgasm hit her without warning and then had no choice but to hang onto him as it poured over her, leaving her weak and dizzy.

Before she could catch her breath, she was flipped onto

her back as he continued the hard tempo. His hands moved over her skin, leaving a fire in their wake. His mouth claimed hers roughly—making Rayne climb higher again. She felt like he was touching and kissing her everywhere at the same time and could only try to catch up to his movement. Lifting her hips, he went to his knees and looked down at their bodies and he thrust into her. She was gasping for air and moaning at the same time. When she felt another wave come over her, she reached out for him to draw him back down to her, but he continued to move with more force and she came screaming his name.

Devin slowed briefly and she felt him pull out of her body and then she was flipped over onto her stomach. Wrapping his arm around her he shoved into her quaking folds as he moved her higher on the bed. He paused, buried deep inside her and leaned her against the wall above the bed. His lips moved over her neck and shoulders, as his hand cupped her breast and kneaded it. With no further warning his teeth sunk into her neck right over his mark on her skin.

Rayne cried out as her muscles clamped down around his. His hips thrust at a furious speed, slamming their flesh together as he grasped her waist to keep her still. He didn't remove his teeth from her shoulder, letting her know that she was claimed from this moment on, while his body ruled over her and he brought spasm after spasm to her. The entire room was spinning and Rayne couldn't find air to bring into her lungs when the third climax slammed through her. She screamed at the same moment he growled deeply and he filled her with a burning heat.

As Rayne tried to remember how to breathe, his hips continued to jerk against her. If it weren't for the wall and his arm around her, Rayne would have slid, boneless, from the bed. He shifted them to lie down on the mattress, his body still deep inside of her. Rayne's head floated as his tongue moved over the mark at her neck. His hand gently cupped her breast and flicked the still hard nipple with his thumb. Each movement brought small spasms through her, causing her to gasp again.

"I could keep doing this for another hour... and your body would comply with my demands." To illustrate his point, he slid his hand down to her tender clit and rubbed over it, making her moan and shake in his arms.

Rayne couldn't speak, only lie there.

"You're mine now, your body belongs to me."

He thrust into her and she moaned again when her sensitive muscles clenched around him. His hands stopped moving and his mouth placed soft lingering kisses against her damp skin.

"You are also my heart and I love you, Rayne."

Rayne smiled, still trying to catch her breath. "And you're mine." She heaved a sigh as he pulled from her body slowly. Shuddering in his arms, he flipped her onto her back and leaned down over her. She touched his face and smiled again. "I love you too." She quietly sighed again. "I could sleep for a week now."

He chuckled. "Considering you invited every leader here to invade our solitude—I don't think that's going to happen."

Rayne laughed. "I knew you'd see it my way."

Devin raised an eyebrow and looked at her with an amused look. "You do know I'm the one that's supposed to rule, right?"

"Like your father does without your mother's help?"

Dropping his head down, he rested his forehead against hers. "I see your point." He kissed her lingeringly, until she had to catch her breath again. "Just let me pretend I'm in charge occasionally."

"Kiss me like that every day and it's a deal."

"Every day, every hour, every thirty seconds..." His mouth covered hers again and sent her world spinning.

Chapter Forty-Four

Rayne lifted her face to the sun and inhaled deeply. She would never get enough of feeling like she was part of the surroundings. Hearing a splash behind her, she turned and smiled at the children antagonizing each other along the shore of the lake. It was a sound that thrilled her. It was a sound that should always be heard here.

One of the girls ran towards her. She was only five or six and smiled as she reached her, holding up her hand, she opened it to reveal a shiny stone.

"This is for you, Rayne."

Rayne knelt and hugged her. "Thank you."

Giggling, she ran back towards the others. Laughing, Rayne examined the stone and closed her hand around it.

Devin stood near the deck with his father, Calum and Gage. She only had to take a few steps in that direction before she had his attention.

As she neared him, Rayne could feel his eyes caressing her and couldn't help to smile at him. She wandered leisurely in that direction and watched as the men spoke to him, but he showed no indication that said he was even listening to them.

Gage laughed and smacked a hand on Devin's back

when she was only a few feet away. "You didn't hear a damn word we just said." He glanced at her and winked. "I think his mind was elsewhere."

Rayne laughed. "Really? Not very leader-like, is it?"

His father laughed and shook his head in his son's direction. "I'd say we need to make sure Rayne is present for all important discussions then."

Calum shrugged. "Or completely out of sight."

Devin glared at him as he wrapped his arms around her. "I was listening." He leaned down and dropped a kiss on the top of her head. "You just weren't saying something I had to add anything to."

She looked up at him and felt a shiver pass over her skin from the heat in his eyes. "I have something to say—to all of you. Will you listen to me?"

Devin grinned, his eyes moving over her mouth. "Always."

"Good." Rayne pulled out of his arms and turned to look back at the children playing by the lake and the parents relaxing in small groups. "I want this." She motioned around them.

Devin rested his hands on her shoulders. "You have this, what is mine is now yours."

She patted his hand. "I know that but you're not following me. I want this camp to be filled with life again. Whether families come here to vacation or we bring those in need of protection here, it doesn't matter I just want life here again."

Devin turned her so he could see her face. "We can do that."

Calum cleared his throat. "Explain the protection part."

Rayne looked from one man's face to the other. All towered over her, all powerful and proud. "I know Aiden's operation, I know his numbers, his associates... I want all those that are trapped under his thumb to be free and safe."

Devin's eyes became serious. "You're not going back there."

Before she could reply his dad put a hand on his shoulder and spoke softly. "She doesn't have to go back to help the Alliance."

She nodded. "I can give you all the information and the strongest from each pack can go and get our people."

Devin's eyes filled with pride, as did the other men when she said that. "If you want to set up shelter here for them, I support that."

Rayne smiled and hugged him again. Sighing, she turned towards Calum. "Will you help?"

Calum grinned at her. "You know it." He cleared his throat and looked at them. "I just have to take care of something first."

"The missing clan members?" Gage inquired softly.

Calum nodded. "I'm pretty sure I've managed to pinpoint the general area that they're vanishing from."

Frowning, Rayne touched his arm. "What do you mean vanishing?"

Devin released her and leaned back against the railing. "Some males from Calum's clan have gone missing and several of their family members have appealed to him to find them."

"That's awful. Of course, you have to."

Calum looked down at her for a few moments. "I will—and now I have somewhere safe to bring them until we know what's going on."

Devin watched her closely. His eyes were burning a path all over her. "With that settled, all of you need to get the hell off my land—I'd like to have a few days alone with my mate before she turns this place into a zoo."

Rayne's jaw dropped open at his words. "You will not be rude, Devin." She looked at his father and shrugged. "All of you can stay as long as you like. Help yourself to anything." Stepping closer to him, she ran her hands up his chest. "Devin and I won't be here of course, our plane leaves in a few hours."

He frowned. "Plane?"

Nodding, she moved her body into his. "It's taking us to some remote fishing cabin for three days."

"Remote?"

"Very, very remote. Your mom is inside packing for us right now."

He pulled her into his body and picked her up. "Guess I'll see you guys in three days."

Rayne shrieked as he headed towards the door leaving the men behind laughing.

KEEP READING FOR AN EXCERPT OF

SCENT

Animal Senses Book 2

JACQUELINE PAIGE

Chapter One

Gage watched the man he passed as he climbed into the truck. His expression was hollow, his eyes void. He had to be close to his own six foot five, but the man stood timidly, posture drawn inward.

Turning, he glanced at Jesse. "What the hell happened Jesse? He looks like he's been broken like a god damned horse."

Jesse sighed and rubbed his jaw, exhaustion clear on his face. "The saddest thing, he's in better shape than the others." Flicking his eyes back to the passenger in the truck, he met Gage's stare. "Devin said it would do him good to be around other shifters of his kind," he shook his head, "I don't know if he'll ever fully recover though."

"What about the others?"

A haunted look flashed in Jesse's pale eyes. "They're at the camp. I doubt any of them will ever be able to integrate back into society."

"What the hell did Tomas do to them?" Gage struggled to keep his anger from showing.

Slamming the door on the car, Jesse spun around shaking his head. "The two women we managed to get out were used as breeders, as near as we can figure. They shrink away from males like they've..." He stopped, clearly unable to continue.

Gage fought the bile that rose, swallowing it down.

"The three men, including him," he motioned to the other vehicle, "were treated worse than slaves. They're not very forthcoming with details." Shoving his hands in his pockets, he looked up, and Gage's muscles tensed when he saw the depth of the anger in the otherwise mild-mannered man. "They've been beaten into complacency and carry the scars to prove it."

"Aren't they all pure bloods?"

"Yeah."

Something in Jesse's tone made Gage's cat want to growl. "Then why are they scarred? Shifting heals fresh..."

"Not if they're prevented from shifting until after the wounds have healed."

"Holy hell." Shuddering at the thought of the torture the man hunched in his truck had gone through, Gage took a deep breath and nodded to Jesse. "I'll see what I can do for him."

Jesse stepped back toward his car. "Devin said to give him a call."

"Will do." Gage watched him get in his car and then slowly walked around to the driver's side of his truck. He had hundreds of questions, but didn't want to bombard the damaged man.

Forcing an easy smile, he looked at the man beside him. "I suppose Jesse should have introduced us." He held out his hand, "I'm Gage Lockman. You'll be staying with some of my clan."

With hesitation, the man extended his hand and grasped his briefly. "Noah Reyes."

"They're getting in touch with your family, Noah, and if later on you want to go be with them, we'll get you there." He watched as several emotions went through Noah's amber eyes.

"No," his voice was heartrending, "I-I don't want to go there." Apprehensively his eyes met Gage's again. "I'll stay with your clan, if that's all right?"

Nodding, Gage put the key in the ignition and tried to appear relaxed, even though he wasn't. "That's fine by me, we can always use a hand at the shop."

"Shop?"

Starting the truck, he put it into gear and pulled out of the empty parking lot. Watching the dust kick up behind them, he kept his eyes from the injured soul beside him. "Yeah, my family owns a large equipment business. We lease all the big rigs and do the repairs and upkeep ourselves."

"I don't know anything about shop work."

Ignoring the fear in his voice, Gage shrugged. "We'll find something for you to do that leans toward your strengths."

"I doubt it."

Glancing at the empty man beside him, he gave him an easy smile. "Why's that?"

Noah turned and looked out the window. "I've only been a guard."

"Like a bodyguard?"

The silence was tense as he waited for an answer.

"No. Like a guard that keeps others against their will."

Shit. "Well, we'll find a place for you." Every muscle in Gage's body was taut, he had to strain to keep his animal under control. He breathed it away during the next few seconds of silence. "I don't want to pry and for the most part I won't, but I'm bringing you into my family and need to know some of the facts." He paused for objections then continued when none were voiced. "How long did Tomas have you?"

"Fifteen years."

It was said with venom that Gage was almost happy to hear, to him that brief tone of hatred meant there was some fight left. He was going to ask more when Noah's tortured voice silenced him.

"Since I was six. They got my sister and I."

He glanced at Noah for a moment to let him know he was listening.

"I don't know what happened to her. I tried to find out when I got older, but..." His voice cracked, "I wouldn't even know her now."

Swallowing, Gage kept his eyes on the road. "Your cat would know family. If she ever crosses your path, you'll know."

"I didn't know that." Noah sighed softly. "I don't know a lot about what I am, or how to function in a group. The things I do know are only from what others that worked…" he cleared his throat, "that were held by Tomas told me."

Gage glanced at him and tried to give him a look of encouragement. "We'll work it out, Noah." He took a moment to look at him. This man was only twenty-one but his physical appearance was much older, and inside, Gage suspected, was aged beyond anything he would ever understand.

"So, are you the clan alpha?"

Gage grinned. "No. The second. My father's the alpha but he's away right now."

Noah nodded and then sat there for a moment, Gage could see the questions going through his mind.

"Do you have a mate?"

Snorting, Gage nodded, "Yeah, only she doesn't know that she is." He grinned, not even knowing how to explain his own personal torment. "I'm sure the boys will love filling in the details for you."

"I found mine…at least that's what the others told me."

The silence that followed his admission stabbed pain right through Gage. "And?"

"When," Noah closed his eyes and inhaled deep for a moment, "when I recovered enough to remember, she was gone."

Holy hell. Is Devin aware of any of this? What the hell do I say to that? "You may still find her someday. Fate is a tricky bitch."

"Yeah."

The word meant he agreed, but the heavy overlay of emotion inside the cab told Gage the man beside him didn't believe it would happen. He tried to keep his tone from revealing anything close to sympathy. "You'll be bunking with four others while you're here. Jake, Gary and Blair are close to your age. Then there's old Cooper, no one can even guess his age, but he's fairly easy to be around." He continued to ramble out the stories of things the men closest to him did in hopes to give Noah a sense of what he could expect. Not once did Noah offer comment or ask for more.

Dropping him at the large house his men lived in just off the shop site, Gage backed out, heading for his own home further along the roughly paved road. He needed to talk to Devin and find out just what he was supposed to do to help Noah.

He didn't even get both boots on the ground when his phone started vibrating in his shirt pocket. Glancing at the screen, he shook his head and answered it.

"I just dropped him off."

Devin's whispered on the other end. "I figured you'd be there by now. Jesse called when he left you."

"Why are you whispering?" Slamming the door, he walked up the path and stomped up the porch. Deciding he needed the air, he dropped into one of his mother's favorite white wicker chairs and swung his boots up to rest on the railing.

"Rayne is exhausted and just went to rest."

He heard a door close quietly.

"She's been helping the two women that were brought back and is emotionally fragile, to say the least."

Gage's shoulders tensed. "Jesse mentioned a bit." Running a hand through his hair, he sighed. "Don't tell me any details right now; I'm still digesting the shit I learned from Noah on our trip back."

"Then you probably know more than I do. I'm sorry I had to send him your way, but the two women were terrified of him."

Gage closed his eyes, feeling the pain he'd heard in Noah's voice. "With good reason, he was probably the guard making them stay put."

"Listen, if he gets out of hand…"

"My instincts say he won't." He kicked his feet back to the porch and leaned forward on his knee. "The boys will keep an eye on him." Rubbing a hand over the back of his neck, he sat up again. "Where the hell is the Alliance in bringing that bastard Tomas down for good?"

"They've gotten a lot of the captives out. We have close to a dozen here at the camp healing. as much as they're able. Some were born into Tomas's organization, Gage, I don't know if we'll be able to get through to them, they've never known of their own kind, the dynamics of a clan and family."

"Yeah, Noah said something to that effect."

He could hear the exhaustion in Devin's tone.

"Look, Gage, I really didn't want to send Noah there not with everything you have going on." He heard another door close and could then make out the sounds of nature at the camp as Devin must have gone outside. "Is Kelsey back?"

Not able to sit any longer, Gage got up and paced to the other end of the large porch. "She was supposed to be here this week, but decided to stop and see my folks on the way home."

"I thought your parents left so you'd have some alone time with Kelsey."

"They did. I'm one hair from going insane, Dev."

He heard the soft chuckle on the other end. "I don't know how you've held out this long my friend. I didn't last a day when I was near Rayne."

Jamming his hand into his pocket, he leaned back against the wall of the house. "Well, she was only sixteen when I realized what she was. That worked like fucking ice water in my pants for a few years. Then she bailed and took off to school, and you know that's been three years of hell for me." Pushing away from the wall, he stepped over to the railing and looked out into the thick trees surrounding the house. "I can't hold on much longer." He closed his eyes and swallowed. "I just hope…"

"You'll do the right thing, Gage, the animal inside you won't let you do anything but."

"I hope you're right because it will kill me to wait this long and then screw it up."

Devin chuckled again. "I can relate."

"Speaking of…how is our Queen now?"

"Surprisingly forgiving. Thank God for that."

Not wanting to dwell on his mate, Gage opened his eyes and stared out into the bush again. "Calum reach you before he left?"

"Yeah. He said he knew the region his missing clan members were last seen. He's supposed to contact you if I'm out of touch when he knows more."

"I'll be here if he needs me. Is the Alliance up to speed?" Turning, he went inside to see if there were any messages on the house phone.

"For the most part, they have their hands full right now trying to bring Aiden Tomas down."

"They don't think the clan members Calum is tracking down are part of Tomas's ring?"

The silence stretched out for a few moments before Devin answered. "It's nowhere near the regions he operates in, but who knows for sure."

Gage could hear voices in the background and knew Devin would be ending the call soon.

"Listen, Gage, keep Kelsey close to home. We've been calling all the clans and warning them. Tomas isn't going to take all of this without striking back."

"Will do."

"Good luck with your mate, my friend, you're going to need it."

Gage sighed loudly and grinned at the phone. "Yeah, thanks for the vote of confidence."

"Oh, I have every faith in you, but I also know the fucking hell you're walking into when nothing you know is as it was."

Gage's stomach tightened. "Something to look forward to."

"I'll talk to you later."

"Will do." He hung up the phone and stared at it for a moment. *Good news all round today.* Glancing at the phone as he walked into the office, he stopped when there were no messages. The tension in his neck was multiplying as it had been for the past month. *Kelsey, whatever games you're playing, you better end them soon.* He felt like a time bomb just waiting to go off.

The cat inside him moved over his skin, wanting out. He'd spent more time in animal form in the last seven years as he waited for his mate to be old enough to claim. Of course, there was no law specifying an age, but his own moral code wouldn't allow him to make a move until she was old enough to understand.

Snorting out loud, he turned on his heels and headed for the door. Kelsey knew nothing of her own heritage. She didn't know what her parents had been before they were killed, or that her family were part of the clan and not just good friends they'd known for years. Many times after she had come to live with his parents, he'd wanted to tell her. She was only fifteen at the time and completely devastated that her parents were gone. His jaw clenched knowing it had been Aiden Tomas's father that was responsible for their death. The more time that passed the harder it got to tell her she was part of a world she didn't even know existed.

Gage didn't know why his folks hadn't told her when she got older, and as the son of the Alpha, it wasn't his place to overstep his position and fill her in. In hindsight, he wished he'd disobeyed and told her. Maybe then he wouldn't be walking out his back door, stripping off his clothes, so he could go run off his frustration.

By the time he reached the bottom step he was in his animal form. Large paws padded across the grass, as he scented the air to choose a direction. Jumping across the creek in one motion, he landed his eight foot, four-hundred-pound body with a fluid grace and turned to look at his reflection. A pale, almost white Bengal tiger stared back at him through his deep blue eyes.

The scent of prey filled his nostrils as he lifted his head. With a low sound from the back of his throat he turned to start the chase.

Come home soon, Kelsey.

KEEP READING FOR AN EXCERPT OF

After
the
Silence
Volume 1

BREE

BY JACQUELINE PAIGE

Chapter One

I was nineteen when the world went crazy, nothing that was would ever be again.

Remnants of a familiar world remained, but not enough to instill those warm, fuzzy feelings you get when life is comfortable and predictable.

I'm Bree Taylor. This is an account of what I remember, how things happened when life changed forever and I managed to survive. There is so much to tell, a thousand pages wouldn't be enough to explain it all, but someone has to tell it. There needs to be a record so if we, as a planet survive, others will have the history. If we don't, then the next species to invade earth will know what we did wrong.

It is now just a few days after my twenty-second birthday, I'm standing looking out the window and wishing my brother, Shawn, well in the afterlife. A seemingly small laceration on his leg became so much more and took him away from me, leaving me to figure out this world on my own. If I have relatives left living, I wouldn't know. All that I cared for are now ashes spread over the dirt and just memories inside my head.

I am alone.

"Bree?"

I turned towards Darren, one of my adopted brothers, and gave him a look to tell him we were done discussing my decision. He didn't heed the warning.

"Are you sure this is what you want to do?"

His voice was filled with grief and worry. *Was I? Yes, at least eighty percent certain.* "Darren, I can't stay here. Being in the city is dangerous enough as a family, never mind a single girl."

A desperate look appeared in his eyes. He was probably wishing at this point that some of the other brothers were still alive, but only Bobby and Darren were left out of my six older brothers.

"We'll move you closer to us, keep you safe."

We, being his very old mother and wheelchair bound brother. I gave him my most stern look. "I think you have enough to worry about, you don't need me to add to that list."

Darren's eyes strayed to the picture I still held. The one of my family and me before life was forever altered.

"Shawn would have wanted me to. I feel like I'm letting him down."

I offered him a smile that said I had accepted it, even though I really didn't. "Shawn is gone and I have to go and try to find my own place now. You guys did all you could to prepare and teach me to fend for myself, your job is done.'

He stuffed his hands in his pockets and leaned back against the wall. "Where will you go?"

I turned and looked out the window. "I think the mountains."

A sound came from him that told me he thought I was too much of a girl to survive that. "The crazies hide there."

I chuckled and slowly turned back, rolling my eyes at him. "And they don't in the city?" His expression pleaded with me. "Darren, I know you have always been close to my family, you're like family. So I know that Shawn probably told you I changed after the virus." The fear in his eyes confirmed my suspicions. He knew the truth. "I have to find out what I've become, before others do. I need to know if

I'm a good thing or a bad thing. And I need space and solitude to discover this."

"Bree, you could never be bad."

My heart warmed from his words. "I hope you're right."

He sighed loudly. "Fine, but you're taking Tremor and Shawn's weapons – otherwise I'm going with you."

I knew he wouldn't, we both knew it, but it was his way of feeling like he had done all he could. "I don't have to take Tremor. I can walk."

He shook his head sending his black hair scattering around his face. "We have LadyBell and her colt; we don't need any more than that. Tremor's fast and loyal and he'll get you through the bad times."

I was hoping the bad times would be few, naive I know, but I could hope. My heart strained as I fought to keep my resolve. He loved his horse and to know he was sending him out there with me meant more than I could express. "Thank you." I wanted to hug him, I really did, who knew when I'd have any friendly human contact again. If I hugged him now I knew I would fall apart, and I needed to keep my head out of the emotional whirl that was already threatening to suck me in. "I should get ready. I want to leave early enough so I can be out of the city before darkness falls."

Darren nodded, even though his entire face told me he didn't agree. "I'll go get Tremor. You get your stuff packed up." He looked at me for a long silent moment before he rushed back out the door.

I stood there looking at the door long after he'd gone. In my head I wasn't at all sure this was a good plan. I was following my heart and it was telling me to get out of town and find out where I was meant to be. Of course my head was saying that was a load of crap, but I was still going to do it. I couldn't explain why I needed to be outside and away from all the buildings and people, it just felt right.

Darren didn't know I was already packed. When I knew Shawn wasn't going to recover I started to gather up what I would need. Before Shawn was too far away from me, we had discussed my plan. He agreed I needed to leave. He had also said he was coming with me as soon as he was on his feet. I think by that point we both knew he would never recover.

I swore to follow the least traveled path. I promised to stay away from crowded places. I vowed to him I would survive and then I tucked the blanket around him and went off to cry by myself until my eyes felt like they were going to split in half.

I'm done with the crying and ready to take on what's left of this planet and the series of trials I know it will throw in my path. Tale of a colony of peaceful people live high in the mountains, it's my plan to find them. I hope the stories of the crazies that live between here and there are just that, a farfetched creation of some idiot's imagination.

Going into my room, I quickly headed to the closet to pull out the packs that had been sitting ready for me. I didn't need a lot. I could live off the land if needed, but one entire bag contained dehydrated food, just to be safe. As I swung the largest pack up onto my shoulder I caught a glimpse of myself in the mirror. Would this be the last time I saw the woman looking back at me? I looked into my now green eyes, a leftover from the virus. I stared until I saw it; determination, hidden just under the surface. Sighing, I ran a hand through my choppy red hair and debated, very briefly, if I should dye it a dull brown and tone it down. I knew that would never happen. I wouldn't trade in my brilliant hair for anything. It was a statement and if I couldn't do anything else I was definitely going to make one.

Closing my eyes, I prayed for my spirit to stay strong. When I opened them I didn't look at the mirror again, just picked up the other two bags and walked out of my home for the very last time

Darren stood outside holding the reins and crooning softly to Tremor. I couldn't see his face, which was a blessing, I didn't have to see his eyes begging me not to go again. The large horse's ears flicked as he listened attentively. No doubt he was receiving instructions to keep me safe and out of harm's way. Darren lifted his face away from the animal and looked over at me. "He's quite happy you're getting him the hell out of this city." A halfhearted grin appeared on his face. With a tilt of his head he motioned to the other side of the porch. "We're going to walk with you until you're outside the city limits."

I turned and looked to see Bobby leaning against the side of the house. I couldn't help but smile when he wiggled his eyebrows at me. Bobby was the clown of the group that grew up together. I often wondered if anyone else ever sensed he was too serious inside and that was why he joked around as much as he did. Bobby was my first crush when I was thirteen. It never went anywhere, for obvious reasons, but I still had a secret place for him in my heart. I was grateful he was coming along; it would prevent Darren from pleading with me to change my mind, again. "Hey, Bobby." He pushed away from the wall and sauntered in his easy way towards me, his long leather jacket making him look like he floated.

"Hey, Brat. You didn't think you were going to sneak off without saying bye did you?"

"Wouldn't dream of it."

He pulled the bag from my shoulder. "Good to know."

Darren came over and took the bags, taking them to secure to Tremor's saddle. "I think you should walk with us for a while and then he won't be too tired to haul ass when you need him to later." He didn't look at me when he spoke.

"She'll be fine, Dare, we taught her." Bobby's tone sounded annoyed.

Silently I hoped he was right.

Stepping in front of me, he looked me over. Without a word he moved and took off the coat that I couldn't ever remember him not having. "You're going to need something to keep you dry and warm." He held the coat out to me.

I opened my mouth to say something, but nothing came out. Pulling my hands out of my pockets I took the jacket and looked up at him. Bobby was a good six inches taller than my five foot five making me wonder if the leather was going to drag on the ground when I put it on. He continued to stand there and say nothing so I put my arms quickly into the sleeves. It hung about three inches off the ground. He gave me a triumphant grin and then moved around behind me, pulling at the material muttering about straps as he did. When he was finished the coat didn't gape away from my body as much as it had.

"There's a nice custom pocket on the inside left." Leaning around me, he flipped the coat open to point to it. "And this…" Bending down to the cuff of his jeans, he pulled up the material to reveal a knife handle sticking out of his boot. "Fits in it perfectly." I knew my eyes were wide as he slipped the knife into the pocket.

He stepped back quickly and jammed his hands into his pockets like he was afraid of grabbing me if he didn't. As he looked down, just before his shaggy blonde hair covered his eyes, I thought I saw a tear running down his cheek. "Find a better place, Bree," he whispered, so softly I almost missed it.

I swallowed the lump that lodged in my throat and nodded. "Thanks."

"Let's go." Darren urged from where he stood. "I want you to have more than enough time to find somewhere to stay when it gets dark.

I wanted to take a huge breath and build the courage to take this final and first step, but I couldn't bring myself to do it in front of them.

"Mom sent a bag of things." Darren patted the small one tied to the back of the saddle. He didn't elaborate what kind of things. Running his hand to the front of it, he flipped open the small pack. "Shawn's hand-gun is in here and there's enough ammo on the other side to last a long time." He looked down at the ground and said nothing further.

I moved around to the front of Tremor and looked up into his big eyes. "We're going to be just fine aren't we?" I ran my hand down the blackness of his coat over his neck and picked up the reins. His ears flicked and he brought his mouth down to nibble at my shoulder. As far as encouraging signs went, that one worked for me.

I couldn't stand the looks Bobby and Darren were giving each other, so without prolonging this any further, I turned and started to lead the way down the street, thankful we weren't far from the nearest border.

I kept Tremor at an easy trot until we were far enough away that I wouldn't be tempted to go back. Stopping, I turned him and looked back to the two men that stood exactly where I'd left them a few minutes earlier. I waved my arm at them, silently thanked them and wished them well. Turning the animal in the opposite direction, I prodded him with my heels to get us out of here. He complied without hesitation and carried us quickly away from the city that was filled with nothing but heartache that I could no longer face.

The Huntress

Alterealm Series Book 1

By J. Risk

http://www.jacquelinepaige.com/j-risk

Chapter One

I didn't even get both eyes opened and focused before I knew something was wrong. Where was the color? I was only seeing sepia? Everything was brown. Blinking rapidly, I tried to readjust my eyes to see if there was any other hue. It didn't change a thing and for the life of me I couldn't figure out why.

Sitting there, I tried to decipher what was going on and why I was sitting on the ground. Looking down I ran my hand over the dried dusty surface. Why was I on the ground? Craning my neck as far as I could in all directions, I looked around. Okay, where was the pavement and cement? The buildings and streets I called my natural turf?

The why's flying around in my brain suddenly decided the top question, was what the *hell* was going on?

Squeezing my eyes shut, I struggled to recall the last thing I remembered doing. I was hunting down a bounty—a nice one with a large dollar sign attached to her. I had tracked her ass down and…

I confronted her? Yes, I was minutes away from calling Frank and telling him to get out his shiny pen and sign my check.

So what happened between then and now? Not to sound repetitive, which is something that drives me nuts, but *what* the hell was going on?

Startled, I started to check for bullet holes or the deep crevices that knives leave behind in flesh. That had to be it, I'd taken a beating and this was that in between place you sit when your near death's door, but not quite ready to see what lies on the other side.

Finding no critical injury, I slumped forward and rubbed my head. There was some rational explanation for this, there had to be. Had I been drugged? It could be some crazy hallucination. Any minute now I was going to either wake up in my bed at home or some hospital with a cheery nurse leaning over me, reassuring me we are going to be *just* fine. I only had to wait it out a little longer and all would be normal.

To kill time until I woke up, I looked around some more. Wherever this was it looked like a burnt-out world. Not the charred kind of burn, but depleted and completely used up sort.

Vacant.

Sitting still wasn't really a strong trait of mine, so I figured I'd get up and take a look around, there had to be something to see around here. If my body was actually somewhere else for safekeeping, what harm could come to me, right?

I staggered like I'd never stood before, struggling to get my balance. Whatever was going on with me, my equilibrium was totally shot. Standing there swaying like grass in the breeze, I turned carefully trying to see if there was anything around me except rust tinted dirt and nothingness.

My heart stumbled around in my chest when I spotted someone coming in my direction. Yes! I wasn't the only one in this soulless place.

The closer it got to me made me the more I questioned my original conclusion. I didn't know, exactly, but it was not some*one* it was a some*thing*. No one label could describe it. Standing over six feet, it had the shape of a man dressed in jeans and a large, very out of fashion gingham snap up shirt. When I reached the face, I can only describe it as part wrinkle puppy dog with floppy skin crossed with Freddy and Jason after the slash scenes.

It stopped in front of me and instinct had me reach around behind me under my jean jacket for my raptor claw knife, which I put on as regular as underwear when dressing; and that would be every day, by the way. Relief washed over me when I felt the small circular handle. At least while waiting to survive I got to bring my toys with me.

Big brown eyes assessed me slowly and I wanted to make

the call that it was harmless, but yeah, having tracked down anything from a sicko killer to a card shark in the last three years, I knew better than to fall for sappy looks.

"Are you a magishian? You juisht appeared."

A male voice, even though he spoke with a heavy lisp that randomly inserted *ish* into his words. Then again if I had saggy lips like he did, I'd be happy to talk at all. I sized him up for a few more seconds, trying to gauge whether he was really in front of me, or if I was having some sort of psychotic episode. Was a magician good or bad? I decided the play dumb, being blonde did have *some* advantages. "A magician?"

Those brown eyes developed a nervous quiver. Magician equaled bad. "No…"

He looked relieved. "Oh good. I didn't want to have to bash you over the head."

I grasped my raptor tightly and shrugged. "Yeah, me either."

The sky brightened and began to glow a rust orange color. When I asked for some color, I'd hoped for something out of the orange family.

"We better go, they'll be coming soon."

"They?" I glanced around quickly, not wanting to take my eyes off him for long.

He nodded and pranced on the spot, the nervous movement had me on high alert. "The daywalkers." He whispered.

Daywalkers? Did I even want to know? I didn't think so, but this bizarre nightmare wasn't going to be complete if I didn't ask.

Looking me over a few times, his eyes widened under the pressure of his drooping forehead; *that* was quite the expression. "You're not one of them, are you?"

I walked in the day, night and even at dusk, but I wasn't going to tell him that. I decided honesty might work, if not violence was always a good backup. Judging by his expression daywalker ranked on the bad list with magician.

"I—I don't know what you'd call me."

Those sappy eyes looked me up and down a few times trying to figure me out. "You better come with me. It's not safe to leave you wandering around." He looked behind him and then motioned behind me and started walking.

I knew in my gut it was a mistake, but as I had no other real options… I didn't know where I was or what was going on and so far he knew more than I did. "Where are we going?"

Pausing he glanced over his shoulder and then lumbered along again. "I'll take you to Troy, he'll know what to do."

My eyes were starting to strain as the sky brightened. "This Troy, he's in charge?"

He stopped so suddenly I almost ploughed right into his back. When he turned and looked at me, his eyes weren't a sad brown any more but were leaning more towards red. It had to be from the strange color of the sunrise. "You're not from Alterealm are you?"

"Is that where we are?"

He nodded.

"Nope."

That nervous jitter of his seemed to return all at one. "How did you get here?"

A reasonable question that I had nothing to offer that resembled an answer. "I don't know that either."

His red eyes darted to the sky. "We have to go."

Turning, he began jogging toward, well, nothing that I could see. Not wanting to find out what he was afraid of, I ran along behind him. All I could think was this Troy person, if he was a person, better have some answers.

He stopped again and dropped down onto his knees. Was he hurt? Surely that short jaunt hadn't winded him that much. He began tapping his hand on the ground. What was he doing? Looking all around us, I kept watch for anything really, not wanting to meet these daywalkers in the slightest. Just when I'd had about enough of his short break, he grasped something in the sand and pulled a door in the ground open.

"We're going to have to use the shortcut. We don't have time to get to the main gates."

Looking down into a hole with a ladder, I glanced around again and despite every muscle in my body telling me to run and get the hell out of here, I started down the metal rungs into a deep hole that would take me, hopefully back to friggin' reality.

About Jacqueline

Jacqueline Paige lives in Ontario in a small town that's part of the popular Georgian Triangle area.

She began her writing career in 2006 and since her first published works in 2009 she hasn't stopped. Jacqueline describes her writing as *all things paranormal*, which she has proven is her niche with stories of witches, ghosts, physics and shifters now on the shelves.

When Jacqueline isn't lost in her writing she spends time with her five children, most of whom are finally able to look after her instead of the other way around. Together they do random road trips, that usually end up with them lost, shopping trips where they push every button in the toy aisle, hiking when there's enough time to escape and bizarre things like creating new daring recipes in the kitchen. She's a grandmother to eight (so far) and looks forward to corrupting many more in the years to come.

Jacqueline also writes under the pseudonym of J. Risk

Jacqueline loves to hear from her readers, you can find her at

http://jacquelinepaige.com

JACQUELINE PAIGE